To Nick
Happy 50th birthday

Peter

Deathbed Confessions

The second Jack Daly mystery

Cover design by
Nina Patel

Books by Peter Larner

Historic Fiction
Farewell Bright Star
One Christmas Past

Jack Daly mysteries
Lost in a hurricane
Deathbed Confessions
The Unfolding Path
Harpoon Force
Deathbed Betrayal

Covenant Series
Covenant of silence
Covenant of retribution

Compilations
The Jack Daly Trilogy
The Covenant Chronicles

In memory of

George Charles Larner

We be of one blood thou and I

The last words of a dying man are like the tooth of a wounded lion, making a deeper impression in his agony than in his most vigorous strength.

The Right Reverend Jeremy Taylor DD
(Holy Living and Holy Dying)

Deathbed Confessions

PETER LARNER

1

Andy's story

Rainbows don't exist. As everyone knows, they are an optical illusion created by the sun and the rain. So quite how the rainbow came to be the symbol of hope seems illogical. What does it say about hope if it is represented by an illusion that is produced by nature to deceive us? It simply reinforces the hopelessness of the hopeful.

It was only nine o'clock in the morning but it was already twenty degrees. It was just starting to rain and the steady drizzle felt refreshing on my face after the long run up the Blackwall Tunnel approach road. My grandmother always called it Brunswick Road. In her day, it was a slowly climbing road, which came out of the Victorian Tunnel and headed up towards Hackney and the other boroughs of North London. It still is, of course, but it is now a six-lane dual carriageway that is only tolerable for a run on a Sunday morning, when the traffic is lighter and the relentless noise of siren city falls below the decibel level permitted at most workplaces.

The innocuous and ambiguous graffiti on the walls outside the Coventry Cross estate, or mugging alley as it is known locally, warned me to run a little faster. They were not the words of the prophets as recorded by Paul Simon, but were, in themselves, prophetic. It was a strenuous run towards a distant and deceptive rainbow and the slow incline took its toll as I made my way, wearily, past Bromley-by-Bow Underground station. My plan was to turn left, at the Bow flyover and head west along Bow Road, then down Campbell Road, where my grandmother had lived, and back through the side streets to my flat above the shoe shop in Chrisp Street Market.

That was the plan. Following the familiar route I walked as a child, whilst renewing memories of my grandmother. Trying not to let those distant memories slip into oblivion. Catching, and holding on tight to that lost relationship by recalling the things she would say. 'Heaven's tears' she called the rain, as we would walk home in a downpour from the local park. 'Heaven's tears' she repeated softly in my ear.

I neared the halfway stage of the run, along the noisy road towards Bow flyover. The flyover, and the underpass that heads north below it, normally carries heavy traffic to and from the City of London, but the roundabout itself attracts few cars on a Sunday and there was an occasional, but temporary, halt to the monotonous drone of the traffic.

The aim was to complete the run in less than one hour, but a session with the boys in the King's Head pub the night before was proving too much of a handicap. I stopped running, filled my lungs with air and clung to the railings that separated the noise intolerant pedestrians from the pedestrian intolerant cars. I made a feeble attempt at some stretching exercises in case anyone might be watching.

An attractive young woman cycled past and smiled at my exhaustion. I recovered myself too late to respond. I bowed my head, took several deep breaths and wondered whether my grandmother ever cycled. I assumed she had as most of her life had been spent at a time when they were at their height of popularity. I looked up just as the traffic noise began to ease and the rain did likewise.

It was the young boy I noticed first. Probably no more than two years old and very smartly dressed. It was just a young child and his dad taking a short cut under the flyover, or so I thought. However, when I looked up again, they were just standing there, not going anywhere. The striking memory I have is how much he looked like John F Kennedy's son at his father's funeral. The Kennedy assassination was long before my time, of course, although I had seen an old black and white photograph and the young boy reminded me of it. He was smartly dressed in his Sunday best clothes. But this wasn't Arlington National Cemetery.

The two of them stood there for a few minutes with their heads lowered in accord, until the man stepped forward and placed a small bunch of flowers by one of the pillars holding up the flyover.

I breathed in deeply and my mind raced. The child had lost his mother and his father had lost a wife. A traffic accident on a busy road. How tragic, she must have been so young. I leaned over the railings, my chest still heaving in and out. I looked up again and they were walking back towards a car parked nearby. A woman sat in the passenger seat and I suddenly realised my assumption had been wrong. My heart sank further. It wasn't the child's mother who had been killed in the traffic accident. Not a young child? I pleaded silently to the Gods. Have they lost a son or a daughter? Can the mother not even bring herself to

8

accompany them?

I could barely hear the car doors slam over the noise of the traffic speeding across the flyover above. Their departure seemed like a signal for the rain to cease and they drove off just as a bright sun reclaimed the sky from the drenching rain. I did some more stretching exercises and set off again along Bow Road. Heaven's tears stopped falling but, in my memory, the morning remained joyless for one young family.

2

Jack's story

The phone rang and I awoke in a vaguely familiar bedroom. I wiped the sleep from my eyes and went out into the hall to answer the call.

It was Ludo. If only I had spoken to her as much when we were together, maybe we still would be. Had I taken my pill? Yes. How was I sleeping? Fine. How was I settling in with mother? Pass.

"Look Ludo, aren't we supposed to be separated?"

"We are not separated," she replied emphatically. "I just said we needed our own space for a while."

"And which TV soap did that expression come from? Or perhaps it was one of those daytime TV self-help programmes. And what does it mean anyway? Space? We hardly saw each other anyway. You work evening shifts at the restaurant. And, when you aren't working there, you attend evening classes to learn English. And when you do get a night off, I am normally working myself."

"Giving someone their own space is a modern colloquialism for a temporary separation Jack." She struggled with the multi-syllabic noun but placed a firm emphasis on the word temporary.

"Colloquialism? Your English is improving Ludo. Are you still attending evening classes?"

"Yes. Well there's not much else to do with you away."

"How's Gavin?"

"Gavin is fine Jack. He's a very good teacher."

"Mm."

"Jack, there is nothing going on between Gavin and me…."

"Gavin and I," I interjected and she mumbled something in Italian under her breath.

"Anyway, Jack. You can come back if you want. I've had as much space as I need."

"Mother's worse," I whispered into the mouthpiece.

"OK, stay," she said abruptly.

"Look Ludo, I was forty last week and the therapist who's helping me deal with that says that moving back in with my mother isn't helping."

"You're seeing a therapist?"

"No Ludo, that was a joke. Hitting forty doesn't bother me in the least. Moving back in with my mother, well that's another story."

A mug of tea is placed on the telephone table from behind me. I hadn't realised mother was up, let alone listening to a telephone conversation with my wife.

"Look Ludo, I'm in one house and you're in another. How exactly is that not separation?" Mother tutted in the background.

"I didn't call you for an argument Jack," she said changing the subject only slightly.

"Well there might be a clue in that Ludo."

"What?"

"The fact that we never argue. You say leave and I leave."

"I didn't say 'leave'. You are always," she paused, trying to remember the right word or the right English expression. "You are always putting words into my mouth. 'You are dumped', remember that Jack? And anyway what about you say 'no children' and there are no children?"

"Careful now Ludo, that might lead to an argument. OK you didn't send me a text saying 'you are dumped', but you did send one that said our relationship 'wasn't working'."

"You know very well," she continued, "that I meant to send that text to Gigi telling him my Vespa wasn't working. And that was five years ago Jack. How long do you hold a grudge? Anyway, I don't see what's wrong with no arguing. We're adults aren't we? Can't we debate an issue without losing control?"

She screamed the last sentence down the telephone before realising that her raised voice rather contradicted the statement she was making. I could almost hear her counting to ten in Italian.

I stopped speaking and took a mouthful of milky, lukewarm tea. Mother had never been introduced to skimmed milk. The last time she experimented with milk was when she changed from evaporated milk in tins.

"What are you doing tomorrow night?" Ludo asked, in a measured attempt to change the direction of the conversation.

"Actually I'm off to Barcelona on business the following day, so I shall be packing."

"Barcelona on business? When did that start? The only place you ever offered to take me on business was

12

Brighton."

"Yes and you passed if I remember rightly. Look we'll talk when I get back at the weekend."

"Cushtie" she said and put the telephone down rather abruptly. I imagined her standing petulantly by the telephone expecting me to call her back to apologise.

'Cushtie' I thought, where did that come from? Ludo had been watching repeats of *Only Fools and Horses*. Quite what a young Italian woman made of Del Boy and Rodney made interesting thinking but what was clear is that her introduction to the Queen's English was becoming corrupted by her addiction to daytime television. Cushtie indeed.

The morning was a heady toxic blend of burnt toast, stewed, milky tea and the damp, stale smell of old age. I reluctantly joined mother in an untidy kitchen. Alzheimer's has a lot to answer for, not least of which is my inability to find anything in mother's house. She looked, disapprovingly, as I filled the kettle. I had more control over my time since I began free-lancing full time. If I had chosen a normal nine to five job like most people, I would have an excuse to avoid the purgatory that was nursing an elderly parent.

Mother's deteriorating condition made it impossible for me to work to any normal routine, and fortunately, there were very few jobs that took me out of the UK, mainly because my boss wouldn't authorise much more than a bus ride. The advantage of working for myself was outweighed by the fact that my 'employers' had no sympathy for my domestic problems. Mother's decline into the deeper recesses of Alzheimer's disease required almost constant supervision now. Ludo was understanding but I should not be surprised if she eventually grew tired of sharing me with an increasingly demanding mother. Unlike me, she had family. Her older brother Sebastiano took responsibility for their mother back in Rome, although she was far more robust than my own mother was and needed only a little TLC, rather than a full-time carer.

Mother was be beset by illnesses. She had stopped smoking some years ago but the legacy of a habit that lasted most of her adult life might still be responsible for her death. I sometimes worried that, growing up in a household where both parents smoked during my formative years, might affect my health, even though I had never smoked myself.

Mother's behaviour had become particularly strange of late. Not the bizarre corollary of her dementia related illness like leaving her shoes in the fridge but a strangely rational irrationality if that is possible. She had become noticeably aware of her deteriorating condition. She was becoming more introverted and spoke less as she began to realise the awful inevitability of her illness.

~~~~~

Ludo and I had been long-term friends before we finally decided to get married a couple of years ago. Once the decision had been made we then needed to consider where we would live. With me being the main wage earner that meant Ludo working in England. The fact that her grasp of the English language was so much better than my ability to speak Italian simply made the decision more obvious. Ludo made regular visits home and I often accompanied her, so her brother soon came to terms with the new arrangement. The compensation for her family was that they hosted the wedding. Just the thought of Ludo getting married in a heathen country was enough to make Sebastiano dangerously violent, so the decision was just as obvious as the previous one.

Italian weddings are smaller affairs than in the UK. They consist of a formal church wedding service, followed by a fairly short champagne reception and the inevitable photo shoot. They do not have the baggage of having to invite 250 people to a gathering of distant relatives, who you have not seen since you were three years old. Not that I have any relatives of course. Both my parents were only children, which left me with no cousins and, as an only child myself, that left my contribution to the guest list best described as minimalist. So the absence of any family members went largely unnoticed at the customary wedding. Having just started a new job at the time, I wasn't expecting my work colleagues to attend so, apart from my best friend Tonka Thompson, who fortunately was not seeing active service with the SAS at the time, I fully expected to be alone. Tonka was not only to be the Best Man; he was to be the only man.

Our wedding followed the Italian tradition. We married in the small church of St Onofrio on the edge of the Trastevere region where Ludo's mother and brother lived. Sebastiano owns a cellar bar off the Via del Corsa, which is the main north-south shopping street through the historical centre of Rome, but his heart was in the Trastevere district where he had been brought up. The bar was a thinly disguised front for the criminal activities of Sebastiano and his unconvincing henchman Gigi. They were artisan gangsters, some considerable way down the food chain that was Roman criminal society. A little fencing of stolen property, added muscle where it was needed or a little chauffeuring of what was left of the Mafioso hierarchy kept them occupied. Sebastiano was a big guy. Six feet tall and muscular, but even he looked small compared with the Shrek-like Gigi, which was an affectionate shortening of the name Luigi. It was not his poor grasp of the English language that prevented Gigi from making conversation but the fact that he simply could not think of anything to say. On the few occasions that he did, he took so much time to construct the sentence in his mind that the subject had changed and his interjection was inevitably out of context. Everyone he met received his opening, introductory gambit where he explains that his name is Luigi, which is one of the only Italian men's names that doesn't end in the letter 'o'.

Running a bar in the tourist centre of Italy seemed completely inappropriate for Sebastiano, who appeared to despise tourists who frequented his dungeon-like hostelry. Il Buco had received a mention in the *Lost Planet* guide so it was often visited by back-packers and others looking for the *real* Rome, which it was if you were looking for the tiny minority of Romans who favoured belligerence bordering on racism. It was his strongly held view that any visitors to Italy should be compelled to speak Italian throughout their trip to his wonderful City. Why should he have to speak English in his own country? His belligerent opinion was often expressed in my company but never directly to me.

16

More often, his barbs were passed as every day comment to his rabbit Gigi, who would nod convincingly in agreement with his commanding officer. I made a special effort to speak Italian at the wedding. Apart from her frequent lapses into the vernacular of *Only Fools and Horses*, Ludo spoke very good English. Whilst this did not prevent me from learning Italian, fluent use of the language was not a pre-requisite of our relationship. However, on our special day, I made the effort for Sebastiano, and Ludo's mother appreciated it too. I learned all my responses for the wedding service in Italian and, rather determinedly, maintained my use of the language throughout the day. The fact that Latin had been compulsory at my school helped the process.

A mixture of guests attended the champagne reception, held in the cloister of St Onofrio Church close to the Children's Hospital. In the end, my new work colleagues did make the trip from England. My joint bosses, Jonathan and Titus, who flew Business Class, used the trip as an excuse to dine at the excellent *Quinzi and Gabrielli* restaurant, whilst Richard Harland, my editor, and his wife travelled over with Ryanair. Tonka made a flying visit, probably dropped off by helicopter knowing him. In fairness, a flying visit was all that was necessary as the whole event lasted just a couple of hours. Some of Sebastiano's gangster friends attended. These largely consisted of those higher up the food chain of course. Although there probably weren't too many further down the food chain who had managed to stay out of prison. A couple of Ludo's mother's friends completed the wedding party, who dined – if one can call it that – on canapés and supped a good quality Prosecco, rather than French champagne, whilst Ludo and I posed for photographs against the frescoes of the ancient hermit Saint Onofrio around the shady cloister.

Titus and Jonathan loved the idea of speaking Italian for the day although I was convinced it was littered with Latin. Tonka joined in too and managed quite well. Unlike me, Tonka had mastered Latin at school and found the learning of foreign languages as easy as leaves come to a tree.

When I introduced Tonka to Gigi, my best friend was subjected to the standard item of conversation from his fellow giant.

"Hi, I'm Luigi but you can call me Gigi," he said in his best English. "Luigi is the only masculine Italian name that does not end in 'o'," he said almost triumphantly.

"What about Giovanni?" replied Tonka almost immediately.

"Si, Giovanni also," nodded Gigi dismissively, as his eyes rolled across his upper lids.

"And Lucca?"

"Si. Lucca too," conceded Gigi dejectedly. "Luigi means 'famous warrior,'" he added in compensation for being thoroughly undone by Tonka's quick wit. However, Tonka wasn't scoring points and the two became good friends once Gigi realised that Tonka spoke Italian very well and completely understood that Luigi was a unique name – well almost unique.

It was only poor Richard and his wife who paddled like ducks out of water in the Italian garden pond of 'Parlo Italiano' that formed at our wedding. *Come sta, grazie* and *bene*, indeed many *bene*, in fact *molte bene*, managed to get everyone through the day. Sebastiano was very pleased to see everyone speaking his native tongue and he even spoke a little slower in order to encourage the exchange of opinions on subjects of world importance, such as Italian cuisine, the importance of Italian art to world culture and how Roma and Lazio were so much superior to AC Milan and Inter.

Gigi looked confused, particularly when encouraged to contribute to a debate on Italian art by Titus. It didn't take much to confuse Gigi, who represented the muscle in the partnership with Sebastiano. For most of the day, he looked gormlessly at events, his eyes circling across his upper lids as he tried to understand why everyone was speaking Italian when he had gone to so much trouble to learn some English. He did so, of course, in an effort to please Ludo. He had formed an enormous crush on Ludovica, as he always called her, since his school days with Sebastiano. It was not reciprocated but he never lost hope.

"No," Gigi insisted to Titus, "you cannot go compare a Constable with a Caravaggio." He was later to be found checking his translation of constable with Ludo and shaking his head, wondering why Titus would go compare a great Italian artist with a police officer. Gigi was obviously learning English via the Ludo daytime TV language course.

On special occasions, Ludo's mother would also refer to her as Ludovica. This was one of those occasions and she used her full name throughout the day.

Ludovica and I met when I was making a study visit from University ten years ago. I was studying Italian literature and we bumped into each other, quite literally, on the very road that leads up to St. Onofrio's church. She was on her Vespa and I was trying to navigate the kerbless streets of Rome.

It probably was love at first sight but, paradoxically, that only occurred to us later. We became friends before we became lovers. A relationship born out of friendship, it always seems to me, is superior to a friendship born out of love. She was difficult to love. Feisty, purposeful and convinced of her own views and opinions. She dominated our relationship, not because of her strong character, but probably because of my weak character. I was happy for her to make all the decisions. I loved my work and preferred the word to the world. Writing is all I ever wanted to do and Ludo knew how important my work was to me. It was implicitly agreed that she would get her way in all things except where it concerned my work.

It wasn't a conscious decision not to have children. It was never really discussed much. We simply postponed the debate whilst we enjoyed ourselves. I had, after all, just started a new job and felt it would be irresponsible to have children until I was sure of a regular income. The subject was largely forgotten then, as we enjoyed the first year of our marriage. Forgotten that was except on those occasions when we visited Rome. For Sebastiano and Ludo's mother, children were an essential ingredient of a successful marriage and fundamental if Ludo was to fulfil herself as a woman. In my heart, I knew Ludo shared that view and so found myself in a minority of one. I did not radically object to children. Not surprisingly for someone who had no brothers or sisters, or even cousins, an independent nature that bordered on selfishness was an integral part of my character. I was also jealous of my time with Ludo, which is why it came as such a shock to me when she suggested we needed our own space. I knew she had no serious intentions of prolonging the separation. In a married relationship that is born out of a long friendship, one feels much more secure of a partner's real intention. I think I knew all along that her suggestion was only intended to provoke my emotions and, perhaps, get me to change my views about having children. In truth, my emotions needed little stirring where Ludo was concerned and I had little real objections to having children. I just needed to get around to it. We both knew that Ludo made the decisions in our household but she just didn't feel comfortable with making this one on her own. Anyway, I always knew Ludo's suggestion of a temporary separation would be precisely that – temporary. After all, she hadn't even changed her status on Facebook.

I convinced myself that mother's situation had been made worse by her trip to Rome for our wedding. I can see now that taking her out of her comfort zone, away from her normal environment, did incredible damage. A visit to the local shops at home was enough to confuse her, so why I thought a few days in Rome would not affect her in a more acute way I don't know. A relaxing holiday and the wedding she had always looked forward to seemed a good idea at the time. In reality, it heightened her sensitivities and increased the frequency of her hallucinatory journeys back to the past. Alzheimer's is not simply having a bad memory; it's an intermittent fault in the brain that takes the sufferer on tortuous journeys into the past.

After five years of living with mother's illness, I knew all this better than most people did. All the help and advice available from the National Health Service is of little use when your mother believes she is living in the sixties and her son, who is desperately trying to administer to her every need, hasn't been born yet. Those moments when she looks vacantly into my face without a hint of recognition are agonizing. How can she recognise me when I don't exist in her world? Those sad, anxious and ever increasing periods of confusion when she fails to recognise me cause us both pain with equal measure. She sits in the armchair, a lonely figure, looking at the wedding album, pointing at photographs of me and telling me that this is Jack. I have hardly changed since those photographs had been taken two years ago but she fails to recognise me, in person. How was it possible that she always recognised me in the photographs but simply could not see that it was that same man sitting before her?

Since I returned to stay with her recently, I had noticed that she took great comfort in the wedding album. Our semi-silent days together would intermittently switch from her living in some distant past time, where Jack was somebody else and I was a complete stranger, to moments of relief, where she recognised me for who I am and she had all the features of a normal, healthy woman. Which of those periods represented the lie in our lives I wasn't sure. On one occasion, when she had wandered out of the house when I wasn't looking, I had to physically link arms with her and force her back into a house that she didn't recognise, to live with the complete stranger who was the son she had never had. Sometimes I could calculate where she was in her nightmare world. Normally it was the East End of London, sometime around the sixties, in a time before I was born, in a world I had never known. Yet I still existed in some way. She would make constant references to Jack as

22

well as my father, Bill. Her mother and father, who I had never known, came into her ramblings occasionally but most of it was my father and I. Always Bill and Jack. How could I exist in that world if I had not even been born? Sometimes, I would indulge myself by entering that past world with her simply to learn something of her past and, perhaps, of the father I did not really know. It left me feeling soiled and guilty of using my mother in that way. For her part, she appeared to enjoy it for she had nobody else who could accompany her on these irrational journeys into her past life.

Mother had been much calmer of late. There seemed to be a stability in her condition driven by a determination on her part to make my time with her a little easier. In spite of my inconsiderate remarks on the telephone with Ludo, mother seemed to be resolved in her patience, as if she wanted to make the most of those periods we spent together where she was cognisant of her condition. Normally she would dismiss the need for me to attend her but, over the last few days, she was happy to have me around her. But we never spoke of her departing this world. Alzheimer's isn't like the cancer that took my father from me. It is a slow decline towards death, rather than a short period where death becomes an inevitability.

I dreaded the thought of leaving mother overnight but her neighbour, Mrs. Joiner, was very helpful. She would always keep an eye out for mother and she had my mobile telephone number so I could be contacted if anything untoward happened. So, when mother had fallen asleep in the armchair I popped across the road to see Yoda look-a-like Mrs. Joiner. She was a kind person and never judged

23

other people, a bit like the real Yoda I suppose. She fully understood that I needed to work and, sometimes, that work took me away. I remember Mrs. Joiner as a child and imagined her sending me off to be a Jedi Knight. She had a higher opinion of me than I did of myself and I felt able to trust her to watch out for mother whilst I was away.

My trip to Barcelona was only necessary because that was the only appointment that Hollywood's latest darling could spare me. Stevie Ray Harvest had been heavily tipped for the Best Actor Oscar for his role in *The Road to Damascus*, a return to the big budget biblical epic of the sixties and seventies.

Apart from my brief encounter with Stevie, I had an interview to conduct with the Foreign Secretary. Presumably, his schedule was just as busy as Stevie's, but I would not have to travel around Europe to meet him. It was still six weeks until the much-awaited Peace Conference in Geneva, but it was a key interview for that week's issue and I needed to see them both at times convenient to them. I also needed to identify a target for the Grand National issue too.

I had worked on *The Main Event* since it was launched two years ago. Titus Barrington-Gill and Jonathan Willshire, a couple of Cambridge-educated entrepreneurs had contacted me when they heard I was leaving my previous job as a PR Manager at Woolly Fold Manor. The idea of producing a weekly magazine that focused on *The Main Event* of the week seemed to work and sales in the UK had been very good. The boys were even considering launching a sister publication on a European theme, or adapting the current publication to meet a broader audience. As the author of the *Daly Report*, a title that was considered a witty pun by Jonathan who had the idea for it, my job was to interview a leading player in *The Main Event* each week. The column proved as popular as the magazine itself and I normally had little trouble convincing the appropriate politician, movie star or sportsman to be the subject of the interview. In fact, I had a fairly constant flow of requests from B celebrities to be interviewed by Jack Daly. I don't think some of them could grasp that I had no intention of interviewing an extra from *East Enders* simply because he had decided to embarrass himself in the London Marathon. No, my aspirations reached much higher than that. Ludo quite liked filling her spare time by writing caustic replies to the misguided individuals concerned. She said it helped her to learn English and she sometimes took letters for students to reply to at Gavin's English-as-a-second-language course. The Foreign Secretary was, obviously, towards the top end of my celebrity list although he was certainly not playing hard to get, as any photo opportunity was presumably a step forward on his path towards Number Ten.

Like all media work, the job had time pressure points during the production. Having a countdown clock as my screensaver, care of Willshire, was not my idea of job satisfaction. Moreover, Titus, or Tight-arse, as we referred to him behind his back, would not pay for a flight to Barcelona if it wasn't entirely necessary. As it was, he insisted that I travel there and back in the same day to avoid hotel bills. I ignored that yellow card in the hope and expectation that my article would be so good he would authorise my expenses for a night in the Ramblas. The constraints and demands imposed by these two focused individuals were only compensated for by the appointment of Richard Harland as Editor. I had worked with Richard previously at the Ron Haggard Sports Reporting Agency off Fleet Street. He was a capable and talented reporter but *The Main Event* was his first opportunity as an Editor.

When I arrived home from Barcelona, I went directly to mother's house after texting both mother and Ludo to let them know that I had landed safely. There was a strange, deafening silence when I opened the front door and stepped into the house. My first thought was that Mother had wandered off again and I was mentally berating myself for leaving her alone when suddenly Mrs. Joiner stepped out of the living room into the hall.

I wasn't surprised to see mother's neighbour. She was a regular visitor to the house. I was just concerned at the silence.

"Oh. Hello Mrs. Joiner. How are you?" I asked.

"You had better sit down son," she said in a worryingly comforting voice, as she stepped to one side to let me enter the living room before her. I looked around the cluttered room expecting to see the result of a burglary or similarly awful event. I dismissed this scenario when I saw the room unchanged, just in the same disrupted state that I had left it in the previous day.

"What's wrong?" I asked, almost anticipating her answer as I narrowed down the alternatives. "Is mother ill?"

I was ushered into an armchair. She was clearly struggling to find her words and wanted me in a seated position before continuing.

"I'm so sorry Jack. Your mother isn't here," she said as she struggled to explain herself.

"Has she wandered off?" I asked.

"I'm not very good at this Jack, I'm so sorry."

She sat down herself and then not knowing how else to deliver the message she spoke softly but firmly.

"Your mother has died."

Having just sat down in the chair at that point I instinctively rose up again.

"Died?" I asked, suddenly realising that I sounded disbelieving.

Apparently, I had been saved from the chaos and cacophony that accompanies any death, albeit unremarkable in the eyes of the world. Mrs. Joiner had noticed that mother had not taken the milk in from the doorstep and so she had used her spare key to gain access.

"I spoke with your mother last night," said Mrs. Joiner. "And arranged to pop over for a cup of tea this morning. But, when I saw the milk still on the doorstep." She stopped mid-sentence, whilst she considered her words, then told me that she had discovered mother lying peacefully in her bed.

"I knew she was dead," she said, "even before I touched her skin. But she looked peaceful Jack. There was no anguish on her face."

"What...?" I said beginning to ask what the cause was. Mrs. Joiner anticipated my question.

"It's too early to know yet," she said, and placed her hand on my arm. She rubbed gently. "I saw her face son. She didn't suffer."

A nice, young policeman had visited the house and arranged to have the body removed. The doctor had confirmed that there were no suspicious circumstances. A heart attack was the most likely cause. A sense of loss was

27

weighed against a sense of relief. I tried to push the latter from my mind. It was difficult to remind myself that this was about mother and not about me.

I wondered, aloud, what I was supposed to do and was surprised to find that the answer was very little. A couple of calls and a visit to the hospital where mother had been taken to obtain a death certificate seemed the extent of my duties. But that was for tomorrow, Mrs. Joiner said.

There was nothing to be done now, except to sit and think about mother, to think about never seeing her again. If only I had taken Titus's instructions seriously, I would have been back with mother last night. Instead, whilst she was dying, I was having a drink in the Ramblas, calling Ludo to tell her how much I loved her and to make her a little jealous of my business trip to Barcelona. Such taunting and teasing is what turns some marriages into sibling relationships and I made a conscious decision, after the call, to stop such juvenile behaviour.

"Call your wife," Mrs. Joiner suggested gently, "I will call your mother's friends to let them know."

Mrs. Joiner left and I thought badly of her for her eagerness to tell her friends the news. I felt guilty for having such irrational and unwarranted malicious thoughts. Mrs. Joiner was a true friend to my mother. Yes, she was the local gossip, but she was also the comforting person who seems to step forward at moments like this.

I poured myself a glass of Jameson, called Ludo, and waited for her in the garden of mother's house.

The garden is a reflection of our life, or at least the relationships we forge in that life. An itinerant and vagabond group of souls inhabited Mother's garden.

28

Magpies, Collared Doves, Wood Pigeons and Starlings visited her garden but chose not to stay. The only residents in the plot to the rear of mother's house were the ants and bees who had work colleagues rather than friends.

The words meet and met pass each other on the pathway of my life, along with has and had. I want to talk about the people mother meets at church and in the neighbourhood. But now it must be met, rather than meet.

My memories of mother have transported themselves to the past tense of my life. I shall no longer talk about what she is doing, but what she did. It is over thirty years since my father died; people are a long time dead and memories fade. The age of mother's few friends suggest that their memories of her will fade sooner than most. They who are remembered never die; such is the great treasure of fame.

The Starlings and Magpies, like mother's friends, were occasional visitors in her life. Such as the friends she met at church on Sunday, if she remembered it was Sunday, or was reminded of it by old Mr. Anderson. And the neighbours she would meet on her way to the shops, like Mrs. Joiner. But there were no life long friendships. Even her husband, my father, occupied her life for only a relatively brief period.

My garden, like my life, reflects different relationships, like the territorial and monogamous pair of Blackbirds that regarded the area around the Oak tree in my garden as their personal territory. Or the inquisitive Robin who would sit on the spade as I planted Geranium and Begonias each year. Or the Green Woodpeckers who, though not resident, lived close by in the wood down by the River Aught, and lunched on the insects who invaded the pond area during the hot summer months. And, of course, the brave and hardy

Shelducks who nested in the forgotten pathway behind my rear fence and burrowed, under the desirable real estate that was my shed, for shelter. Resilient and resourceful creatures who, in spite of the love of water, chose to live nearly one mile from the river, just to enjoy my garden.

When I have a son or a daughter, I will lift them up, above the fence, to see the Shelducks busying themselves. And we will name each one of them and wave goodbye to those who choose to leave with the warm weather, or stay with those who remain.

I share the garden with these creatures as I share my life with Tonka, Ludo, Richard Harland, and others to whom friendship is not a transient commodity but one to be treasured.

The blue tits were just beginning to occupy the bird box and chaffinches and other small birds fluttered about in the hedge at the rear of mother's garden. It was a sign that winter was ending, a signal of new life. Truly the new buds of Spring slept in the earth's dark core. Wherever we might arbitrarily place the New Year in the calendar, nature itself placed it firmly where February meets March. The flowers and birds declare the arrival of spring, not a date chosen by humankind. But, for every beginning, there must be an end. My world was changing and my life with Ludo would make a new beginning too. What would we make of the strangely unwanted freedom created by the loss of my only living relative? Mother's death convinced me more than ever that Ludo and her mother, and Sebastiano were all right. It was time for us to have a baby.

Ludo was, as expected, terribly supportive. As I had seen so often, she was magnificent in a crisis. Our temporary separation had been forgotten. It had as much life as a cut flower anyway. No one who knew us could imagine us apart. Nor could I imagine us apart, and the last few days had simply been contrived by Ludo to inject some new life into our relationship.

We returned home and discussed what we needed to do the next day. Neither of us had dealt with this situation before. My father had died when I was only eight years old. Some boys live in their father's shadow but I lived in nobody's shadow. My father cast no shadow at all. He had been largely forgotten through my childhood and I had assumed it was because his loss held such heartache for my mother. So I participated in that subterfuge and, as a consequence, his memory had been lost to me. I remembered he was cremated. Unlike mother, he had no wish to be buried, or at least that was what mother told me. At least I knew that much about them both. Mother was a devout Catholic, so a Requiem Mass and burial seemed a post requisite to her death.

I do not remember visiting the cemetery after father's death. I assume we had made, at least, some token visits as I had some recollection of the cemetery. There was a rose bush, I recall, close to a pathway. But that was all I remembered. Was it such a torture to mother that she could not even bring herself to visit his last resting place? Or was it because he wasn't really there? After all, most crematoria don't even give you the ashes of the departed one. The ashes are, in fact, a combination of departed ones. So what is the point? A burial is different. If he had been buried, there would have been bones. The last remains of William Daly.

My father had been several years older than mother and

a heavy smoker. That is about all I remember of him apart from his interest in boxing. Not that he looked as if he had boxed. He didn't look the type. He was small in stature with no particular features that I recall. Certainly none that would suggest he had taken up boxing. I don't remember looking like him or being like him either. And I certainly didn't remember what happened when he died.

How does one know what to do when someone dies? Not emotionally, but practically. I was to find out the following morning. It is not difficult because the system takes over. My visit to the hospital to obtain a death certificate was like throwing a six to start playing a game. The death certificate leads to the registrar, which leads to the undertaker, which leads to the church. Perhaps I should have gone directly to Father McNally in the first place. He was, after all, a close friend of mother, who attended his Mass without fail each Sunday, until she started to forget what day of the week it was.

I called the office and spoke with Titus, who conveniently forgot I was self employed and, rather patronisingly, told me to take a few days off adding, just before putting the phone down, that I could email drafts of my forthcoming interviews from home.

Making the arrangements for mother's funeral was surprisingly easier than one might imagine. After all, these things happen every day. Ludo kept her eye on the expenditure. I was hopeless in that sense and it is easy to dismiss cost as an issue in such circumstances. So the type of coffin and the number of cars became sensible and appropriate, rather than extravagant and expensive.

The funeral was deferred until the following week in

order that Ludo's family could attend. They had never visited England before and I was a little surprised that they wanted to be with us at the service.

Ludo decided that we should do some comfort shopping to take my mind off my mother. I think she had noticed a danger of my drifting into the morbidity of guilt.

"I know" she declared enthusiastically, "You can buy a new suit." Although I knew she actually meant 'you *will* buy a new suit'.

"You have become very scruffy since you went to work with those two ex-students," she said demeaningly of Titus and Jonathan. "You will need a suit for the funeral."

She took advantage of my hesitation.

"Why don't you treat yourself to some new clothes for the funeral, Jack?" she said again, with an imposed tone of selflessness born out of the opportunity for her to renew her wardrobe and shoe collection.

"It'll be nice to see you in a suit again. Since you became self employed you have reduced the expression 'smart casual' to a new low. I haven't seen you in a suit for months. Yes," she continued, "You shall buy a suit. You know it makes sense." The end of the sentence was delivered with a distinct Peckham accent.

I yielded under the barrage and agreed to go shopping the following day.

I voluntarily ended a disturbed sleep back in the marital bed before the sun rose the next day and crept downstairs to finish off the article on Stevie Ray Harvest. Five minutes later, whilst occupied in intense thought, I was startled by Ludo's voice from the doorway.

"You are supposed to be taking a break," she said with a

grimace, "so why are you working?"

I saved the document and put the lid down on the laptop. We chatted over tea and toast and planned our day.

~~~~~

"Let's go" I said around ten o'clock, believing a spot of shopping would do us both good.

Ludo's suggestion that I buy a new suit wasn't entirely selfless, for she had every intention of buying herself a new little black number for the service. She hated shopping for clothes with me lurking in the background, so when we arrived at Langton's Department Store in town I went off to the Menswear department and she took herself off to Ladies Fashions.

Rather unenthusiastically, I picked up a black suit and examined it. If I bought a black suit, she might not insist I wear it after the funeral. Grey? Grey was sombre but a little too light for a funeral. Navy, I thought as I picked up a suitably funereal looking suit and went to the changing room to try it on. Ten minutes later, I had purchased the suit, a black tie and a crisp white shirt and went off to find Ludo. After a further ten minutes of fruitless searching, I decided to call her mobile but there was no answer.

Feeling rather embarrassed I went to the Customer Service department to see if anyone had handed in an attractive 35 year old red head. The assistant remained silent, seemingly unable or unwilling to answer my simple question. She stuttered and fumbled with some documents on the counter whilst continually looking, rather knowingly and furtively, off to her left. In the end, she didn't need to speak and I decided that this is where Ludo must be.

From behind a closed door in the direction she was looking, I suddenly heard Ludo's voice. I could not quite make out what she was saying but it sounded like "I am not a Romanian and do not go compare me with a Serb either."

I rushed over and opened the door. Ludo was sitting at a small table with her back turned to me. A young man sat on the other side of the desk taking notes and a second man, about the same age as me, stood with his back against the far wall.

"Ludo" I said as I swept through the door "What is going on?"

The young man at the other end of the room moved quickly towards me and said "And who are you mate, her pimp?"

My reaction was spontaneous. It was certainly not premeditated, although presumably some plan had formed briefly in my mind before I smashed my fist into his face, knocking him backwards on to the floor. The room fell silent for a few seconds. He sat up and blood from his nose trickled over his lips. He wiped it away with his hand and instructed his colleague to call the police.

"Do it now," he screamed, as if he expected me to continue the assault on him.

"Oh great," said Ludo.

In the few minutes it took for a heavily built policeman to arrive, Ludo told me that she had been arrested for shoplifting.

"That's ridiculous" I insisted to the bloodied young man,

who was now taking his colleagues chair, as the policeman came into the room.

"We have CCTV evidence," he said confidently to the new arrival, who looked bemused.

"Aiding and abetting a known Serbian shop lifter," he continued telling the policeman whilst remaining in his seat.

The policeman took out a notebook and pen. Pointing to his name badge, the bloodied man finally introduced himself to the policeman as Damian Lewis the Store Manager at Langton's and was quick to add that I had assaulted him in the course of his proper duties.

"And do those duties include insinuating that my wife is a prostitute?" I asked.

I was told to be quiet by the policeman and Mr Lewis and PC Etherington began examining the CCTV footage. It clearly showed Ludo passing ladies clothing to a furtive looking man of swarthy complexion behind her.

"I was simply looking at the dresses when a man behind me asked me to pass him two dresses on the next rail. How can that be shoplifting?" my wife questioned defiantly.

"Well" said Constable Etherington, "perhaps because the man you are passing the dresses to is well known to the police as Radovan Karadzic, a Serb leader of a determined and, as yet, uncaught band of criminal shop lifters." 'Uncaught?' I thought. Is there such a word? I then suddenly realised I knew the name of the wanted man.

"Radovan Karadzic?" I questioned. "Are you sure?"

"Well" the PC corrected himself "Radovan Stodkovic. Same thing."

"Not really" I suggested, "one is a mass murderer and the other is allegedly a petty crook."

PC Etherington was not impressed with my knowledge of world affairs and only allowed us to leave after ensuring we could prove who we were and that we lived at a permanent address locally.

"We will be in touch with you in a few days. You will be asked to attend the local police station to be formally charged", added the stocky police officer after reporting in on a scratchy two-way radio.

"What with?" I asked naively.

"Well you with assault and your wife with theft, or aiding and abetting a theft," he answered, as if stating the obvious.

Later that evening Ludo spoke to her mother and brother via the web cam on Skype, as she did at least three times each week. Only this time, the events were a little more unusual. 'Come sta, Ludo, tutto bene?' Well, not exactly Mama, I've been arrested for shoplifting and Jack is going to prison for assault.

Perhaps her explanation was a little more subtle than that but it didn't stop Sebastiano exploding. The web cam showed him leap from his seat and smash his fist into the wall behind him. I had learned quite a lot of Italian since marrying Ludo but I had not completed the advanced course that included obscenities and exclamatory swear words.

"It was not me" Ludo insisted loudly to her mother who took over the conversation whilst Sebastiano recovered himself.

"Si, si" Mama sympathised.

"It was some Serbian crook called Radovan Stodkovic," which only sent Sebastiano back into a rage and the second round of his fight with the back wall.

Wanting to temper the discussion a little, Ludo confirmed that my mother's funeral would be on Thursday of next week. I could just about translate Sebastiano's mumblings from 'Stodkovic doppia settimana' as 'and Stodkovic the following week'.

Suitably, but only partially, calmed, Sebastiano told Ludo that he and mother would fly over on Wednesday, along with his friend Gigi.

~~~~~

Every adult member of Ludo's family of childbearing age had the reproductive energy of the Von Trapps. As a consequence, they looked at Ludo sympathetically, as if the absence of offspring was an illness, not a positive decision not to have children.

Childless at 35 attracted the same expression as the black plague or leprosy in Ludo's family. I was reminded of this by Ludo when I suggested to her that I would be spending the night at mother's house so that I could make an early start to the tidying up process the following morning. I was assaulted by a threatening diatribe of Italian words uttered under her breath which, roughly translated, consisted mainly of 'how was I supposed to have children if we sleep in different houses. Different beds would be difficult enough, but a different house makes it absolutely certain, absolutely clear. You never want children.'

"I do and we will," I answered reassuringly as I left,

adding "I'll be home tomorrow."

It was Titus's generous insistence that I take a few days off for the funeral and to tidy up my mother's affairs, that prompted the idea of removing some clutter from the old family home. But, his generosity was beginning to wane, much like Ludo's tolerance of my recurring absence and lack of enthusiasm to father children. In truth, it was not very generous of Titus, seeing that he paid me by the word not by the hour, although Ludo's waning tolerance was more understandable. How were we possibly to start a family if we were living apart?

So, having promised to return home the following day, I slept at mother's house that night and set the alarm for an early start.

The following morning, after taking a shower, I dressed in some old clothes, ate some toast, and set about tidying up. I wasted the first hour wandering from room to room trying to decide where to begin.

Eventually I decided to leave my childhood bedroom and the kitchen until the end, so I could, at least, continue to sleep and eat if necessary, although any consideration of sleeping needed to be looked on as an emergency in view of Ludo's threats. After some good progress and a short coffee break in the untidy but now largely uncluttered kitchen, I began to wonder what might be in the loft.

I hadn't been in the loft since I was a child, when mother lifted me up to retrieve the Christmas decorations each year, and my recollection was of a large empty space.

My hopes that it had remained in that condition since I reached manhood were misplaced. In one corner by the water tank were two suitcases. I remembered them from my youth. A holiday in Weston Super Mare in the company of my mother, with donkey rides, candyfloss and an ice cream sundae. It must have been just after Dad died. I think Mother thought we both needed to get away from the house. We needed to get away from the damp clinging smell of death that hung about the house.

I remembered mother sitting on a deckchair puffing away on a Senior Service cigarette, picking the loose tobacco from her bottom lip, and looking mournfully, in deep recollection out to sea. On reflection, it was more a period of exile than a family holiday and I don't recall the suitcases being used again.

Those days must have been difficult for a mother alone with a young son who kept needing new clothes; forever growing out of trousers and shoes. Not that she ever made that apparent to me.

I didn't miss holidays because they were largely unknown to me. My education was more important to mother. I remember her watching Tonka and I doing our homework on the kitchen table before he went home to the right number of parents. Both Tonka's parents worked in London and they were terribly grateful to mother for looking after him in the late afternoons. She would never accept any of the gifts they offered and the only other holiday I recall is when I went to Lloret de Mar with Tonka and his parents for a week when I was about ten years old.

They offered to repeat the treat on several other occasions but mother would never agree. She had already lost someone close to her and the thought of losing me was just too much for her.

I can see that more clearly now because she has gone and

I now realise how she felt. Perhaps Ludo feels the same. Sometimes, people simply cannot live alone. University and a bachelor life, enforced by having a girlfriend in Italy, made me accustomed to it. But perhaps Ludo felt differently.

I decided to use the suitcases to transport other items from the loft to the local recycling depot. My expectation that the suitcases would be empty was as misplaced as my hopes about the loft itself, and I found myself struggling from one problem to another.

I opened the suitcases and there were those exact clothes that I had, by degrees, grown out of. I started to think that, if mother hadn't disposed of these useless items, what other rubbish would need to be disposed of. This was going to be a long day. I lowered the suitcases through the loft hatch and dropped them as gently as I could to the floor below. Two large cardboard boxes filled with familiar Christmas decorations followed them.

In the far corner of the loft were two cardboard boxes of books. Some biographies, some novels. I suddenly had a clear memory of Dad sitting in the armchair downstairs, reading a book and talking to me about it. I searched the box and found what I thought was the actual book, a biography by Jose Torres, a world light heavyweight boxing champion in the sixties. I flicked through the pages of Muhammad Ali's life before deciding I was wasting time. I had to climb down the steps to take the cardboard boxes of books down. Returning to the loft there was a large pile of old sheets and curtains that I dropped through the loft hatch. Camping chairs and a couple of prints in frames also need to be carried down.

Progress up in the loft had simply been replaced by a

heap of rubbish in the narrow hallway at the top of the stairs below. Still, the loft was almost empty and one trip to the recycling plant would soon dispose of the unwanted heap that represented my mother's past life. I returned to the loft for one final visit and it was then that I noticed this lonely light green shoebox positioned just under a timber rafter. Dolcis shoe shop, ladies' court shoes, size 6. I didn't expect it to contain shoes and this time my expectations were realised. Letters, a photograph, and other items seized my attention. These looked very old and as frail as I was beginning to feel from working in a confined workspace. I decided to stop for a break and take the box downstairs.

Skipping over the heap at the foot of the loft steps, I went into the kitchen and made myself a cup of tea. I placed the shoebox on the kitchen table and, rummaging through the cupboards, I found a packet of digestive biscuits before settling into a chair. I resisted the temptation of looking inside the box until I was sitting comfortably at the kitchen table with a dunked biscuit in my hand. The table was empty, apart from my cup of tea, a packet of biscuits and the shoebox.

A few minutes later it was littered with the contents of the box. Two letters, one old newspaper cutting, one green rosary, a Mass card that was the shape of a bookmark, a marriage certificate, two birth certificates and a black and a white photograph of three people.

One of the people I recognised as my mother. She must have been around twenty years old and attractive in a simple, old-fashioned way. She was with two men, one who was clearly older than the other one. I don't remember seeing too many photographs of my dad but one of the men was clearly him, although he looked very young.

It is a strange paradox that death can be a conduit for so many beginnings and I had an overwhelming feeling that this shoebox was to prove a beginning in many senses for me. Mother had rarely spoken of dad or of her past life. My grandparents were unknown to me. In fact, her entire life before I was a child was unknown to me. My only excursion into mother's past had been created by her descent into Alzheimer's disease. How much of that was real and how much was the meanderings of a madness brought on by her illness was impossible to say.

The other man in the photograph looked vaguely familiar. Mother wore a large floral dress with straps over her bare shoulders. She wore high heels, which made her slightly taller than dad. Dad, if indeed it was him, looked quite dapper in a dark suit with wide trouser legs and what I suppose must have been a trilby hat. The other man wore jeans and a denim jacket over a loose T-shirt. I couldn't make out the design on the T-shirt but I think it said Lonsdale. He wore what looked like an old-fashioned pair of baseball boots.

I put the photograph down. The green rosary brought distant memories from my youth and there was a small prayer card with the picture of a saint on one side and a prayer to St Jude on the other.

This left two letters and the newspaper cutting. The newspaper cutting had been cut so that there was no evidence of the publication or date. It was worn and discoloured.

Police fear gangland feud

A Scotland Yard spokesman warned of gangland reprisals following the execution of an East End nightclub boss Charlie Harrison and his son Michael yesterday. Police were called to Diamonds nightclub in Mile End after the pair had been gunned down in what appears to be a professional killing. The bodies of Charlie and Michael Harrison were discovered by employee Donald Rhodes in the bar of Diamonds nightclub. Police confirmed that both men had been shot in the head and body several times by a handgun. Detective Superintendent Staddon said that significant evidence had been retrieved from the scene and he was hopeful that an arrest would follow.

I convinced myself that I had never heard of any of these people and dismissed the newspaper cutting as irrelevant. Mother had never mentioned anyone called Harrison or Rhodes from her days in London's East End although, in truth, she had spoken very little about her life before we moved to Essex. She had never shown any interest in going back and, even on the few occasions when we passed that area on the train into London, she never showed any signs of recognition.

The first of the letters was no more than a handwritten note on a sheet of ruled paper that had been torn from a writing pad. It was undated, shabby, and the handwriting appeared slow and deliberate, almost childlike. It was a note to my mother and was signed by someone called Liam.

Mary,

Those feelings that we agreed to keep locked in our hearts cannot be hidden any longer. My love is too great. I cannot bear the pain any more. I'm so, so sorry, but I cannot live like this. You know how I feel. We share a great love and I must do something about it. I know you and Bill might suffer by my actions but it must be done. Jack is my responsibility. I love him too much to deny him this one thing.

Liam

I read the note twice. Who was Liam? Mother had never mentioned him to me. I sat looking at the words, trying not to reach what was an obvious, but incredible interpretation. Was I Liam's son? What else could these words mean? 'We share a great love'; 'Jack is my responsibility'. 'I love him too much to deny him this one thing'. What was this 'one thing'? I churned the words over in my mind and came to the conclusion that 'this one thing' must be a better life with who I thought was my father. What else could it mean?

I unfolded the second letter, which, this time had a date on it. It was neater, although it was written in the same childlike handwriting. The sentences were short and to the point. Deliberate statements in equally deliberate writing.

45

10th January 1969

Dear Mary

I have reached a decision. I don't want to see you any more. Seeing you hurts too much and I think you and Jack should get on with your lives with Bill. Bill is a good man. He was a good friend to us both and I let him down by doing what I did. It is best that little Jack knows nothing of me. Please grant me this one request. Forget me. I have the photo you gave me. This is all I need. A last kiss for Jack. How can anyone not know who his real father is?

Liam

There were no kisses on the bottom of either letter. The absence of these and any closing reference to love seemed out of context with the letters themselves.

If I had any doubts after reading the first note, the second letter made it quite clear. Liam was indeed my father. The date on the second letter was around the time of my first birthday. I looked back at the photograph and realised why I thought the other man was familiar. He looked like me.

The solution was obvious. My mother had an affair with Liam and I was the embarrassing result of that affair. The supporting evidence was contained in the same shoebox. The marriage certificate for mum and dad, or mum and Bill, showed that they had married only five months before I was born. I had never really known the date of their anniversary as my father, or Bill, died when I was just eight years old. My mind raced as I started to work on the clues. It was like a jigsaw puzzle with most of the parts missing. But it took little imagination to determine what picture it produced. Mother became pregnant by Liam, but married Bill. Yet Liam is clearly in love with her. Was Liam a married man? He intended to take some action but this didn't prevent my mother marrying Bill. But then she continued to see Liam for another year. Did Bill know about this? Why didn't she destroy these letters? One thing was certain; I needed to trace Liam, if he was still alive. My birth certificate showed Bill as my father, so he either did not know or chose to lie about my parentage to the authorities.

I looked at the photograph again. There was something about the pose. Mum appeared very affectionate towards the younger man, but my dad, or Bill - and I was now sure it was him, seemed the outsider. And what was the significance of the newspaper cutting? Gangsters Charlie and Michael Harrison gunned down. I switched on my laptop and searched for the names. I eventually found details of the shootings, which occurred before I was born, in the sixties. It didn't take very long before I found the connection. Liam Calnan was convicted of the murders of Charles and Michael Harrison in 1967. Further searches for Liam Calnan established that he was serving his full life sentence. No parole for him it seemed. And then I discovered a small recent newspaper article on line. It revealed that murderer Liam Calnan was to be released from Sanderlings open prison in Essex, after serving more than forty years for the murder of three people, in two separate incidents, in the sixties.

Further on-line searches failed to reveal where Liam was now, although I did find evidence of why he had served the full term. The other murder victim of Liam Calnan was a police officer. My knowledge of the Harry Roberts case reminded me that cop killers are rarely granted parole.

~~~~~

The A414 is a long, winding road that runs just north of the M25. It made a more interesting journey than the motorway. At Chelmsford, I took a two-lane country B road that eventually arrived at a desolate section of the Essex coast. An even smaller road led me directly to Sanderlings Open Prison, a windswept but totally unguarded building. No perimeter fencing, just a wall that barely reached head height. There was nothing to stop the inhabitants leaving this place, other than the loss of their privileges and conditional liberty. The Victorian building overlooked a less than docile North Sea. It was cold and the receding tide had left a blanket of marshland that formed an unattractive coastline. It was eagerly inhabited by Redshanks, Oystercatchers and the Sanderlings that the prison was named after. Closer to the white-painted walls of the prison, Brent Geese and Swans fought other lesser birds for the food left by the ebbing waters.

I should have telephoned but thought a personal visit might produce quicker results. It didn't. It was not the policy of the prison service to give information on the whereabouts of former inmates, Governor Stimpson advised me before despatching me from his office. My search for Liam had met a premature and unsuccessful end at the hands of belligerent authority. My trip appeared to be a futile one. How would I explain my wasted day to Ludo? And if the local recycling depot had closed, how would I explain the need for a further night's stay at mother's house? I was beginning to think I should have brought Ludo with me. Her determination and resourceful character would not have baulked at the first obstacle.

As I drove disappointedly through the open gates of the prison I remembered passing a pub at the junction where I turned off towards the prison. I was feeling hungry and it represented an oasis and an opportunity to think about my next step.

The special of the day was a less than spicy curry with rice. I allowed myself one pint of cold lager to take the taste of the curry away. A middle-aged couple sat at a table discussing their morning bird-watching excursion. Two men were standing at the bar talking and it became apparent to me that they were prison officers. I then noticed the Prison Service emblem on a holdall at the foot of the bar stool that the men stood next to. One of the two men finished his pint of beer, said his goodbyes to his colleague and the barman and left. The other man remained to finish his drink and was engaged in a spasmodic conversation with the owner about the daily delivery of bird shit on his car when parked at the prison. He spoke loudly enough to offend the two birdwatchers. It was an opportunity I could not resist. The weather was sufficient to engage him in conversation when I went to the bar to refresh my glass, but I needed to get to the point quickly as he didn't look like he was planning to stay too long. I had no intention of drinking the second glass and when he refused my offer to fill his empty glass I thought my opportunity had been lost.

"I've just been to see your boss," I declared boldly in desperation of starting a conversation.

"Have you?" he replied in an uninterested tone as he went to pick up his holdall.

"Yes, Governor Stimpson and I have been discussing a project I'm working on." I offered my hand, which he shook reluctantly but vigorously

"I'm Jonathan Willshire. I work for the City Gate Centre, an exhibition hall in London. We're planning to exhibit works of art by convicted criminals later this year."

"Oh, I suppose old man Stimpson was singing the praises of young Vincent Prendergast was he?"

"Yes" I replied less than convincingly, "and Calnan, Liam Calnan."

"Liam Calnan?" he asked disbelievingly. "He may have painted the walls of some prison canteens in his time, but they were hardly works of art. Are you sure?"

"Oh yes" I said more confidently, thinking I had at least stopped him leaving.

"It was quite a few years ago but he was pretty good. In fact I'm going to see him next week at...." I fumbled in my pockets in an imaginary search for a non-existent piece of paper.

"The Maidment Centre" he intervened. "That's where most lifers go when leaving here."

I nodded knowingly. "Yes, yes, that's it. The Maidment."

"Well good luck" he added as he left, shaking his head and mumbling 'Liam Calnan, who'd have believed it?'

After waiting long enough for him to leave the car park

and leaving a full pint of lager for the barman to puzzle over, I left too. Once in my car, I logged on to my laptop and searched the web for the Maidment Centre. Fortunately, it was only about twenty miles back inland. However, my hopes of finding Liam Calnan were, once again, dashed. Unfortunately, he was not at the Maidment Centre and I was beginning to believe that if he had been this evasive forty years ago, he might have avoided a long stretch in prison. But, as luck would have it, the receptionist was more forthcoming than the Prison Governor and, once I had convinced her that Calnan was a relative, she managed to give me the next clue in this strange adaptation of the egg hunt that mother used to organise each Easter. Mr. Calnan, she explained, had received an admission medical and was found to be unsuitable for a regular day care centre. He had been moved to a specialist unit for the aged and infirmed, which cared for those with dementia.

"Dementia?" I questioned. She frowned and I tried not to look worried that she had uncovered my deceit. I failed.

"I haven't seen him for a long time," I explained as she began to doubt the authenticity of my story. "I visited him in Sanderlings last year though," I added in an attempt to convince her of my relationship with him. She looked less than convinced.

"Dementia you say," I continued unnecessarily but with pathos.

"Dementia, Parkinson's, Alzheimer's something like that" she added with ill concealed indifference, as she finally dismissed any untoward doubts about the motive for my visit.

You wouldn't be so vague if you had to care for someone with Alzheimer's I was thinking to myself. Anyway why is she so vague about such complicated diseases? Most hospital or surgery receptionists I have met consider themselves intimate with such medical terms. This one didn't seem interested.

She finally agreed to give me the address of the Imperial Nursing Home. I drove directly there, a journey of some ten miles back towards home. It was late afternoon but the rush hour traffic had not started.

It was perhaps the first really warm afternoon since the day mother died, when I sat in her garden, waiting for Ludo to arrive. This day was windier but the bright sunshine signalled the beginning of March as the countryside began showing the first evidence of a new spring. I parked the car in the visitors' car park and walked across the gravel drive towards an imposing building, raised above ground level and accessible by some rather elegant and wide steps. The front of the building overlooked a large ornamental pond that contained signs of the new life that Spring would bring. The immense clumps of frogspawn indicated that no fish had survived the winter, if indeed it had contained any before the winter, otherwise the offspring of the would-be princes would have provided a banquet for them.

Enjoying the unusually warm day, I left the car and walked slowly around the outside of the area containing the stagnant pond. The Pussy Willow was in flower, attracting some Comma butterflies and a small swarm of bees at the beginning of their service to a long and hopefully warm summer. The Catkins were already turning a dark shade of green.

The unnatural heat inside the building contrasted with the fresh mildly warm air outside.

A young nurse who had little to say led me through the building. As I entered a sparsely furnished room, there sat a man old beyond his years, clawing at his ragged hair and grinding his teeth in the silence. Liam sat with his back to me, agitated, silently bobbing and weaving like a punch-drunk boxer, barking mumbled instructions.

"Who knows? Who knows?"

I walked over to the window and turned to face him. He looked somehow, strangely familiar, but I thought I must have been imagining that. Perhaps he did look like me, or I like him. He continued to look at the floor, bobbing and weaving like an ageing boxer but without leaving his seat.

"Who knows?" he repeated. He was speaking loudly but not sufficiently loud to disturb anyone outside the otherwise empty room. After a few minutes he looked up. His translucent eyes were glazed over, like someone subdued by drugs. I may have imagined all this but, in spite of a face made expressionless by a combination of age and medication, there was a strange look of recognition in his eyes. He fell silent for a moment as if he was waiting for something, waiting for an opportunity to speak. He seemed to me like a soldier waiting for permission to speak. As if he was constrained from speaking. It was almost as if he was counting to ten before speaking. I remained silent. His condition suggested that questions would be a waste of time. The nurse had left the room and I just stood there quietly whilst Liam composed himself and prepared to speak. I pulled up a chair and sat next to him, looking directly into his glazed eyes.

53

"Jack" he said and the word came like an electric shock, although it was directed into space rather than at me. And then he returned to the bobbing and weaving of a shadow boxer.

"Be first Jack, be first," he added as he continued to bob and weave, ducking under imaginary punches from an invisible opponent. He stopped and, almost as if he had time to consider matters further, he looked back into my face. It was less a look of recognition than one of questioning.

It should be possible to learn a considerable amount about someone from the scars they carry, both the visible and the invisible ones. Liam had several scars over his eyes. The result, it would seem, of a less than successful boxing career.

"Be first Jack, be first" he called louder, causing the nurse to return.

"Who's Jack? Was he a boxer?" I asked the nurse.

"I don't know, I'm new here."

There was an unmistakable look of recognition each time he stared at my face.

"Jack?" he asked pleadingly. "Jack?"

"Yes, Liam it is Jack," I said speaking directly to him, but without leaving my seat by his side. The nurse looked confused. I wondered how he could possibly have known me. This was the Liam in the letter, of that I was for sure. He began to cry.

"Jack. I'm sorry. God I'm so sorry."

The nurse temporarily stopped her chores and looked over her shoulder at me.

"He doesn't make any sense at all I'm afraid. He's been like that since he arrived. But at least he recognises you."

She paused as if she was trying to remember something.

"Who did you say you are?" she asked.

I mumbled a subconscious reply 'I don't know'.

"What?" she said.

"My name is Jack. Jack Daly," I said and handed her a business card. She showed only slight interest, even though an otherwise psychologically damaged man had spoken just that name a few moments ago.

"He talks about you all the time. He's obviously very fond of you."

"I don't think so."

"How can you be sure?" she responded, suddenly becoming a little more interested. You are a relative aren't you?"

"I'm not sure," I whispered.

She went to intervene but Liam suddenly began swaying again.

"Be first Jack," he mumbled burying his chin in his chest and swivelling his shoulders forwards and backwards. He went silent for a few minutes. We sat there, the still, warm air in the room disturbed only by the nurse busying herself and the muscle spasms that produced involuntary movements from Liam's limbs.

A chain of unconnected words trickles, with the saliva, from his mouth. Then, suddenly, he began to speak louder again.

"Raining. Rain. Truly sorry." Each word or phrase kept apart by a moment's thought of the patient if, indeed, he was capable of reasoned thought. Then suddenly he smiled and his eyes brightened.

"England. England Jack", he looked at me, or rather

through me. At the word 'Jack' there was a glimmer of recognition, just as there had been when he first looked on my face. Then he began mumbling again: "Garden, Jack. Mustn't be seen. Powlees." He jumped slightly out of the chair and slumped back into it. "The Powlees, Jack. He's called the Garda." I had to strain to understand the words. He retained a distinct Irish accent, which betrayed his birthplace.

He closed his eyes and sat there quietly, not sleeping but not moving either. I spoke to the nurse but was interrupted by him singing quietly.

"Nick, knack, paddy whack, give a dog a bone," he sang gently, almost in a whisper.

"No Irish, no dogs. I'm hungry Jack. No food. One apple since two days gone."

He looked through me again. Then directly into my eyes, almost in disbelief, as if he knew me but didn't recognise me.

"Garden, Circus" he laughed uncontrollably, before shrinking into a ball whilst still sitting on the wooden chair.

"Don't hit me. Don't hit me. Jack, Jack," he called louder.

He moved his right hand from his lap and touched my sleeve, prodding it, as one might prod a dead body to check for life. Then looking directly at me again, he showed definite signs of recognition.

"Jack. Jack. You can look after yerself Jack." He paused again then suddenly shouted, irrationally: "Seconds out. " He looked directly at me again and repeated a common part of his diatribe. "Who knows? Who knows?" he repeated almost deliriously.

He went quiet again but stayed awake, looking directly in front of him, giving me time to examine his features. There were certain elements that convinced me that he was my father. I had always wondered why I was not like my dad. Now the answer was literally staring me in the face. Liam was my father. Look at the shape of the face, the nose, and the eyes.

"Me Jack me," he began again, adding to the determination of my thoughts. "Seconds out. Be first Jack. Be first. Feign, feign, jab, jab."

He went quiet for a minute and I rose to see if I could find the nurse again. She had left to continue her work along the corridor. Liam started to laugh as I left the room and I paused, stood in the doorway and tried to make some sense out of his ramblings. At the same time that I was convincing myself that Liam was my father, I was becoming just as convinced that I wasn't the 'Jack' of Liam's ramblings. It didn't make sense. Whoever Jack was, he seemed to be a boxer. I racked my memory to see if my father had ever spoken about a Jack. He loved boxing, so there was certainly a connection between Liam and my father. Jack Dempsey was once the heavyweight champion of the world. That was the only link I could make. However, that didn't seem to make any sense whatsoever.

"Nora" Liam cried out, "Gabby. No not Gabby, not Gabby." He laughed hysterically again.

I began to reach premature conclusions. Liam and my father, or the person I thought was my father, were friends. Liam betrayed his friend by trying to steal his girlfriend. Well, not so much tried to steal his girlfriend but did betray him, as my mother seems to have done, by having sex. I was the product of that union. It is easy to imagine how things might develop from there. What was apparent was that my mother stayed faithful to Bill. She and Liam were strong and decided to leave things as they were, in spite of the pending arrival of me. What wasn't clear was what drove the rejected Liam to commit murder. Two East End gangsters and a police officer all murdered by someone very close to my otherwise dull mother. Liam did not look particularly dangerous now but he must have been in his youth. None of this contributed to my investigation and I thought about leaving.

"Mr. Levy. Mr Levy. Sorry. Sorry. I'm so sorry. 'Sprechen Sie Deutsch? Sprechen Sie Deutsch?'" he suddenly added in very poor German.

A few seconds elapsed and he turned slightly away from me on the chair and began singing a song that I vaguely recognised. *Big girls don't cry*. I remembered my mother playing it. It was sung by Frankie Valli and the Four Seasons. I patted him on the arm and he appeared startled, as if a ghost had touched him. But he just kept singing that same line over and over again.

"Big girls don't cry. Big girls don't cry." After a few minutes, he stopped and remained calm again.

The heat in the building was becoming unbearable. Quite how the nurses put up with the heat and the relentless ramblings of the patients was beyond me.

"Nora, Nora," Liam said as he continued his mutterings. "Mary, Mary. Where's Jack. Wait, wait. Find him find him. Feelings Mary, feelings."

The nurse obviously felt comfortable leaving Liam in my care whilst she continued with the rest of her duties. I removed a notebook from my jacket and began writing down Liam's words. I thought, more in hope than expectation, that I might be able to make sense of them later. It was a simple task because he seemed to be on a loop, continually repeating certain elements of his repeated message. The names, Mary, Jack, Nora, Gabby, Mr. Levy, but strangely not Bill. The repeated words like 'be first', 'garden' and 'circus'. Garden and circus seemed to be places. Some garbled words could only make sense in a single context, like 'seconds out'. The movement of his body confirmed that he was obviously present, in his mind, at a boxing match. Then there were the songs like 'Nick, knack paddy whack' and 'Big Girls don't cry'.

He began to get very tired. His voice became weaker, quieter. He called quietly, but violently, at someone called Terry, and the last words he spoke before falling asleep were "Face fears, face fears."

He had the marks of a boxer; therefore, he must be a boxer. Perhaps he boxed in prison, although these memories seemed to be before that time. If they weren't, Jack could be someone he met in prison.

Then, just as he was drifting into a deeper sleep, his body shook in a spasm.

"Who knows?" he cried louder than before. Not me I thought.

I looked again for similarities between Liam and myself and remembered the incident in the store. Was it something in my genes that produced that spontaneous response? I wasn't normally violent. And I wouldn't call myself a violent man. It was not premeditated, nor was it a conscious decision. It seemed that something so deep in my being that it cannot be identified caused my reaction. Liam was a boxer, or, at least all the evidence suggested it. Surely that cannot be genetic. Punching someone isn't genetic. But aggression is, I suppose. He recognised me. He called me by my name. How can that be? How could he recognise me now?

My mind went over and over the facts. The letters; the secret that my mother and Liam had to bury deep in their hearts; Liam's features; the aggression gene. I shook my head and thought, 'who knows?'

Most of the time, Liam had been incoherent and unintelligible but sometimes, particularly when he looked directly at me, he became lucid, as if he had recognised me. There was a look of childlike horror in his eyes. Was I mistaken? He clearly recognised me, but how could he? That wouldn't make any sense at all, unless he had seen a recent photograph of me.

I was still writing down as many of his words that I could remember when the nurse returned to the room.

"What are you doing?" she asked curtly. "You're not a reporter are you? You told me you were a relative. Who are you?"

I tried to explain who I was and what I was doing there but this only served to reinforce her opinion that I was an impostor. It didn't make any sense to me so how must it sound to her? I was ushered from the building unceremoniously by the young woman, who opened the main door to the building and stood in silence. Her missing goodbye was a deliberate omission to reinforce her disappointment at my behaviour.

The fresh air came as a welcome relief to the unnatural

heat inside the building. And, as I walked to my car, the day had awoke to the sound of a new season. A woodpecker could be heard thumping away at a nearby tree, whilst magpies and blue tits fluttered on the edge of a nearby wood and chaffinches chased each other through the branches of a hedge. I paused for a moment and bathed in the freshness of Spring.

As I drove through the country lanes back towards home, I kept thinking about Liam. Could he be my father?

A Friesian calf stood close to its mother in a field by the side of the road. It was identical in every respect other than size. Liam's features seemed to remind me of myself in so many ways. His aggression and my sudden bout of spontaneous violence in the store seemed to me to be born of the same genetic material.

I telephoned Ludo before leaving the Imperial Nursing Home. I just wanted to hear a familiar and friendly voice and I was hoping she would ask me to return home after my brief return to the house of my childhood. I didn't relish the thought of spending another night alone in mother's house. Ludo did, indeed, ask when I was coming home and I agreed to do so after collecting some items from mother's house.

~~~~~

Ludo and I live in the village of Beadsman's Cross, which has a population of about one hundred people if you included the local farmland that surrounds it. Some of the

61

local families had lived in the village for generations, just as they had done where mother lived. But not the Daly family. I knew my parents moved to the area from East London in the sixties but that was a recent history compared with some of the locals. Some of mother's friends still referred to her as the Londoner or the Cockney woman. My family history went back a relatively short time.

Ludo worked in Loch Fyne, a fish restaurant, in Evestown, which was about eight miles away. She had originally been employed at an Italian restaurant called Ristorante Darsene, which was situated near the marina just outside Evestown. But her constant criticism of their sensitive Sardinian chef meant that one of them had to leave, and it wasn't going to be Giovanni. I had learned from my frequent visits to Italy that the parochial nature of Italian cuisine provides a source of eternal disagreement in that country. Unless, by some unalterable event of providence, or decree of heaven, dependent on your religious persuasion, Ludo and Giovanni shared the same mother, the chances of a Sardinian and a Roman agreeing on how a simple seafood risotto should be cooked are only slightly better than Osama Bin Laden sharing a political platform with President Obama.

I drove directly from my visit to Liam to my mother's house. There were still some items to be tidied up but my real reason was a selfish one. I just wanted to feel close to mother and seeing her body in the undertakers didn't do it for me. I made myself a cup of tea and rummaged through some of the paperwork in the shoebox before gathering the contents together to put in the car. The doorbell rang and I was surprised to find Tonka Thompson at the door.

"Sorry to hear about your mum Jack" he said sincerely.

"Where have you been?" I asked, ignoring his statutory condolences.

"ETD" came the acronymic reply that I was supposed to understand.

"Erm. Extra Terrestrial Dignitaries?" I guessed jokingly, but he didn't seem to be in the mood for jokes.

"Extended tour of duty," came a rather tired response.

"Anywhere nice?"

"Six months training in a friendly African state followed by six days work in one of the other kind."

"Where's that then?" I asked as we both walked into the kitchen and he threw his backpack in the corner of the untidy room.

"Somalia" he said rather dejectedly, but managed to continue. "Voted by the lads as the shittiest place in the world and, believe me Jack, we've been to some shitty places. Not a Michelin star restaurant to be found."

I turned round and leaned against the sink as we waited for the kettle to boil.

"The locals were nice though," he added a little more jollily. Kept leaving us little presents."

"Really?" I asked stupidly.

"IEDs mainly," he quipped.

"Oh, no" I said flippantly. "Now I know that one." "Improvised explosive device."

Tonka sank his heavy six-foot frame into a chair. He looked completely shattered.

"So they're not nice people then Tonka?" I asked.

"Christ, Jack, just telling the lions from the Christians is an achievement. Which is a good thing actually, because you can go to sleep at night convincing yourself that you haven't actually killed any Christians today." There was emotion and anger in his voice and he was struggling to keep the lid on both of them.

"You can kip down here if you like," I offered. He looked keen but explained that he was on extended leave.

"It's not being used Tonka, so you may as well stay here. I don't even know what I'm going to do with it yet. Sell it I suppose but I'm not really in any hurry, so just bed down here for as long as you like."

We sat and drank our tea. It was great to have my oldest and most durable and resourceful friend back. And it was good to be there for him for a change. We both enjoyed school days together but Tonka wanted that institutionalised regime to continue in his life. I went off to Fleet Street, he joined the army, and we lost contact. That was until about five years ago when he appeared back in my life just at the right time. I didn't even know I needed help but, somehow, he did. And there he was, arriving just in time, like the Fifth Cavalry. And here he was again, standing on my mother's doorstep as if he had simply called round to accompany me to school. The short trousers were gone but the look in his eye was unmistakable: *I'm here. What do you want me to do?*

I was suddenly transformed to a time, long ago. A moment in time, when I was eight years old and my father had just died. Tonka arrived at my house, just as he had done today. There were no statutory condolences that day. He wasn't old enough to understand the formalities of adulthood. He said nothing and did nothing but he was there, because that is where he thought he should be. Other friends avoided me, not knowing what to say. But not

64

Tonka. I suppose that is why he joined the Army and then transferred to the SAS. He always wanted to be where the problem was. Right up close, looking in its eyes. He could never just stand by. He could never remain detached from a situation. He felt vulnerable by not having direct involvement in a problem. He was much more comfortable walking alongside danger, in the daylight, rather than having it lurking, unseen, somewhere in the shadows.

Tonka was obviously covered by the Official Secrets Act but it never seemed to constrain his conversations. He was certainly less concerned with breaching the Official Secrets Act than prejudicing the safety of his colleagues in the field.

There were details of missions he could never speak of and he never mentioned his colleagues' names. He was more interested in my mundane life than his exploits in the war zones of the world. Perhaps that brought him back to normal life. But he was always more interested in other people than he was in himself. That is probably why he was so good at his job.

"Anyway," he suddenly said, "a little bird told me that you and Ludo had split up. That doesn't sound right mate."

"It's not right Tonka. Well not completely. She wanted a little space for a while but that's over now."

"So you're back together then?"

"Well, we would be but this cropped up. You know, mum dying. I was intending to be back home tonight."

We spoke about my mother for an hour and while I was washing up, he fell asleep in the chair. I left him there and took some rubbish to the recycling depot before it closed. I telephoned Ludo to let her know I would be staying overnight at my mother's house again. She sounded disappointed but when I explained that Tonka had turned up and appeared to need a friend, she offered no objections. It was understood that the temporary disconnection was over and we would be back together tomorrow night.

That evening, without mentioning names of people or places, Tonka told me something of the mission. He and five colleagues were dropped into a remote area of Somalia to infiltrate an Al Qaeda training camp.

"And kill them all I suppose?" I said too knowingly.

"No Jack, this was a bloodless mission. This camp held the names of a terrorist sleeper cell in the UK. We needed to go in, get those names and details of the planned attacks, and get out without anyone knowing we had been there."

They had succeeded and the operation provided key intelligence about terrorists working in mainland Europe and in the UK. Four UK-based terror cells had been identified, disrupted or destroyed. Simply killing the suicide bombers was not enough. Identifying those spread out across a network of terrorist support units was more important.

"So what about the terrorists in Somalia? In the camp you raided?"

"They were taken out by an air raid a couple of weeks later," Tonka explained.

"Much safer" I said, "than having to send you guys in."

"Oh," he said, "our job isn't over at that stage, another team of covert SAS guys go back into the camp after the air raid to identify the dead."

"What on earth for?" I queried.

"Oh, don't worry" he said. "They take DNA samples and report straight back to a US aircraft carrier off the coast. A team there identifies the samples against the US and UK terrorist records, to see who has been taken out. Essential work Jack."

The rest of the evening was taken up with reminiscing about our childhood. In the morning, Tonka stayed on at my mother's house and I returned to Ludo.

~~~~~

Titus's offer that I should extend my few days' break was only made on the basis that I had already submitted my column for the next two weeks anyway. I relished the chance of making the most of my extended period of absence from Ludo. After all, absence makes the heart grow fonder and the testosterone flow stronger as Willshire once told me.

I worked at home that day whilst Ludo did her shift at Loch Fyne. I needed to prepare my article on the Foreign Secretary for the Peace Conference issue of *The Main Event* in five weeks time.

The President of the USA intended to apologise for the injustices of slavery, which was, in itself, an incredible development. The US had waited hundreds of years for their first black President and, once he was in office, he found himself apologising for slavery. What next? Obama apologising for the atrocities of the Klu Klux Klan?

The Peace Conference would open with a message of regret from the Pope about the Catholic Church's failure to condemn the holocaust. Most of the second morning had been allotted to the German Chancellor. But all this paled in comparison with the UK, who would be responsible for the whole of the third day. Even then it was expected that the British Foreign Secretary would probably make everyone late for the Dinner of Reconciliation. He not only intended to provide an apology on slavery and go on to express his regret for the Imperialistic fervour of Victorian and pre-Victorian Britain. But, later, he would be joined by the current Dukes of Marlborough and Wellington to apologise for a catalogue of destruction by British Forces over the centuries. The Boer War, Zulu War, Crimean War, Sikh Wars, Afghan Wars, American Revolutionary War, the Wars of Austrian Succession, the Wars of Spanish Succession and finally the Seven Years War and the Hundred Years War. The last two emphasised Britain's love of a long drawn-out fight, particularly as the Prime Minister of Israel followed immediately after the UK to apologise for the four-day war. Much more cost effective.

The French would dispense with their apologies rather swiftly, covering off the Napoleonic wars and the Norman Conquest. And the Italians could fit theirs in between the dessert and coffee over dinner, with an act of contrition for the monumental activities of the Roman Empire.

Richard would insist on a far more sombre preview of the Conference being featured in *The Main Event* than my comic assessment. He would also insist that my interview with the Foreign Secretary grasped the gravity of the formalities too. I found that a great challenge, particularly as the killing continued in several parts of the world, as Tonka could testify.

Ludo and I were only to have a few days alone together

before her family arrived from Italy for the funeral. We made the most of our time trying to successfully produce a baby. I began to wonder why I had resisted for so long. But a long weekend of repeated, noisy, sex had to stop for the arrival of the remaining members of the Vittuci family.

According to Ludo, Sebastiano intended to speak only English when they visited the UK. Apparently, he was goaded into this by Gigi, who reminded him of his belligerent views on non-Italian speaking visitors to his beloved Rome. So the two made a pact to speak English and Sebstiano's preparation for this was a telephone conversation with his sister, in English, every evening. It proved to be the highlight of my week.

When Sebastiano, Gigi and Ludo's mother arrived the following Wednesday, I misguidedly decided to take them to Ristorante Darsene. I hadn't been aware that Ludo had shared her disagreement with the restaurant's chef with her brother but that became clear over the first course. As I had learned to my cost in the past, Sebastiano held conservative and parochial views on Italian cuisine, so the idea of taking him to a Sardinian restaurant was flawed. At least the food in a Chinese restaurant would have been completely alien to him and, by definition, beyond comparison. He continually glanced at Gigi, desperately wanting to revert to his native tongue to tell the Sardinians what he really thought of their attempt at Italian cuisine.

"A carrot in a dish of vegetable antipasti," he said as he struggled to fulfil his commitment to speak English throughout his visit. "How long have you been in Engaland?" he said adding an extra 'a' to the middle of the final word. After the waiter had walked away in disgust,

Sebastiano turned to me.

"You can no go compare Sardinian cookery with Roman. What a plonker."

I had resigned myself to the fact that Ludo's use of the English language had been significantly influenced by her infatuation for British television, particularly the advertisements, which presented an opportunity to learn English in small, easily digested, portions, and her injudicious love for repeats of *Only Fools and Horses.* Now, it seemed, she had corrupted her brother's interpretation of the English language too.

I had got used to an affirmation like 'Oh Yes' being delivered with the assured intonation of a puppet dog made to resemble Winston Churchill. However, it was extremely unnerving and took on a completely different connotation when spoken by a still nubile and husky voiced Italian woman, who could never simply say 'yes' but insisted, for some bizarre reason, on 'oh yes'. Rather than a gruff Churchillian tone, it was unmistakably Latin, delivered with what the Italians called 'La Passione' and with all the nuance of a mutually successful sexual climax. This was fine, and quite attractive, when we were on our own but, when delivered in a public place, 'oh yes' often attracted similar responses to the famous *When Harry met Sally* scene. In restaurants, it was invariably followed by a stifled 'I'll have whatever she's having' from an adjacent table. If Ludo could do this with an insurance advertisement, I was simply grateful that Cadburys didn't run their *Flake* advert anymore.

In addition, I now had to contend with Sebastiano's similar interpretation of the English language.

Throughout the meal, other words were constantly preceded or followed by a constant companion word. Nothing was ever compared with anything else but was always 'go-compared.'

Occasionally, Sebastiano would forget to speak in English and, much to his annoyance, was sharply rebuked and reminded of his commitment by Gigi. We eventually left the restaurant to the strains of Sebastiano telling Giovanni where he could put his meatballs.

"Sardinians are not Italian", Sebastiano assured me as we got into the taxi. They are more French than Italian."

The following day the funeral cars arrived at the house. Tonka, Sebastiano, Gigi, and Ludo's mother had all gathered at the house and were joined by several of mother's friends. The Yoda look-a-like Mrs. Joiner and mother's friends from church Mrs. Griffiths, in her big black number, and her friend Ivy O'Brien, or the widows Twanky, as I called them. Then there was Old Tom Anderson, he of the new hip and Mr Greaves, who spent most of his time like a banished soul smoking outside in the garden. Mr and Mrs Jackson, who lived even closer to mother than Mrs. Joiner arrived after everyone else. We drove to the church in a cortege and were met at the door by Father McNally, who had been very helpful in selecting mother's favourite hymns for the service. Tonka gave a reading from St. Paul and I managed to say a few words about a dedicated and beloved mother.

Conscious of the fact that we had numerous men with bladders weakened by age and infirmity, we paused for some time after the service before proceeding to the cemetery. God was generous with the weather, as Mrs. Griffiths pointed out. It was a dry but cool day, which was more like spring than winter.

Not everyone accompanied us to the Horse and Hounds pub after the burial but there were enough of us to enjoy a prolonged spell of reminiscing. Unfortunately, nobody seemed to remember anyone called Liam. Mother had never mentioned him, nor had she spoken of Nora, Gabby or another person called Jack. Nobody could recall that she was particularly fond of Frankie Valli and the Four Seasons, although several remembered singing 'nick, knack, paddy whack' at school. But as mother had not attended school with any of them, this was hardly relevant. Ivy O'Brien had a vague recollection that one of the Carmichael children was called Liam. Once it was made clear to everyone who the Carmichael children were, and it turned out they were members of a large Irish family who sat in the front pew at church each Sunday, the churchgoers in the pub set about recalling their names. I was reminded of many Friday nights in the pub with Tonka trying to recall the names of the Seven Dwarves or the Magnificent Seven. Incredibly, the Carmichael children consisted of a sleepy one and a dopey one and it was generally agreed that there was one called Liam. Contrary to Mr. Anderson's strongly held opinion, Steve McQueen's character in the Magnificent Seven was not called Liam. Ludo searched the Internet on her mobile telephone and confirmed that it was 'Vin'.

"Vin what?" bellowed Sebastiano, "Vin rouge or vin blanc." He said laughing into his twelfth Peroni.

"No" clarified an expressionless Gigi, "Vin, as in Vincenzo."

I tried to call a halt to the proceedings at several points through the noisy discussion but to no avail. They were all a little disappointed when I told them that their contribution had been of no use to my enquiries. Ludo told me she thought this comment had been a little uncharitable.

"Who is this Liam chap then?" asked an inquisitive Mr. Anderson.

"Oh" I answered, "some distant relative I believe Mr. Anderson."

"Tom," he said.

"No, Liam" I replied.

"No, please call me Tom" he corrected me.

"Oh right. Tom. Yes a distant relative, or perhaps just a friend I think, but I'm not even sure if he was connected to mum or Bill."

"Bill?"

"Sorry," I corrected myself, "mum or dad."

Tom looked puzzled and returned to a previous conversation with Mrs. Joiner. Believing I was out of earshot, which was unlikely as he was deaf and spoke with all the delicacy of a foghorn, he told her that he thought I was still in shock at the loss of my mother.

Around four o'clock some of the older ones began leaving the pub but I felt I should wait until everyone had gone before suggesting to Ludo that we leave ourselves.

Just as Gigi left to get our coats before leaving, my mobile phone rang. The tune was a little too jolly for a funeral gathering but then one doesn't normally download something more sombre whilst in mourning.

"Hi, I'm Elana Balcescu. You don't know me."

She was right, I didn't.

3

Ω

Liam's story

Hoon knows. Hoon knows it wasn't me. Hoon knows.

An impatient, but rainless thunderstorm rumbles loudly in the distance, occupying the space in my mind that I need to clear. I need to clear it in order to think. I need to think in order to remember.

Hoon knows. I remember that much.

I long for silence, that crisp, snow-laden, virgin field of silence that was solitary confinement. That steadfast companion of peace, that sheltered me from the on-coming storm. That unwavering silence that protects me from the incessant noise that is prison life. The incessant noise that prevents me from remembering. The distant storm rumbles threateningly like an ominous stranger furtively waiting in the shadows of my mind.

Perhaps, if I try to think of a time before it all began, a time when life was simple. A time from my childhood, in Ballycraich, when I was accompanied by the lost grace of contentment. If I can just picture myself in that small village, alone, with no noise, no thundering human verbal traffic, no incessant voices.

I shall return to the streets of my childhood to try to find that peace. A peace that will enable me to think through the events of those distant days so that I may understand what happened yesterday. The end of childhood or at least the beginning of the end of childhood. I need to piece together the evidence about what happened to Jack. Only then can I try to understand how it is possible for him to still be alive. And, if he isn't alive, if that wasn't really him, to understand what is happening to my mind. I saw him and it looked like him. I touched his arm and it felt real. But if I no longer understand what is real, perhaps, I simply dreamt it. How can Jack still be alive, unchanged by time? All flesh is perishable, even Jack cannot escape the inevitability of death or the ravages of age.

Perhaps I can ask Gabriella when she next visits. She will know whether Jack is really alive. She will make sense of it for me. I can explain everything to her. I can explain about Mary being raped by Michael. She will understand. She was raped too, she told me. She was raped by Serbs or border guards. She will understand why Mary is like she is. She will understand why Jack had to act like he did. Once she understands what happened she can tell me whether it is possible for Jack to still be alive.

Twas Himself I saw yesterday, or was it a few days ago, or maybe weeks. It doesn't make sense. I did not speak directly to him for fear he would dissolve. In case he was a mirage that would disappear if I acknowledged it. But I touched him and you cannot touch a mirage. If only I could remember what led up to his disappearance. I must go back to the beginning, back to Ballycraich.

~~~~~

It is a summer's day, warm and compliant, as I am now, subdued by a rainstorm that has since withdrawn to some distant place beyond the horizon. Thundering ominously, distantly, threateningly, but gone. It is peaceful, but it is not Ballycraich. It is not even Ireland. I have passed beyond the shores of my homeland, just as the rainstorm has done. For a moment, my mind is at peace. I treasure the moment, consciously deciding not to think, in case the silence ends. In case my peace is fractured by thought.

The storm has passed now and my thoughts settle on something of my own device for the first time in so long. I decide to stay there, to stay within that solitary moment in time. I mustn't endanger the moment with a return to conscious thought. The story must start from wherever I am at this moment in my past. Perhaps then I can understand how Jack can have returned. Perhaps I can determine whether it was simply a dream or whether Jack is really alive and I murdered two people for nothing. Not innocent people perhaps, but not guilty of killing my brother.

All those years of intransigent belligerence. Never able to say I was sorry. But, if he is alive, then I would truly be sorry for my actions and I might then meet my maker in peace.

And so, the rain has stopped, the thunderstorm silenced and I return to a moment in time, a moment in my past, a moment where life began and life ended.

The money that the Mammy gave us lasted only as far as Fishguard. The ferry tickets and a bowl of soup at the dockside accounted for all but a few pennies. For my sake, Jack remained cheerful throughout the crossing, although I was sick for the greater part of it. It was just as well that we didn't eat before we left Rosslare because the precious food would have been bequeathed to the waves for sure. Watching two weatherworn old Irishmen drinking Guinness before dawn did little to appease my rolling stomach. Apart from a fishing trip on Uncle Timmy's boat down at Kinsale, I knew nothing of the sea. I'd always wondered why we should sing for those in peril on the sea at Mass on Sunday, but now I understood.

"Are you OK Liam?" asked Himself as I gorged on my vegetable broth. I smiled and nodded. Twas only once I had a full belly that the sense of adventure seized me. I had rarely left Ballycraich and only twice visited Cork, but now here I was, supping soup with my big brother and not knowing what God or foul fortune held for us.

"Have ya got nutting to say for yerself?" he asked me.

I thought and shook my head. My fifteen years had taught me to keep my own counsel in our household. You wouldn't want to be upsetting my Pa with a quenched thirst on him.

"England, Jack" I said excitedly after contemplating the risk of talking for a few moments. "England."

"We're in Wales actually Liam, but I don't expect you would know the difference."

"We haven't gotta make anudder of those sea crossings have we now Jack?"

"No, you're safe on dry land now Liam," came the

consoling reply.

It was early afternoon as we left the small café on the dockside at Fishguard. The streets had been left wet by the same rain that had lashed the ferry on our crossing. But the rain had passed and the sun was breaking through causing dry patches to appear on the rude kerbstones at our feet. A stout man with a beard was leaving the café at the same time and asked Jack where we were headed.

He shrugged and said "London, I suppose."

"Then you're in luck" he replied. "I have fifteen tons of veg to deliver to the Garden. There'll be no pay for helping me unload but I'll get yers to London." He spat in the palm of his offered hand and Jack took it with his.

"John" said my brother in introduction.

"Aye" said the bearded man, so Jack didn't bother to introduce me.

Eight hours of rattling around in the noisy cabin of the lorry and a sign informed us that London was another 52 miles. The driver told us that he had to reach the Garden by five a.m. or he'd have to wait a further 24 hours to sell his wares. He assured us we'd make it but there was no time to stop, other than to relieve ourselves at the roadside.

Two more hours passed slowly by and, as the sun rose on the distant horizon, we drove into the heart of a great metropolis that took my breath away by its size. Even Cork had a beginning and an end but London appeared to have neither.

"Welcome to the Garden" the bearded driver said as I woke up from a disturbed and restless sleep. It was about four o'clock in the morning, although it didn't seem like morning and it wasn't like any garden I had ever seen. The streets were filling up with people and lorries. The driver showed me how to undo the knots on the ropes that held the load under the tarpaulin and he and Jack then folded the heavy sheets.

As daylight came up men started to arrive with wheelbarrows and the driver traded his wares. As dawn arrived slowly over the top of the warehouses full of fruit and vegetables, the streets filled with more people than I had ever seen in one place. Jack and I loaded up box after box of cabbages, carrots and the like, and sack after sack of potatoes. And the men hurried them away to their warehouses. Shortly after six the back of the lorry was nearly empty.

Once the remains of the load, which consisted of broken boxes and torn sacks, were sold off to the scavenging bargain hunters, the driver insisted on buying us our breakfasts. We'd not eaten since the bowl of soup in Fishguard more than twelve hours earlier. I was famished and devoured the sausages, beans, bacon and egg and mopped up the plate with several slices of heavily buttered bread. It was a rare treat for me because dripping had replaced butter in our house since the first of my sisters arrived. Twas all washed down with a big mug of milky tea and as much sugar as I could take without embarrassing Himself, who had taken to giving me a stern look when the fancy took him.

The bearded man rose from his seat, slapped his stomach and shook our hands.

"Good luck ter yers both. May yer be in heaven before the devil knows yer dead." It was as many words as he had spoken since we met him in Fishguard.

"See ya all of a sudden" called out Jack as the man stepped into the street.

~~~~~

My brother never mentioned the scrap with our father and I wasn't going to be the first to speak of it. I don't think Jack was entirely convinced that I had seen those sad events. I'd been sitting on a bench on the other side of The Bull pub, munching on an arrowroot biscuit that Pa had given me, when I heard the argument start.

Little Tommy Flynn, who was playing nearby, seemed to sense the danger in the air and scuttled back inside the pub to the waiting arms of his Ma.

"Yer've laid yer hands on me Mammy fer the last time," Jack called as he approached the pub. Pa was just leaving with Father Kennedy. The priest was half the height and half the width of my Pa. Pa stood a full six feet with a big round face, reddened by prolonged bouts of drinking. The palms of his hands were as big as house bricks and felt just as craggy. He'd worked with bricks all his life and, eventually, his hands took to feeling like a brick themselves. He held out the palm of his right hand to push my brother away but Jack just swayed to the left, ducked under it and landed a right hook to Pa's midriff. He gasped and wheezed. Father Kennedy protested but Jack called him again.

"Yer word now Pa. No more."

Father Kennedy said something about every marriage

being its own mystery, as if he was preaching from the pulpit at Sunday Mass. Pa laughed at Jack's attempts to knock him down.

"Is it I who'll be beholding to you is it? Was it not me who wiped your arse all those years ago? Be off wid yer boy before I send ya to yer maker." The last syllable had barely left his lips when Jack hit him with a blow to those same lips. I kept ducking behind the wall so that nobody could see me. But that of the fight that I did see never included a landed blow by my Pa. Jack ducked and weaved effortlessly, striking my father at regular intervals until, as if like a wild beast shot by a poisoned dart, he slumped to the ground under the weight of punches and sheer exhaustion.

"That's enough" called the priest, "or I'll be calling the Garda."

"Yer heard ma words," called my brother as he walked away, "don't test me Pa or I'll send yer to your grave." I sat back down on the bench hoping that nobody had seen me peering around the corner. Jack's fortune and fate were graven on his heart from that moment hence. The Bible tells us as much. Honour they father and thy mother. But, for all his failings, my love for my brother was unconditional. I ate the last piece of arrowroot and heard my Pa call out to Flynn the landlord to call the Garda. Father Kennedy protested.

"But he's ya son Patrick. Tink on it man. Yer own son now."

"Flynn. Call the Garda now," he repeated even louder.

They stumbled back inside the pub and I ran off down Gowan Street towards home. I ran so fast I arrived barely thirty seconds after our Jack.

"Mammy, Mammy" I called, "Pa's calling the Garda to

81

take our Jack away."

Jack and Ma were in the pantry. She was telling him like it was. Mammy seemed to know the consequences of his actions. She pressed a green rosary and some loose change into his hand.

"Will ya be after thinking about the consequences of yer actions John? To be sure yer fists will be the death of ya. Ya can't go hitting ya own farder. That's assault that is John. And that'll mean prison for you. Now pack yourself some tings in this bag and get yerself away before the Garda gets here."

"He'll not be calling the Powlees Ma, not for his own son," said Jack casually.

"But he has Jack" I interrupted, "I heard him telling Flynn to be doing it."

"What" said Ma, "were you there?" she screamed. I didn't have to answer.

"Be Jasus John the little fella's an accessory too. Yer'll have to be taking him wid ya." Jack pleaded, taking Ma away from me to ask quietly in her ear to be allowed to leave me.

"Da ya want him in prison for your actions John? Am I to be visiting the littlun in borstal?"

Jack shoved a shopping bag in my hand and told me to put some clothes in it. Mother's face suggested that she was having second thoughts about leaving me in Jack's company. In any case, I hardly had any clothes other the ones I was standing up in.

"He can't go to London with a shopping bag John," she declared, and she handed me a small and very worn, red attaché case, that held barely more than the spare set of clothes that I could muster.

And as the night overpowered the day, with the household in complete disarray, Jack and I left. Our younger sisters were crying and the Mammy was trying to hold her feelings in check until we left. I kissed Theresa, Biddy and Nora goodbye, thinking we would probably be gone a few days.

That night was dry and we slept in a field before setting off again the following morning with little more in our bellies than a couple of apples we picked from a tree by the roadside.

~~~~~

Covent Garden wasn't a garden at all. It was the biggest fruit and vegetable market I have ever seen. Jack had put some apples in his pockets as we were leaving one of the trader's premises. It wasn't really stealing, they had millions of them. And so we set off to find our fortune. I suppose we only chose east because that's the way we had been heading since we left Ireland. It made no sense to go back the way we came from. We could just have easily have headed west or north or south and maybe our lives would have ended up completely different. I remember a tinker telling Mammy that everyone's life is already mapped out for them when they're born, so Jack and I were always going to be heading east I suppose. We thought we would walk until we reached the outskirts. Rooms would be cheaper to rent on the outskirts of London for sure. And so we walked and we walked, endlessly onwards, through a town without end. By the afternoon I was feeling exhausted and hinted that we might consider stopping.

"It's just a stretch of the legs," says Himself, "we'll stop soon enough."

With each mile the streets became dirtier, more damaged by the bombing. The people in the street looked poorer and there were more stray dogs. Each neighbourhood looked increasingly more dangerous than the last. The natives grew more threatening with each mile we covered.

As we passed one group of young men, they began singing "Nick, knack paddy whack" with the emphasis on the 'whack'. With no hesitation, Jack turned and walked back to them. Marching straight up to the biggest of the four he said, loud enough for all to hear: "Are you the leader of this little gang then? Or are you just the one with the biggest gob?"

With fear in his eyes, the scruffily dressed young man simply shrugged his shoulders and stammered: "It was only a joke."

"Yeh" said another lad sitting on the wall beside him, "can't you take a joke?"

"Not as well as you can take a punch, I bet" says Jack and he walks back to me and we continue on our way.

Each time we passed a shop my stomach would rumble. Outside a newsagent's shop a poster said that the Prime Minister had left the country to join the peace talks. Harold Wilson had just won the election Jack told me and he was going to put everything right in England. From our journey, I could see there was a lot to be put right and I wasn't quite sure why he thought he needed to solve problems in

Vietnam before he started.

"Hasn't he got enough problems to solve here Jack?"

"Plenty," he replied looking round at the bombsites where houses used to be and children with no shoes or socks on their feet.

"Is Moscow in Vietnam then Jack?"

"No."

"Then why is he going to Moscow?"

"Look Liam, can we have less questions, it's been a long day."

I had difficulty keeping up with Jack at times, so determined was his step, but he never got too far ahead as to lose me. He was always just ahead of me on the road to our new home, as he was in life.

It was a bright sunny day and we had been walking in a straight line for so many miles that I'd lost any sense of time when we came to a seamen's mission in East India Dock Road, in a place called Poplar. This was on a section of the road where there was a bend and the sun was now setting behind the imposing building that faced a park. I had never seen such a large park. It had tennis courts, a bowling green and a large playground with swings and a roundabout. A cloudless sky hovered above it as the day started to think about clocking off.

To Jack a seamen's mission meant that there may be rooms and, even better, there may be the possibility of work in the docks. The lorry driver who brought us to London told us that all the workers in the docks were casual. You simply turned up at the dock gate and offered yourself up for work. What could be easier than that? It was called 'the lump' he told us.

Even if there had been a room at the Mission, which there wasn't, we didn't qualify for accommodation, as we weren't seamen. And, after the journey across the Irish Sea the previous day, I wasn't thinking of becoming one either. Apparently, there was a seamen's strike on and the mission was full. The combination of the lorry driver's advice and the election of a new Labour Government gave Jack false hope for work. He wasn't the most optimistic of men, so I concluded that he was acting so for my benefit. The man at the mission said we should look in some of the side streets where there may be rooms to let. So we followed the advice he gave us and we did indeed find some tall houses with a basement and three floors above that had rooms to let. But underneath the word 'vacancy', in every case we found, were the words: "No blacks, no Irish, no dogs."

Eventually Jack knocked at one of the doors and tried his best to lose his Irish accent. I thought it was a convincing attempt but the door was almost closed before we heard the words: "can you not read?" Jack told me it was a rhetorical question, she knew we could read.

It would have been a waste of time anyway because we had no money to pay for the rooms. We weren't alone in seeking a refuge for the night. Several tramps appeared to have built a camp on a debris site opposite the houses. Most of the streets in this part of London had suffered from bombing in the war and little or no work had been done to replace the houses that had been lost. By the Lord's good grace, it was a dry night and we slept in the park opposite the seamen's mission with one or two others who seemed to be regular residents. The park was locked and the swings and roundabout had been chained up. What did they think would happen to a roundabout?

"Do they think somebody will steal the roundabout Jack?" I asked Himself.

"It's to stop idjuts like you playing on it Liam."

The entire park area was protected by a fence, so you had to be relatively fit to gain access. But we waited until dusk when the park shut and climbed over the fence. We managed to secure the benches in a wooden shelter in the children's playground. A previous resident was quite surprised to see the two of us and, if he had been a little more hospitable, I'm sure we would have shared. But hostility was met with hostility and the young man was no match for Jack. My brother worked at Gilligan's blacksmiths in Ballycraich and the work had transformed his features from someone who looked not too dissimilar to me, to a strapping young man who now had the physique to back up his occasional moments of ill temper.

It was very late before the sun finally disappeared and was replaced by a crescent moon. By turning away from the streetlights, it was dark enough to get to sleep. I was exhausted and took just a few moments to fall asleep.

When I woke up it was bright daylight and Jack was already awake and reading a newspaper that had been left by a previous inhabitant of our temporary dwelling. It was a few days old but, with the exception of learning that Mr Wilson had joined the peace talks, we hadn't seen any news since we left our home. The headlines said that the ban on black workers at Euston railway station had been overturned.

"Does that mean it's just us and the dogs now Jack?" I asked.

"Ah, you're awake young Liam. We can be off to find some work now."

There was no mention of food and I was beginning to feel a little faint at the thought of another day without a meal inside me.

As we approached the dock gates my heart sank. If they had work for two hundred men that day, there still wouldn't be enough to go round. As the man responsible for recruiting stood on the box and called out his requirements, Jack was quick to call back and throw his arm up heavenward like a schoolchild who knew the answer to his teacher's question. A voice called from deep inside the throng: "Ged 'ome to ya potato picking ya Irish fucker." Twas only the anonymity of the voice that protected it from a thrashing at the hands of my brother. But there was more support for the voice and none for us. Prejudice prevailed and we found no work that day.

"What are we going to do for food?" I asked as we walked away. Jack reassured me that he would think of a solution.

"But I've had but one apple since two days gone" I answered.

"Now stop your whinging Liam. It'll be alright soon enough."

"Here" said a voice from behind us, "take this two bob. There's a pie and mash shop across the road there. This will feed you till you find something."

He was a kindly looking man who was at least ten years older than Jack was. He was short but with an amiable nature that was difficult to resist. Although my brother was determined to try.

"We're not a charity case," answered Jack impolitely.

"Nobody says you are," said the man sympathetically. "But you can't see the boy starve now can you? What part of Ireland are you from?"

"Ballycraich" I answered eagerly.

"Isn't that near Cork" he countered

"Tis so" I answered, only to be silenced by a glare from Jack.

"We appreciate the offer, but..."

The man cut Jack off mid sentence. "Take it as a loan then. Pay me back when you see me next."

"London's a big place," answered Jack "I'd be surprised to see the same person twice in the same year."

"It's not that big," replied the man. He paused, and then continued, "You're a strong looking lad," he said to Jack, "Have you ever boxed?"

My brother admitted that he had never boxed but was not afraid to use his fists if he needed to. I thought about confirming that fact but the glance was still fresh in my memory and I remembered it was normally one glance and one slap across the head.

"Well tomorrow's Saturday. Take yourself down to the Circus and see if you can earn yourself a dollar."

"Is it in America," I asked wondering why my brother would be paid in dollars. The man apologised.

"Sorry young 'un" he said, "a dollar is five bob round here, or five shillings to you. You'll get used to the language soon enough."

"Are you from Ireland?" asked Jack reluctantly.

"My dad was," he answered, expecting a conversation to begin. It didn't. My brother was a man of few words.

The Circus turned out to be no more a circus than Covent Garden was a garden. Ludgate Circus is an area we had walked past the previous day and a dollar turned out to be the reward for the boxer who won the fight.

After another night in the playground, we were up early and walked to Ludgate Circus. It took us a couple of hours. Signs directed us to the Golden Lion pub where boxing matches went on throughout the day, with the winner earning five shillings and the loser going home with nothing. Having seen Jack in action with my Pa I was brimming with confidence. T'will be a hearty meal for us tonight for sure I thought to myself.

Jack went off to see a man about a fight and I noticed an empty ringside seat. The elderly man next to me was smoking a cigar and was accompanied by a very attractive young woman who was about the right age to be his daughter. He looked disdainfully at me as I leaned back in the comfortable seat. He looked over towards a giant of a man standing near the corner of the ring. The big guy needed no instructions, nor was he given any. He walked over to me and, with one hand, lifted me up from the seat.

I had never seen Jack move so fast in my life. He was back down the stairs and stood by my side in a second.

"Put the boy down" he said, looking upwards into the big guy's face, "or I'll put you down." The smartly dressed cigar smoker nodded to the big guy and he put me back

90

down on the ground.

"He's in the wrong seat," says the big guy.

"Then I'll put him in another" says Jack.

A cigar is stubbed out next to my foot, and the look says 'that's enough'. Jack points out a seat to me about four rows back and he heads off to arrange his fight. I'm too far away to hear what is being said but Jack is remonstrating with a man in a dark suit and bow tie. Suddenly I notice the smart looking man in the front row nod his consent to the man in the bow tie, who leaves his conversation with Jack and walks over to receive some instructions from the man he was now calling Mr. Harrison, who then whispers something in the big guy's ear. The big guy smiles and walks off towards the dressing room.

Just at that moment, I recognise a face walking over towards me. It's the kindly man from the previous day. He holds his hand out to me and I feel quite adult as I shake it firmly.

"William Daly" he says as he sits next to me. "Bill", he adds, correcting himself.

"Liam Calnan" I reply.

"Where's your brother?"

"Trying to organise a fight."

"It's a boxing match Liam, not quite the same thing. Who's he up against."

"Well" I answer, "if I'm not mistaken I think he might be fighting him." I point over towards the departing giant.

"Is he mad?" asks Bill, "that's Digger Rhodes, Charlie Harrison's minder. Even if he wins, he loses."

"I don't think he knows yet," I answered. "And, in any case, our Jack can look after himself."

Jack didn't know who his opponent was until they both stepped into the ring. He spoke with the referee and then called me over. "Fill that bucket with water and get that towel over there Liam, I need a second in my corner." I accepted the role with pride.

The first round was even. The crowd were largely cheering for Digger but I listened to what they were saying and countered with the same instruction for Jack.

"Be first Jack, be first," I shouted, urging him to get the first punch in.

Digger had a longer reach and Jack had to find a way inside the big man's punches in order to land one of his own.

"What do I do now?" I asked as Jack came back to the corner at the end of round one.

"Just give me some of that water and leave the rest to me," he answered confidently. With nothing to occupy me and eager to learn, I looked over at the other corner for some guidance. They seemed to be getting advice from Charlie Harrison on how to get the better of Jack. I decided that Jack needed some encouragement.

"Joe Louis beat Primo Carnero Jack and he was enormous, so I reckon you can beat this guy. I bet he doesn't punch his weight."

"If he did, I'd be dead Liam. Now shut up and give me that towel."

The bell went and Jack stormed into Digger landing a straight left and a right hook. Digger moved back to the corner where I was standing. As Jack approached him, he spun him round and looked over his shoulder for orders from the ringside. The cigar smoker nodded. With Jack in the corner of the ring above me and the referee behind the both of them, Digger rammed his thumb into Jack's eye with force enough to knock it out of its socket. It didn't come out but, effectively blinded in one eye, my brother couldn't see the right hook that everyone else in the pub saw a minute later. He fell to the canvas with a crash and Digger, who towered above him, looked over at me and smiled.

Jack rose to his feet about two seconds after the referee had counted him out. He remained silent as we left the pub. Bill followed behind us and offered to walk back to Poplar with us. Before doing so, he took us across the road to Shoe Lane where there was a café that sold a large bowl of minestrone soup for eight pence. He bought three bowls and the silence wasn't broken until Jack said, "we're beholden to you."

"William Daly. Call me Bill," he replied and Jack held his hand out. Bill shook it heartily and made me nearly spill my soup when he said, "Of course, you would have won if you'd had me in your corner. No disrespect Liam but there's a little more to it than dispensing water and towels." I heard the legs of Jack's chair scrape against the tiled floor as he started to rise. But he sat back down again.

"Liam did OK."

"He did handsomely," replied Bill "but you could have done with some advice out there. That way you would have been buying the soup and not me."

It was the wrong thing to say. Jack was already indebted to Bill and his reaction was instant.

"Listen, I don't take charity…" But Bill cut him off and apologised.

"Nonetheless" continued Bill "you would have won with

we me in your corner."

"And how would that be?" asked Jack.

"Let me take your corner next Saturday and I'll show you."

"I don't want any more of your help. We'll stand on our own two feet and we'll be repaying you for the money you've given us already."

"Oh" said Bill "I'll not be doing it for nothing. I charge a tanner for acting as second. But you'll still be four and six better off."

"One condition," answered Jack "tell me what I should have done today and it's a deal."

"Well two things would have changed the result. Firstly you were punching him on the nose and on the chin."

"I thought that's what I was supposed to do in boxing" interrupted Jack.

"Well its not" answers Bill, and he gets Jack to stand up opposite him. Jack stood about three or four inches taller than Bill who stepped around the table to be next to his pupil. He stood me up too and held my shoulders in his two hands.

"This" says Bill "is Digger." God I thought, I hope he isn't going to hit me. He put his hand about six inches behind my head.

"You have to be aiming at a point about six inches behind his head Jack."

"John" my brother corrected him. Bill looked quizzical but seemed to understand that only I called my brother Jack. To everyone else he was John.

"OK. John. Aim for a point six inches behind the opponent's head and hit that. Punch through his face not on his face. OK?"

"And the second point?" asked Jack impatiently.

Bill hesitated, trying to remember what the second point was. "Oh yes" he said, "always, always, take advantage of your opponent's weakness."

"And what was Digger's weakness?"

"He can't think for himself. Didn't you notice the way he looked to the corner for advice every now and again? You should have picked that weakness up in the first round and then capitalised on it in the second. He can't think for himself John. As soon as he turns his head to get instructions, hit him. If he looks over his left shoulder, it's a left hook and if it's the right shoulder, it's a right hook. Simple as that." He paused. "Oh, remembering to hit through his head. OK?"

The two were still talking tactics for next week as we left the café. Almost as an afterthought, Bill said there was a company recruiting messengers near Shoe Lane recently. With the World Cup taking place in England over the next few weeks, there were news agencies around Fleet Street needing extra help. We crossed the road to a small office next to the Evening Standard newspaper building and stopped. I waited for instructions.

"Well, we'll not be coming in with you Liam," said Bill. "In you go and ask for a job. Tell them you're experienced and happy to work weekends and evenings. That should do it."

I'd never been for a job interview before. I had only just finished school at home and would have been working as a farm labourer if we'd stayed in Ballycraich.

It was nothing like I had imagined an interview would

be. I offered my services and an elderly, well-spoken man, accepted. Five pounds per week was the wage and I was told to report for work on Monday at nine in the morning. After that it would be evenings and weekends.

I stumbled down the last few stairs as I joined the other two outside.

"I've got a job."

"Well done Liam," they both said.

~~~~~

The following Saturday Jack and I returned to the pub in Ludgate Circus. I was not on duty until late afternoon and my dutiful brother wanted to keep me in sight. He picked my seat and told me to stay there until he returned. He then went off to put his name on the list for a fight. Bill was sitting next to me rummaging through the contents of a small holdall bag of liniments, bandages, styptic pencils, scissors and smelling salts. They looked like the instruments of a loser to me and it was difficult to reconcile this with his confidence in Jack.

Jack returned with a name. Bill looked surprised and mumbled something about Jimmy throwing him out of the club if he found out. Jimmy Anderson ran a local boxing club and, according to Bill, he would expel Jack's opponent if he discovered he was boxing for money. But Bill was familiar with the young contender. Terry Marsden was about the same age as my brother but boxed and trained regularly at one of the best amateur clubs in London. Rumours were he had been sacked from his job and needed to earn some money. Bill had never seen him box but was aware of his reputation.

It was a three round contest and the local boy had plenty of support. At the end of the first round, I left my seat and stood at the ringside to listen to Bill. I was intrigued by his absolute confidence of victory. Even I knew that Jack was behind on points after round one. Jack was telling Bill what he thought was going wrong.

"John. For fuck's sake stop talking and listen," not noticing me standing below him otherwise I'm sure he would have moderated his language.

"I've only got one minute to straighten you out. This bloke is a counter puncher John. Every punch you throw at him is an opportunity for him to hit you, and he's being very successful at it. You have to cut off his supply."

"What, do you want me to do, stop hitting him?" answered Jack sarcastically.

"Will you listen John? Shut up. No talking. Just listen. Feign. Feign. Then one punch. Pick your best chance. Land one punch when it's safe and then step back. Retreat. Then same again. Feign. Feign. One punch, retreat. OK, go."

It was against Jack's nature but he stuck to the plan and I have to say he won the round. He may only have landed six or eight scoring punches but his opponent didn't land one. The crowd didn't particularly appreciate the skill involved and as the bell rang there was some booing from those at the back.

"OK" said Bill at the break. "Now do the same again. Don't get impatient. The same again and you've got five bob. Understand. The same again and you and young Liam can eat tonight." He continued to repeat the incentive until the bell rang to begin round three.

To his credit, Jack followed Bill's instructions to the letter. It was his opponent who lost his way. The frustration grew until eventually he had to go forward. He had to take the fight to Jack. He was clearly a good counter puncher but when he had to take the initiative it was completely foreign to him. And as the final bell got closer and closer, his patience disappeared. He lunged at Jack with a left hook that missed by eight inches and sent him off balance slightly. The opportunity was not missed and Jack sent him on his way to the canvas with a thumping right hand that seemed to be aimed at a point six inches beyond the point of impact. Terry Marsden lay there until the referee had finished the count and sat up in time to see his second and Jack standing above him, both grateful to see he was unharmed.

Billy earned his tanner that day and Jack earned what was left of the five bob. The knockout ensured that Jack would get a fight the following week too, which appeared unlikely when the booing began at the end of the second round.

~~~~~

Our situation improved in the days that followed. Bill became a good friend to us. He had the ability and energy to make things happen. In Ireland, or perhaps just in Ballycraich, because I had travelled little outside our small village, things happened without any real effort on the part of its inhabitants. We accepted the pace of life, if indeed it had any pace. Ballycraich ran on inertia, if that were possible. The people of the East End, however, felt unable, or unwilling, to simply accept what life delivered. They were compelled to make things happen and nobody was a greater example of this than Bill Daly was. The grace of contentment had been lost on them, probably as a result of the war. There were reminders everywhere of that period in each person's life. Those of my age only felt the residue of its effects. Some slightly older than me remembered rationing. The younger ones simply remembered the war in their play, by fighting imaginary Germans.

Eventually we secured accommodation in a street behind the Seamen's Mission where Jack and I had first decided to stop after a long walk from the Garden that wasn't a garden.

It was an old wreck of a house with a basement and three other floors. Jack and I occupied the attic, which consisted of a large bedroom overlooking the street and a smaller one at the rear, and a small landing where a lonely armchair sat waiting for someone to take up occupancy. Just why anyone would want to sit in such a dark, dreary, place was beyond my imagination. I imagined the chair was the sole remaining item from a bombed house and it had been retrieved and given a new purpose in its damaged life, albeit a lonely one. Like the Irish, the East Enders felt unable to let any half-useful item go to waste. So, the chair stood, less than half-useful. Perhaps it had been carried up the many stairs with the intention of it being placed in the large bedroom to make it more complete. Clearly it could not pass through the door and so it had been left, strangely reticent of its reduced status in life. Jack claimed the larger bedroom but even the smaller one was too large for the few belongings I brought to the house.

The landlady was a generous, if slightly bawdy individual who took us in willingly. At first we thought that someone had simply stolen the 'No dogs, no blacks, no Irish' sign for firewood, but Nora had no such prejudices. There were few neighbours to disagree with her surprisingly liberal views as most of the houses in the street, along with a church, had not survived the blitz.

Nora's pragmatism left little room for prejudice of any kind. Like Bill, she worked hard and had little respect for those who failed to apply themselves in a similar fashion. My shift work meant I often saw more of Nora than Jack did. Himself had found a good job on a construction site in the City. It was called the Barbican and, when it was finished, would include theatres and office buildings. It seemed to me that Mr Wilson had his priorities confused if he was in Vietnam whilst his colleagues at Westminster were building theatres for people who had no homes. And those who did have homes lived in buildings like we did, bereft of the basic amenities.

Living in Ballycraich, Jack and I were used to an outside toilet so the one in Plimsoll Street was not inconvenient to us, even if the journey from the attic to the basement became a nuisance in the night. I convinced myself that Jack pissed in the sink in his room and, when he was not there, I often availed myself of the facility too. When I did take the long journey to the basement, it was not unusual to find Nora sitting there, with the door agape and her dressing gown likewise, reading the newspaper. Avoiding this experience in some way justified my pissing in the sink occasionally.

Nora had several jobs. She worked in the fish and chip

shop in Chrisp Street Market at lunchtime. She cleaned the house of the owners of the shop twice each week. She worked in the bookmakers in Commercial Road on Saturdays and, for the rest of the time, she would make dresses on an old Singer sewing machine in the basement of the house. It was no wonder that Jack and I had such difficulty finding employment when the likes of Nora had four jobs.

There was little for me to do when I was working the late shift in Fleet Street, so often in the mornings I would help Nora with the dressmaking in the basement. She would produce dresses from a large roll of material left by a strange little man each week. During the summer months, it would be bright coloured floral dresses and these were later replaced by the more sombre colours of autumn. Nora would sew up the cloth belts and leave them in a pile on the floor for me to turn them inside out with a knitting needle and then get them as flat as I could before she would run the iron over them and I would then push them through the waist loops of the finished dresses. Then, if I were there on a Thursday, we would pack the dresses into polythene bags ready for Mr Levy's arrival.

Each week Nora would leave one dress hanging in the corner of the basement room away from the window in case of prying eyes. We would go off upstairs to open the door and she to argue with him, and me to stand in admiration of her brazenness. Mr. Levy had met Jack on a couple of occasions before he found work, so when the little old man appeared at the door Nora would ask him to be quiet in case he should wake 'Big John', who had been working night shift.

At first, I would look confused but soon understood the motive in her lies. It did her no harm for others to believe that there was a strong lad upstairs and it minimised the length of the argument she had with Mr. Levy each week. Mr. Levy insisted that he had given her enough material to make twenty dresses and she would explain that the pattern only enabled her to make eighteen.

"There was an awful lot of waste in that pattern Mr. Levy," she was saying, as convincingly as possible.

"Nonsense," he would insist, as quietly as he could in view of the fact that he was obviously passionate about the loss of some dresses, but didn't want to upset the young man asleep upstairs. Sometimes she would look at me for assurance and I would nod unable to tell a lie, even for Nora.

"You steal from a poor old man like me" he gesticulated to Nora.

"Well I wish I was as poor as you" Nora would respond.

And so the argument would continue, with Nora occasionally pointing up the stairs if Mr Levy's voice rose too loud. He, convinced that she had made nineteen dresses, so insisting that twenty had been made, and she explaining that only her unmatched skill as a dressmaker made it possible to make even eighteen. He would leave, cursing under his breath, and she would close the door with a whispered one in return. She spoke quickly, joining all the syllables together into one long unbroken word.

"Buggeroffyouoldmiser."

I had to try to separate the syllables to understand the riposte.

Sunday was not a complete day of rest for Nora, as she

102

would sell her 'overs', as she called them, at the pub. If Mr. Levy had spent more time in Poplar and less time at his warehouse in Whitechapel, he would have discovered the extent of Nora's extra curricular activities, as almost every other woman in Poplar must have worn a Levy dress at some time. This wasn't really stealing Nora insisted. It was the proceeds of her endeavours. Others, she told me, would struggle to make sixteen dresses from the material she was given, so it was not unreasonable for her to enjoy a share of the profits. And, this aside, she was, indeed, an honest woman. I'm sure she would not consider stealing from the home she cleaned or the bookmakers she worked at. And, apart from giving me an extra large portion of chips whenever I visited the fish and chip shop, she never took more from any of her employers than she was entitled to, with the exception, perhaps, of Mr. Levy.

In many ways, Nora became a surrogate mother to me. She sometimes made lunch for me but I rarely saw her eat herself. Sometimes she shared some of the sandwiches she made for me, or supped at a bowl of soup. She had a light frame and an appetite to match. Jack somehow knew about our clandestine lunches in his absence and at the weekend, he would search her out in the local pubs and buy her a drink to show his appreciation of her friendship for me.

Jack worked as a hod carrier. He had to explain what a hod was and, when he did, I saw the muscles in his face flinch. Not from the burden of his labours but the object carried in the hod. Our father had made his living working with bricks and now here was Jack carrying them. He tried so hard not to be like our father. Any small nuance of similarity was met with a conscious effort to change. Every time he fought in the ring, he would look at his fists and convince himself that he was not using them in the same way as Pa did. They were not to be used in anger but as a way of putting food on the table. Jack had the ability to avoid fighting and the strength to deal with a situation if it failed to avoid him.

We made few friends outside Bill and a local publican's daughter Mary and there was a strange absence of any discussion about returning home. I resisted any temptation to raise the subject, assuming Jack would do so when the time was right. His blossoming friendship with Mary, who worked in her father's pub, suggested a discussion was getting less likely with each passing day. For my part I had little objection. The news agency had kept me on after the World Cup. They employed a transient population of young men ambitious to become sports reporters, full of eagerness and absent of the necessary talent.

Unlike Bill, the grace of contentedness had never left me. I was happy in my work. I wasn't fearful of hard work or slow when an opportunity to earn extra money arose, although Jack kept a close eye on my activities. On one occasion, a dubious character called Terry Hoon, who we met occasionally in the pubs around Poplar, suggested I could earn some easy money by helping a friend of his. Bernie Woolaston was a professional gambler whose success was born from his ability to resist taking any risks. In fact, he would object to being called a gambler at all. He worked hard at his scam and it deserved to be rewarded. Bernie frequented Clapton dog track just north of Poplar and neighbouring Mile End. As the preparation for his scam, he took photographs of all the local greyhound trainers and most of the owners. Then he set them to memory. He then took up his position in the members lounge above the winning post and enlisted the help of a young assistant like me.

My job was to position myself behind any of the trainers and owners known to Bernie to find out which number dog they were betting on. Bernie would simply nudge me to indicate which people I had to stand behind in the queue. Then, when I got to the bookie's stand, I would act as if I had changed my mind, or forgotten my money. I would then report back to Bernie on who that particular trainer was betting on and he would store this information away in his very capable memory. Amazingly, he never wrote anything down.

For most races during the evening, there was nothing unusual or suspicious about the range of bets being placed and he, himself, did not place a bet on these occasions. But, usually, at least once at each meeting, he would discover either a significant bet by a particular owner or trainer or several of the trainers and owners would be betting on a particular dog. Bernie would have his bet for the evening, often thousands, which he spread around the track to avoid any undue attention.

On the three occasions that I accompanied him to Clapton he never failed. Often the winning greyhound was very short odds but Bernie made a good living out of it. His patience, planning and restraint were always rewarded. And he was a generous man too, particularly if he knew he could put his confidence in you and trust you. Obviously there had been helpers in the past who had seen the scam as an opportunity to line their own pockets but I was too simple to take this option. As such, Bernie rewarded me well. He paid me fifteen pounds on the first two occasions and on the third, he gave me twenty pounds, telling me that he would not need my services any longer. He went to great lengths to tell me he was pleased with my work but he had to keep changing his assistant to ensure that the managers and trainers didn't become suspicious.

Nora said that Bernie was an astute gambler. I didn't know what this meant but he was successful at what he did, so astute must have been good.

I was too afraid to spend the money that Bernie had given me in case Jack asked questions about its source. I placed the fifty pounds in the little red attaché case that the Mammy had given me when we left Ireland and thought about telling Himself about it. I didn't have to give it too much thought before deciding not to tell Jack. In fact, a few weeks later, somebody said something about Bernie's activities and I was given a stern warning not to become involved in any such scam or with undesirables like Bernie Woolaston or Terry Hoon. After giving my word that I never would, it seemed a less than sensible thing to do to tell Himself about the fifty pounds. So there the money sat in the little red attaché case, with me frightened to use it.

~~~~~

My job as a messenger required little application. I was happy to deliver the news by hand and had become familiar with the short cuts around London that made my job easier.

The Daily Herald was the only newspaper that required a bus journey but I walked and claimed the fare. Nobody questioned it and it was no more than a good stretch of the legs. My willingness to work late shifts and my deferential nature enabled me to become a stalwart of the staff. I would do all the jobs that others evaded. Making tea, running errands, and reading endless copy over the telephone.

Thursday was a quiet day. There was little sport to speak of. I would sit and listen to the reporters concocting stories from nothing. Twas not too different from Uncle Timmy's tales back in Ballycraich, telling stories that had been stretched beyond the boundaries of probability. A telephone call to Tommy Docherty about the likelihood of a particular player's transfer would always provide a story in the absence of any real news. Then off I would traipse around the newspapers and the following morning it would be "Docherty denies Bonetti rumours." It was often job and finish on Thursday evening. Normally I would work until ten at night but Thursday was earlier. Deliver the post and head home.

Jack must have forgotten it was Thursday that night. I climbed the stairs to the attic and it must have been around nine thirty. I reached the landing and thought I heard Jack call me. I opened the door to find Himself and Mary almost naked on his bed. I closed the door, apologising profusely as I looked away, realising it was a groan more than a call. I sat on my bed, rigid, considering the consequences of my hasty action. Ten minutes later Jack knocked and walked in. He stood there and knocked on my door again in the full view of myself.

"Remember this?" he asked, referring to the knock.

"Sorry" I said, "I thought you called." He sat on the bed next to me.

"Are you OK Liam?"

"Sure, I'm fine Jack," I paused. There was a short silence.

"Are we ever going home Jack?" I asked without thinking about the question. There was another, longer pause.

"We will," he assured me. "Just not yet awhile."

And a while it was too. When the leaves began to fall I felt it may, indeed, be a long while.

Nora occupied the basement and ground floor of the house. A foreign gentleman occupied the first floor. I saw little of him and, when I did, he was engrossed in his work. He sat on the landing working a fret machine, not dissimilar from the Singer sewing machine in the basement. He made jigsaws. Printed wooden pictures would be cut into a hundred pieces with great skill and dexterity. His long, old, fingers moving the wood one way and another, whilst working the treadle. For the rest of the time he sat in his small living room stroking his cat. Or at least that is how I imagined him because the door was always closed. I never recall meeting him on his way to, or from, the lavatory.

"Mr. Felstein keeps himself to himself," Nora explained to me as she busied away at her sewing machine.

"He's not one for a chat" she said, "so best not to ask these things. After all, I don't ask about you or your brother do I? Most folks just want to be left to themselves, Liam. Best left that way. But if he were, you know, a German, he's not one of those Nazis. If anything he left the place to avoid them if you ask me", she said confidently.

I hadn't asked her. I was just wondering if he suffered from the same prejudice as Jack and I did, as I had heard he was a Jew or a German, or both if that was possible.

The signs didn't say 'no Irish no dogs, no blacks and no Germans'. So presumably, we were worse than the people who had bombed them. Their hate for us was unreasonable and illogical. What had the Irish done to them? Twas times like this that I longed for home even more.

It wasn't prejudice with the Harrisons. They simply hated the idea of anyone who might possibly pose a threat to their empire. Not that Jack or I did that. It's just that Michael simply wanted what Jack had. Self-confidence, courage and, of course, Mary. Michael's courage came from his father. Nobody dared threaten Michael, so Michael never had the same self-esteem, or independence, that Jack had. If a simple man like me could see that, then it must have been obvious to Michael. I think it wore away at him. It is difficult having respect when you haven't done anything to earn it. You must feel like an imposter.

And so a mutual dislike fermented below the surface of the silent relationship that developed. Jack saw increasingly more of Mary and I worked as much overtime as I could. I saw Jack at breakfast and in the evening.

~~~~~

That Autumn Bill, Mary, Jack and I spent the weekends visiting Greenwich Park or taking a Green Line bus to Ongar or some other remote and romantic place. As the

109

weather grew ever colder we spent more time together in the local pubs and we became inseparable as a group. Jack won more bouts than he lost and we had enough money to survive. Almost inevitably, talk of Mary and Jack getting married crept into our conversations. Their deepening love for each other was apparent to anyone with eyes to see. We didn't see much of Bill on Saturdays. He liked to spend that particular day at the betting shop and, as I recall, he was fairly successful. Well, he always seemed to have plenty of money on him, so he must have been. I once told Bill he was an astute gambler but I'm not sure if he knew what it meant either.

Christmas approached. That fateful Christmas and New Year when, in every sense, the seeds were sown that would determine all our futures. In the bars and pubs we would sing along to the latest records. The Beatles and Rolling Stones of course, but more popular with us were the Beach Boys and Frankie Valli and the Four Seasons. We would drink and sing into the early hours before taking Mary home. On New Years Eve, Jack insisted that we visit Diamonds Club. Bill, Mary and I were all reluctant but Jack persuaded us. As it happened, we were welcomed personally by Charlie Harrison who waived his over 21 rule for me. A gesture he hoped would afford him some power over us.

I didn't see what happened that night. There was clearly an argument or a fight in the toilets, out of the sight of Charlie Harrison or Digger Rhodes and his team of club bouncers. The first I knew was when Billy dragged me up from my seat and led me to the door, where Jack was waiting with Mary. Whatever happened, it caused us to stay away from Diamonds.   I don't recall going back there until that fateful Whitsun night some months later.

Jack and Michael had seen each other occasionally in pubs but always managed to avoid contact.   When we finally decided to return to Diamonds the following May, Michael seemed to offer an olive branch, or at least a bottle of vintage Champagne. Like father like son, every gesture was designed to impress both Mary and Jack. Michael and his father wanted us to know we were on their turf, in their territory.   The old man particularly didn't want any problems in his club.   Later in the evening, Michael arrived at our table to ask if everything was OK. We thanked him for the Champagne.

"Perhaps we can have a dance later?" Michael asked Mary.

"I'm not dancing tonight Michael," answered Mary.

"That's a pity" he replied as he turned and walked to the bar.

That short conversation haunted me in the weeks, months and years to follow. A dance, a simple dance may have avoided everything that followed that night.

About an hour later, I recalled those words for the first of many occasions as I sat at the table and looked across an emptying club to see Jack dancing with Mary and Michael glaring at the two of them, overpowered by their obvious love for each other. Maybe that was the moment Michael decided she would be his, even for only the briefest of moments, and even if it was without her consent.

It must have been around this time that Mary found out she was pregnant. It may even have been that night that they told me she was having a baby. She and Jack applied for a council flat and, through the intervention of Bill, received an offer of a maisonette near the market in Brunswick Road, close to where we were currently living. It had two bedrooms so Jack insisted that I joined them, at least until the baby arrived. Perhaps then I would think about returning home. The flat was a bit noisy and had a main road running past it.

I said my goodbyes to Nora. She hugged me in an act that seemed foreign to her nature. My emotions were not lessened by the fact that I was probably still going to see her every day - in the chip shop, in the market and I might even visit her for a cup of tea.

"You should think about going home young Liam" she said wisely. "Your mother will be worried about you."

"I'll wait for the baby. Bill will let me use his camera to take some photos and I can take them home to show my mother and sisters."

"And your father," she corrected me. I nodded, wondering whether he still wanted to have me imprisoned for witnessing his fall from grace.

"Oh go on with you," she answered, dismissing me with a revealing tear on her cheek.

Mary continued to work, for a while, in her father's pub. A wedding was planned at the local Catholic Church. Mary, Jack and I moved into the flat and Mary spent the greater part of her time cleaning it and turning it into a home. Jack and I did our best to paint and paper the walls.

The events leading up to the destruction of our little piece of paradise are not as clear to me now as those that preceded them.

Time is, indeed, memory's enemy. So it is strange that

the days from leaving Ireland to us moving into the flat are as clear to me now as those that happened yesterday. Clearer in fact, because I cannot believe the events of yesterday. Seeing Jack again after all these years doesn't make any sense at all. Yesterday was a dream or hallucination. A change in my medication since leaving prison must have caused it. Something made Jack appear to me. I am not long for this life, I am sure of that. The beatings I took in prison from both sides damaged my liver and most other organs. Now the drugs are playing mind games with me.

What I remember of events at the time is largely anecdotal. Only the ending, or the ending of our lives as we knew it, was witnessed first hand. Indeed the ending was devised, created and executed by me. Yesterday has made me wonder about what is true and what is not. Can I believe anything anymore?

Michael went to the flat when Jack and I were working. That much must be true, for Mary told me as much. Well, she told me eventually, after much crying. She had told Jack when he returned home or, at least, he guessed from the fragments of information gleaned between her sobbing. This too must be true for she was still sobbing when I arrived home in the evening. She begged me not to leave her, so I stayed. I should have gone. I should have helped Jack. We were still sitting there several hours later. Darkness had fallen and there was no word of Jack.

Mary eventually stopped crying. I just assumed she had been raped. She was a strong character. Not physically but mentally. I knew it had to be something very serious for her to withdraw into herself in this way. I think we sat there all night. Perhaps she wasn't even conscious of the time, because she didn't ask where Jack was, although I was thinking of little else. It was early morning when Bill arrived. I had to wrench myself out of Mary's arms to answer the door. I rushed to the door expecting to see Jack. Bill saw the disappointment on my face. He rushed into the sitting room to Mary and I followed him hastily.

"Put some things in a bag. Do it quickly. We have to leave here now." He stared, in amazement at our inaction.

"Listen to what I am saying you two. We have to leave now. All our lives are in danger." He began searching in cupboards for bags and eventually found two holdalls. He threw them at us.

"Please" he pleaded. "We have to go till things settle down." He grabbed my shoulders and spoke quietly but firmly. "Liam. Do it now. For Mary's sake Liam."

"Where's Jack?" I asked.

"We'll talk about it when we are on our way."

"But shouldn't we wait for him?"

"Liam, listen to me," his voice dropped several decibels." In all probability" he paused, "John is dead."

The concept was lost on me. Everything was fine this morning. Jack was here. He was alive. How could he possibly be dead?

"No" I said, "I have to find him."

"Not now Liam. Now we must look after Mary. It's what John would have wanted you to do."

I suddenly noticed that the couch was empty. Mary had got up and had gone into the bedroom, hesitating at the doorway for a moment. She was in a daze and was putting clothes into one of the holdalls. I wanted to ask her what she was doing but she seemed oblivious to me. She mumbled to herself as knickers, tights, shoes, skirts, tops were placed into the bag as she mechanically followed instructions. Bill had begun packing some of my clothing in the other bag.

"But where are we going?" I asked.

"I'll explain on the way. We need to use public transport, keep changing trains, buses. We mustn't leave a trail. Just keep heading in one direction."

"What direction" I asked as if it made any difference. "East doesn't seem to help. I can't go west, not without Jack."

"North then" said Bill abruptly. "We'll go north."

We walked through the back-doubles to Limehouse. Then a bus to Mile End. Then the underground. Then a train. Then a green bus. There was no destination in our plan. I'm not sure how Bill knew when to stop.

Along the way, each time we were left alone in a train carriage or elsewhere Bill would tell us firmly: "Those feelings that you have in your hearts now, keep them there. Lock them away."

After an uneventful overnight stay at a less than hospitable pub, eventually we came to a small town somewhere in Hertfordshire, where we stayed for a couple of days. Bill busied himself getting to know the locals whilst Mary and I began to talk about what had happened and the probability that Jack was dead. The word 'dead' was never actually used, as if it had been extinguished from our language. Jack had clearly gone to find Michael, gone to seek revenge. He would probably have gone to Diamonds. We concluded that, whatever happened, he failed to make his escape. Charlie Harrison would not, could not, let his son be beaten or harmed by anyone without extracting revenge. Bill eventually told us of the rumours he had heard. That Jack had, indeed, gone to the club and beaten Michael to within an inch of his life. But Charlie Harrison had killed my brother and disposed of the body. For several weeks after we left the East End Bill read the newspapers each day for news. There was none. After reading each newspaper, he would allow us to read it too. It was as if Jack had vanished from the face of the earth. How could he be dead? There was nothing in the newspapers.

Bill had found out that the landlord of one of the two pubs in the town was hoping to emigrate to Canada and was looking for someone to take over the lease. A deal was tentatively agreed and all three of us started working in the pub whilst the arrangements were finalised. We never spoke to the locals about our past, managing to avoid such discussions, or simply passing off our backgrounds as ordinary. It had been anything but ordinary for me. But that is exactly what it was becoming. Life became ordinary, or as ordinary as we could make it. The pub did little more than provide us all with a modest income. The previous resident had good cause to leave, as the takings were barely sufficient to pay the lease and put food on the table. Mary's experience of working in her father's pub was invaluable but she was not the same person who left London. She refused to talk about Jack. It was too painful for her.

Of course, Mary wanted to make contact with her father and Bill said that she could do so but should not tell him where we were now living until the situation had settled down in London. Her father had no more news for us but was able to tell Mary that there was sufficient gossip to indicate the rumours of Jack's killing must be true. Mary dismissed her father's views as vicious lies. He spoke out of spite, she said. It was clear that in the absence of any evidence she would never accept that Jack was dead.

Occasionally when strangers appeared, particularly men on their own, we raised our guard and defended any questions that came our way. Gradually our posthumous lives, as Mary called them, became more and more ordinary. Mary's pregnancy became increasingly obvious and she sought help from the local midwife. People just assumed that the baby was Bill's. He wasn't so much older than her to make it unlikely.

Then, one morning, Mary and Bill appeared at breakfast and declared that they were getting married. Bill was elated but Mary looked resigned. I didn't know what to say. This was taking the deception too far. It stood like an acceptance, or even a declaration that Jack was dead. Perhaps it was this that triggered the chain of events that was to change my life. The plan, if indeed it could be elevated to such a status, for it was little more than an idea, was to kill the Harrisons, to avenge my brother's murder with two more murders. I had never spent Bernie Woolaston's £50 and had even saved some money, for we spent little on ourselves since leaving the East End. Whether it was enough to buy a gun, I had no idea.

I suppose the act of revenge had been in my mind for some considerable time. At first, it was instinctive. It was something that should be done, something that needed to be done, a fulfilment or an act of honour rather than retaliation. But, once the concept was nurtured through brooding anger and a sad resignation that these people had denied me contact with my brother for the rest of my life, I became resolved in the matter. The Harrisons had denied me even the basic right to say goodbye. So yes, it became obvious, an undeniable resolution. The plan was simple. Kill them both. It was only a question of how long I could postpone the inevitable. The idea sat like a latent desire awaiting something to provoke it into action.

~~~~~

The day was fixed for the wedding. It was just a few days after what would have been Jack's birthday. He would have been twenty-three. The combination of all these things - the approaching birth of Jack's child, the marriage of Mary and Bill, and the birthday that Jack was never to have - was the catalyst. What had been an idea that could dwell in my mind and be activated at my command now became a reality. It could not be deferred any longer.

I only knew one person who might be able to provide me with a gun and that was the weasel, Terry Hoon. Disposing of guns was probably a regular occupation for him, along with all the other soiled objects of his customers' crimes. Crimes, which he hadn't the skill or courage to commit himself but crimes he could help to conceal. It hadn't occurred to me that he might see this as an opportunity to dispose of a murder weapon. All that was to become clear in the days and months to follow.

Terry would have been aware of the rumours about Jack's death. He may even have been involved in the disposal of his body, although I'm not sure Charlie Harrison would allow a treacherous individual like Terry to have such intimate knowledge of a crime which led directly back to him.

I packed a few things in the old red attaché case, which had remained empty apart from the £50 that I had kept there for so many months, afraid to use it for fear of Jack. And I left a note to Mary and Bill saying I was going back to Ireland. I was sorry to miss the wedding but suddenly felt an urgent need to return home. I knew that Bill would follow me if I told them the truth. This small deception would afford me some time, for I knew not how long it was to take me to execute the killings.

I returned to the park opposite the Seamen's Mission and spent the night there, just as Jack and I had done the year before. Then, the following evening, I waited across the road from the pub to see if I could see Terry. I sat in the shadow of a doorway and waited. Eventually, just after eleven o'clock Terry came out of the pub and began the short walk to his home. I raced around the streets to get to his house before him and waited by a hedge till he walked past.

"Terry" I whispered.

He was startled but made no sound. I told him I was in fear of my life. I told him that, whoever killed my brother might now want to murder me. Did he know where I could get a gun? He began to say he couldn't help me, and then a look of sudden realisation appeared on his normally blank face. He suddenly, and surprisingly, agreed to help me but asked for a ridiculous amount for the gun he said he could get me. £500 was the first figure mentioned, which gradually came down until he simply asked how much I had. I had no idea what was a fair price for a gun so I told him I had £50, or rather I showed him the £50. He took it eagerly from my grasp and he told me to meet him at the pub tomorrow. I shook my head and said that the gun had to be supplied tonight because I was leaving before morning. I feared that Terry might double cross me. He might decide to take my £50 and then collect another £50, or more, from Charlie Harrison.

"Come with me," he said and I followed him for about twenty minutes till, eventually, we arrived at a block of lock-up garages by a large estate of multi-storey flats on the road that led on to the Isle of Dogs. He made sure nobody else was around. It was about midnight and, apart from some traffic noise in the distance, it was silent, or as silent as London can be at any time. He lifted the garage door and went inside. He returned with a shaving bag. He opened it to reveal an automatic pistol. He released the magazine and showed it to me so I could verify it contained bullets. He then slammed it back into place and showed me the safety catch.

I felt in my pockets to ensure I had some money left for my getaway. He wiped the gun clean of his fingerprints with an old rag and gave me the bag with the gun inside.

I returned to the park shelter but didn't sleep. It was too late to go to Diamonds nightclub tonight and, in any case, there would be too many people present. I left the small attaché case with my belongings under a bush behind the shed and took only the gun in the bag. I went to the club the following morning and found a vantage point on a balcony of a block of flats nearby. From here, I could see people arriving and departing.

There were no movements for the first hour except for some cleaners leaving. Then a familiar car drew up outside and Charlie and Michael Harrison got out and went into the club. They appeared to be alone. I ran quickly down the stairs, looked around and crossed the road to the club. The door was unlocked, so I took a chance and entered. The foyer was empty, but I could hear voices behind the double doors that led to the large bar area. I hid behind some long velvet curtains and listened. I could hear Michael's voice and then Charlie's. I was breathing heavily. It all seemed to be too simple. The moment had come too soon, before I had time to think about it, but it was an opportunity not to be missed. Then suddenly I heard a third voice. I didn't recognise it. Perhaps he had been in the club all the time, or perhaps he went in whilst I was coming down the stairs of the flats. I was trying to decide what to do when Charlie bellowed an instruction.

"Davie, go and find out where that lazy bastard Digger is. I've got a meeting across London this afternoon."

"Right boss," came the answer and I felt this person walk past the other side of the curtains and leave. I stopped thinking and acted. I took the gun out of the bag and burst through the double doors into the bar. Charlie was sitting on a stool at the bar and Michael stood a few feet away from him. They looked surprised but not alarmed. This changed when they saw what I had in my right hand. Charlie went to speak. I lifted the gun to shoulder height and fired at him. The bullet removed a small part of his left ear before smashing a large mirror behind the bar. I adjusted my aim and fired a second time. The bullet clipped his right hip and buried itself into the wooden bar that he then leaned on as he tried to get off the stool. I adjusted my aim again and pressed hard on the trigger. Two bullets slammed into Charlie's chest with a double thud. It was such a dull sound that, at first, I thought he might be wearing a bulletproof vest. But I saw blood ooze through his white shirt. All the time, Michael seemed incapable of movement. Charlie grimaced and appeared almost to be smiling. Before I dismissed the possibility of an armoured vest, I had pointed the gun at his face and fired again. This bullet smashed through his clenched teeth and the velocity knocked him back against the bar and he fell from the stool. I had almost forgotten about Michael, who had remained rigidly still throughout the shooting. I pointed the gun towards him and noticed a puddle of water at his feet. He had pissed himself. I was holding the gun much steadier now. Michael just seemed to walk onto the bullets that I fired into him. He appeared to be caught between a decision to run and a belated plan to grab me. In the end, he did neither and slumped to the ground as the two bullets entered his chest.

It was clear that they were both dead. I thought about making sure but, instead, ran from the club putting the gun back in the soap bag that I found I had been holding in my left hand all the time. After I had run for about ten minutes, I saw a broken manhole cover in the pavement and dropped the gun and bag into it. After collecting my belongings from Poplar Park, I headed for Victoria Coach station and climbed onto a coach heading to Cardiff. I would work out how to get to Ireland from there.

Eventually I was picked up by the police just outside Fishguard. They assumed I was making my way to Ireland.

I tried to tell them the truth but they just laughed. I had in fact, reached Ballycraich and seen my mother and sisters. My mother had insisted that I return to face the consequences of my action. She genuinely believed it would be seen as a crime of passion and I would serve only a short sentence. Back in England, the police were searching for a gangland assassin, a professional hit man. They had found the gun and this confirmed their belief that I was such a person. The 'baby-faced killer' was the most popular headline. The gun, supplied by Terry Hoon, had been used to kill a police officer a few months earlier, so I was charged with this murder too. So Hoon knows. He knows I didn't kill that copper.

In court, I admitted to saving up for the gun, which demonstrated premeditation. I refused to say where the gun had come from, so I received the maximum jail sentence permitted. The newspapers condemned a society that could produce a 16-year-old 'Cop killer'.

The evidence of the gun was enough to secure a guilty verdict on both counts of murder. For the deaths of Charles George Harrison and his son, Michael Charles Harrison. And, in a separate hearing, I was convicted of murdering Police Constable Derek Underhill, who I had never met.

I spent a considerable amount of time - certainly in the early years - in solitary confinement, among the paedophiles and rapists, because I was in danger of taking beatings for my crimes. But there was an inevitability about it. Some beatings metered out by friends and associates of the Harrisons and other beatings purchased by the police fraternity for a few cigarettes. It proved to be a friendless existence and it was possibly the Lord's blessing that I grew immune to the punishing treatment. There were more important issues than some pain or a little injustice. Making sense of what had happened to Jack. That was more important. It totally occupied my mind. It didn't make sense. It was such a complex puzzle that I became totally pre-occupied with solving it. If I could justify what had happened I might find peace.

One day all men look in the mirror and see their father looking back at them. I did but it had no effect on me. But Jack. Jack would have looked in that mirror and wished he was dead.

~~~~~

My life sentence was punctuated with disappointment. I could not be released for either of my parent's funerals as they were outside the UK. And, after indications that I would be released for Bill's funeral in 1976, my application was finally rejected because he was not a blood relative.

In the beginning, my only visitor was Nora, who in spite of my protests, continued to visit me several times each year for many years. Then, one day, Gabriella, who had visited me with Nora a couple of times, arrived on her own, to tell me that Nora had died. The one thing prison protects you from is death. Death doesn't happen in prison or, if it does, it is hidden away. People don't die in prison; they are released to die at home, Iffy Gallagher told me that. I was in prison because of death but once there, I was protected from it. So it was a shock when Gabby told me about Nora. I had forgotten that people die you see. I had simply forgotten that people died. I had never felt so lonely at that point. I even thought about writing to Mary because I didn't think I could stand the loneliness, which she had suffered since Bill died. Then, one day, I was summoned to the visitors' room and there was Gabby. I wasn't sure why she had come back to see me. I don't think she knew why she had returned herself. It was Gabby who witnessed my deterioration. From her intermittent visits she must have noticed how I was losing the power to communicate, losing the will to live.

The beatings in prison dulled my brain and this, together with the long periods of solitary confinement left me just a few degrees from a vegetative state. A mind that could think, a mind that continually challenged reality, but a mind that, to everyone else, just meanders and mumbles inarticulately of little more than nonsense. A happy release awaited me, until yesterday, or was it last week, or perhaps it was something I imagined or saw in a dream.

Certainly I had dreamed of it many times. Now my damaged brain has simply, cruelly, made that dream seem a reality. Jack is alive. Now I can say sorry for my crime, for I truly am sorry. If the Harrisons didn't murder Jack, then I am truly sorry for what I did. But how could it be? How many years have I been in prison? How old am I? How old would Jack be now? How old was Jack when I saw him yesterday, or last week, or whenever it was? I cannot seem to stop my mind from thinking. It never settles, never stops for a moment. I feel weak. I feel old. I seem to have been moved to a new location. This doesn't feel like prison. There are nurses here not guards. There are doors here, and windows without bars. There are no bars here, so it cannot be a prison. Perhaps I have already died. Perhaps this is some afterlife, or alternative universe, where Jack exists because we are both dead. I always believed he was only ahead of me on the road as he was that day when we arrived in London and as he was in life. It seems, in the end, I caught up with him.

'Face up to your fear Liam'. That's what Jack told me. 'Knock it over more times than it knocks you over. Nobody lost a fight by getting knocked down. They lost by not getting up'.

I don't know what day it is. I'm not even sure what year it is. I only know the seasons. If it is hot, then it must be summer. And each summer it hurts more. Whenever the dawn came up on a bright June day, I knew I would never forget. Every June day would henceforth be filled with his absence. A void filled with emptiness. How fortunate the man who lives his life unfettered by fraternal love.

My head is full of thoughts but none of them are of my own creation. So many, it seems that I am unable to think my own thoughts. I am incapable of emptying my mind so that I may think for myself. The torrent of instructions and abuse that controlled my existence for so much of my life has not stopped simply because I have changed locations. Not the same instruction received from the Mammy, or the verbal abuse of my father. That was tolerable, perhaps even necessary. But the instructions of the prison guards who, for so many years, monopolised my thoughts. Those instructions were different, compulsive. They controlled what I could do and, eventually, what I could think. Those poor misguided guards, who believed I had killed a police officer. I had been convicted, so what more proof did they need? I have forgotten how many years I was confined in the Scrubs and Maidstone. I have even forgotten how old I am. It doesn't matter now anyway for I am not long for this world.

And then there were the prisoners, none of whom could befriend me. For to be my friend was to become an outcast, like me. I killed the Harrisons. I had been found guilty of murdering two East End gangsters. And, yes, I had killed them. But murder? Up until this week, I never believed it was murder. But there are forces at work in this world that we cannot possibly understand. I simply avenged the murder of my brother Jack. A life for a life, how can that be murder? But if Jack is alive, then it would, indeed, be murder. Seeing Jack this week, after so long, has only added to my confusion. Surely he died all those years ago; Bill told me he was dead. So he must be dead. If not, why did I kill the Harrisons? Why did I spend so long in prison? The baby-faced cop killer.

Perhaps if I speak my thoughts I can overcome the confusion. Think of a moment in time and pause there. A time when Jack was here; the last time I saw him. But I can't remember when that was. I need to make sense of Jack's return. I need to think back to those distant days. Jack boxing and me by the ringside. Billy in his corner but no Mary of course. Mary would never watch him fight. "Be first Jack" I would shout, "be first." Billy looking disdainfully at me. On this occasion, he didn't want Jack to be first with the punch; he wanted Jack to be patient, to counterpunch the counter puncher. I bobbed and weaved with him. Ducking a swinging punch or moving to one side to avoid a straight left. "Go on Jack." But my attempts are in vain and I am taken back into Maidstone.

Now all I can hear is the shouting of the prison guards and all I can feel is the fist of a prisoner or, several prisoners as was often the case. It was not personal, but friends of the Harrisons would bring small gifts in, which were entirely permitted, to any prisoners on the same block as me. For a few cigarettes, I could be beaten and bruised. I could be left in this wretched state. For my body, I care little anymore. But if only I could take control of my mind.

If only I could switch off the voices for a few moments, so I could retrace what had happened, or what I believed happened all those years ago. For the events of this past week have thrown confusion and doubt over my recollection of those events. And, even though I am now removed from that prison to a place with windows and not bars, with nurses and not guards, I still can't stop the voices in my head.

I need some pills for this headache. I need some pills to stop this noise in my head. I call the nurse but she does not answer, so I get up and go to look for some pills. I just need to make sense of seeing Jack again.

Perhaps Gabby can explain, but I'm not sure if she is alive. Nora is dead, yes, but what about Gabby? When did I last see Gabby? When was it I saw Jack? I wanted to ask him so many things but I was so afraid that, if I spoke with him, he would disappear. But he disappeared anyway. Maybe it was a dream. It must have been a dream. After a life that was a nightmare, I must have been due a dream.

I finally find some pills. There is nobody around so I take them. I must rid myself of this headache. I just want some silence. I just need some quiet place, a place of solitude, where I can think again. The beating in my head drifts slowly away, like a thunderstorm retreating into the distant sky. The rain has stopped and the sun has come out. It is a hot day and I am sitting on a bench outside the pub waiting for my father. I feel sleepy. The arrowroot biscuit makes me feel dry but I'm not feeling brave enough to ask for another lemonade. You wouldn't want to upset my pa with a quenched thirst on him. There seems to be some movement in the pub and I look round the corner to see Himself, my brother Jack, walking over towards me. His eyes seem fiery. He seems preoccupied with something and he doesn't even see me. Little Tommy Flynn runs inside the pub to the comfort of his mother's arms.

I'll just sit here beneath the warmth of an Irish sun. What's the worst that can happen? It is suddenly silent; Tommy has stopped crying, there is no bird song, no shouting, no instructions, and just absolute silence at last. I sit back in the warm sunlight of my youth and feel myself dropping off to sleep.

4

Jack's story

"Hi, I'm Elana Balcescu. You don't know me."

On the evidence of the opening line and the fact that I did not recognise the number, I wrongly assumed it was a sales pitch and made a pre-emptive strike.

"I'm not buying anything..."

"I'm not selling anything," came the immediate reply.

"That's what they all say."

She had a foreign accent, so I presumed it was an overseas call centre, although her grasp of English was good, if a little fractured. She seemed too nervous for a sales person.

"Sorry" she said, "I am Romanian. I call about friend. He is criminal."

"Look" I said defiantly "if you know anything about that shop lifting bastard who got my wife into trouble, you had better speak up." There was a pause.

"Erm" she said after the brief period of silence. "Can we start this conversation again? I am not sales person and I am not shop lifter or friend of shop lifting bastard, who got your wife pregnant."

"No, not in trouble as in pregnant," I explained, "in

trouble as in trouble with the police."

I called over to Ludo and her family that I wouldn't be a moment and, being incapable of rudely dismissing a woman in unchivalrous fashion, I allowed the caller to start over again.

"My name is Elana and I am friend of Liam. He called me Gabriella," adding "Gabby."

"Liam Calnan?" I asked in a surprised tone. "I'm sorry, do you know Liam Calnan?"

"Yes" came the monosyllabic response.

"How do you know him?" I asked.

"I visit him in prison," she answered in poor but recognisable English. I hesitated, wondering if this was an elaborate scam.

Elana or Gabriella explained that she shared a house with someone called Nora when she first arrived in the UK. Nora visited Liam in prison and, after a while, Gabriella joined her. When Nora died a few years ago, the Romanian woman continued to visit Liam, albeit infrequently, firstly in Maidstone Prison and later in Sanderlings Open Prison. There were so many questions that I wanted to ask but everyone was ready to leave the pub.

"Can I meet you?" I asked, "Where do you live?"

She agreed and I arranged to meet her the following day in a Starbucks, near Mile End Station in the East End of London.

For some reason I didn't feel comfortable with telling Ludo what had gone on so far, so I told her I had a business appointment the following day. I hardly slept that night going through all the questions I wanted to ask of this strange Romanian girl.

131

Elana, or Gabriella, did not look anything like I had imagined. I thought she would be younger but she was older than her voice suggested, but still a waif-like individual who might be considered attractive by many men. She was about my age and spoke English with a strong eastern European accent. Her grasp and delivery of the English language improved the longer we spoke. It was clear that her Romanian accent returned whenever she was nervous. She had clearly been nervous on the telephone and her anxiety continued when we first met. She obviously needed time to feel comfortable about the person she was speaking with and I felt her becoming more relaxed as our conversation went on.

My response on the telephone must have worried her considerably and this had induced the broken English from her not too distant past. But, this aside, she appeared to me as a determined and single-minded individual and her fondness for Liam became more obvious as our conversation continued.

I remember my English teacher, Mr Kelly, posing the obscure question to me that, if I was an egg, what sort would I be? Then, challenging me to write about my life from that perspective. He was a little surreal to say the least, but he was a very interesting teacher. Ever since then I always tend to look at other people in that way. Clearly, Liam was scrambled in more ways than one. The nurse who looked after Liam was poached – slightly underdone, insipid and watery. I was the hard-boiled variety. Someone you can cook and put to one side; someone who might make a tasty snack later but didn't require any urgent attention. Someone who could be forgotten about for so long that you then have to dispose of them wastefully. Someone who appears tough on the outside but, unless you were prepared to put enough time in at the beginning would let you down.

Gabriella was an omelette. Her voice sounded young on the telephone and I hadn't realised that she had been visiting Liam for many years. I had mistakenly assumed that this was a recent development. Why had she remained so faithful for so long? What had kept her friendship for Liam so strong? Elana, or Gabriella, and I still wasn't sure which name was her real one, was not underdone in any way. She was an omelette. Her character had texture.

A petite 40 year old with a robust character that provided hearty support when it was needed. A woman of substance. I had known her just a few moments before her determination became obvious to me. She was, in a word, unwavering.

I was not surprised when she told me that Liam had dismissed her many times. He had told her to stop visiting; told her to live her own life; told her to forget him. But, like a loyal dog, she just kept going; not frequently, but regularly without fail. It seemed so selfless but, in her eyes, it wasn't. She did it for very selfish reasons she said but was reluctant to explain what those reasons were. She told me everything, or it felt like everything, in that first meeting.

She spoke, not with pride, but almost in reparation for something. A previous failing on her part that needed to be recompensed for. For her, Liam represented a penance - a catharsis.

Gabriella, as she wanted to be called, had been born and raised in a small town called Jimbolia, which was about forty kilometres from the city of Timisoara in Romania. She was an only child and had lived her formative years under the corrupt, repressive and economically disastrous regime of Nicolae Ceausescu. She had been about twenty years old when she managed to escape the horrors that were becoming daily life in Romania.

When she arrived in London, she rented a room in Poplar, in the East End of London. The landlady was an older woman called Nora, who didn't own the three-storey Edwardian house but, as the oldest resident there, acted as the spokeswoman for the tenants. It was Nora who convinced the landlord to let Gabriella rent the flat on the middle floor.

Gabriella got to know Nora as a friend and learned that Nora visited a man in Maidstone prison. His name was Liam and he used to live on the top floor of the house. Nora had become a surrogate mother to Liam, who had run away from home in Ireland when he was just fifteen. Then, one day, Liam was arrested for killing some people. He was convicted and Nora began visiting him in prison. She visited him every month to begin with but less frequently as she got older. When Gabriella arrived in 1986, the visits had fallen to three or four each year. Up until that time, Nora was making the journey into London to get a train to Maidstone, then a bus to the prison. She would be out all day and the visits were becoming more arduous as she grew older.

Gabriella took driving lessons and, after securing work locally, she bought herself a second hand car. She couldn't sit by and watch Nora make that long journey so, one day, she offered to take Nora to Maidstone. The visits continued for a few years, with Nora always applying for visits when she knew Gabriella was not working. When Nora died, Gabriella explained to me, it just seemed natural for her to continue the visits. At first, she just went to tell Liam that Nora had died. They had both grown to love and respect the old woman and they shared their grief that day. Liam didn't ask her to come again and Gabriella didn't offer to continue the visits. But, three months, later, Gabriella arrived at the prison as usual and Liam didn't ask why, or question her motives. Liam was, of course, much older than she was and there certainly were no romantic intentions on the part of either party.

Over the years, they spoke about Nora and the house and about some of the neighbours that Liam could remember. But they spoke little of why Liam was in prison. It wasn't a taboo subject; she just didn't need to know what had brought about this awful situation for Liam. She thought he must have been about seventeen or eighteen when the trial took place.

On the few occasions when the subject was raised, she recalled Liam denying responsibility for murdering one of his three victims. It was a police officer. His denial was not delivered with any rage of injustice but just calmly saying that he did not kill the copper. He had never denied the murder of his other two victims. Gabriella thought they were a father and son. She had heard local people talk of them in the pubs from time to time. She thought they had been gangsters who owned a nightclub, which was now closed. People still spoke of the Harrisons, she said, and whenever anyone mentioned the local cinema, they always added: "where the Diamonds nightclub used to be."

"Did he have any family?" I asked.

She shrugged her small bony shoulders and parried my question with one of her own.

"Everyone has family, don't they?" she asked rhetorically. "But none that he ever mentioned to me. He just wanted to be left alone but, for some reason, Nora was an exception to the rule and when she died, I sort of inherited that privilege."

I shrunk at the word privilege and suddenly realised the sincerity in that expression.

"Why do you do it?" I asked.

"Why not?" she answered with another question, "few of us have motives that are entirely selfless Mr. Daly. Few of us undertake anything without some ulterior motive. I have very selfish reasons for visiting Liam."

It was clear from her intonation that she didn't want me to ask her to explain. Her reasons for visiting Liam were her own. The reason for her behaviour was a secret that she was not prepared to reveal to a stranger. In fact, I am not sure it had ever been revealed to Nora or Liam.

"Jack" I said, "please call me Jack."

"Gabriella" she replied and we shook hands.

"Why not Elana?" I asked.

"It is unimportant. You would not understand."

"Please?" I asked.

"I was Elana Balcescu in my homeland. When I left, I changed it to my Confirmation name, Gabriella."

"Why?" I asked again.

"You are not familiar with Romanian history are you Jack?"

I shook my head.

"Nicolae Ceausscu was an indescribable tyrant, as was

his wife, Elana. She was a plague on our country and I could not go through my life with that name. It would have been a constant reminder of the pain they caused me and my family."

I pressed her further but she was unwilling to disclose more of the tragedy that resulted in her departure from her homeland.

When I returned home, I found Tonka stirring away at a homemade curry. I told him about Gabriella. He wanted to meet her but I wasn't sure either of us would ever meet her again.

~~~~

Sebastiano, Gigi and Ludo's mother flew home to Italy on the Sunday after the funeral. It was a relief to return to work the following day, although a considerable amount of time was still occupied with my mother's will and, of course, clearing the house in preparation to sell it. Tonka continued to stay there for the remainder of his leave.

After a prolonged spell of living away from home, I still managed to find a clean shirt and I joined Jonathan, Titus and Richard at the monthly diary meeting to decide what *The Main Event* would focus on over the next few months. The programme was decided some weeks in advance, which gave me sufficient time to organise interviews with the main characters. Some events were pencilled in and others set in stone. Wimbledon was an annual feature, as was the Grand National and the London Marathon. *The Main Event* was published ahead of the event, rather than as a commentary on the event itself. Several of the national Sunday newspapers tried to put us out of business by producing free supplements on events but our sales were maintained and there appeared to be a demand for the magazine. After all, everyone actually attending an event would buy a programme. So, with the increase in those watching on TV, there seemed to be an opening for a similar publication for the armchair viewer. Follow up articles were made impossible by the nature of the publication. So my articles on Giant Killers Stapleford Rovers in our annual FA Cup third round issue ended prematurely. Their giant killing had dispatched two lower division league sides in the first and second rounds. With *The Main Event* being produced in advance of their meeting with Premiership big boys from London, I rather missed the scoop when they stole a narrow victory at their marshy field of a pitch against their top-flight opposition. I pleaded with Richard to let me write a follow-up piece about the ebullient Rovers Manager but my pleas fell on deaf ears.

So, I spent the day building contact lists for the various events and tried to establish how and when I would interview my guests. I also managed to contact the Foreign Secretary's PA and arrange a date for the interview, which was to be published in the Peace Conference issue of *The Main Event*. The first day back at work was a long one.

That evening I finally decided to tell Ludo about Liam and my meeting with Gabriella. After the initial disappointment that I had not confided in her immediately, she was very supportive as usual. She suggested that we should visit the Imperial Nursing Home. Perhaps, she thought, that she might be able to make some sense out of his ravings. And she was convinced the nurse would be less dismissive of a couple than someone she suspected was a reporter.

"Why would she suspect that?" I asked.

"Because you are one," Ludo replied, adding, "I don't know why you simply cannot tell people the truth from the beginning. It makes life so much easier. You know it makes sense."

We decided to visit Liam the following Sunday when the traffic was quieter. Ludo was determined to find the underlying cause of this matter.

"If Liam is your real father, then you need to know. How can you go through life without knowing who your father is? It is ridiculous."

I agreed.

~~~~~

We took the country road to the Imperial Nursing Home, avoiding the main roads so that we could take in the Essex countryside as it welcomed the Spring Equinox. It was a different route to my previous visit, along the little-used B1739, which took us past my old place of work at Woolly Fold Manor. We travelled over the River Aught, past the village of Withersedge and up towards the Crouch estuary. The pretty white Anemone, the white chickweed and inappropriately named blackthorn and the yellow celandine accompanied our slow journey towards the nursing home.

Chiffchaffs, blackbirds and the scavenging magpies signalled the onset of Spring and the promise of warmer weather to come.

It didn't seem to matter what season it was inside the nursing home. The heat was relentless and the smell of old age fell rancid on the nose. There was a different nurse on duty and she seemed unduly shocked when we suggested we were there to see Liam Calnan.

We were escorted to a waiting room where we endured a long wait of over twenty minutes. I tried to ignore my impatient wife and resorted to reading the wall posters giving advice on anything from sexually transmitted diseases to Alzheimer's disease. I read the latter one and learned nothing that I hadn't come across over the last five years. Ludo was pacing with short strides up and down the room, clicking her heels on the tiled floor. She grew impatient before I did and got up at one stage to see if she could find the nurse. I suggested we should wait but Ludo insisted that she should make at least a tentative search for assistance. But there was nobody in any of the rooms along that corridor and wandering around an unfamiliar building might only waste more time. Just as Ludo was losing what remained of her patience, a Doctor and the nurse returned.

"I'm sorry," she explained, "but I needed to call Doctor Nagpal. We don't have a doctor on duty on Sundays," she explained further, "so Doctor Nagpal had to be called."

"Why?" I asked.

"Mr. Calnan" the doctor began to explain.

"I'm not Mr. Calnan" I replied.

"Are you not a relative Mr....?" He paused.

"Mr. Daly" I answered, "Jack Daly. It's complicated," I

140

continued. "I believe Liam Calnan was my father."

"You believe he is your father?" he asked with the emphasis on the word believe. I nodded and he paused to consider the suggestion.

"That's not very likely Mr. Daly," the doctor eventually replied, as he rummaged through the notes he had in a folder. He finally found what he was looking for.

"Mr. Calnan has been in prison since he was 17. How old are you Mr. Daly?"

"Forty" I replied.

The doctor sat down opposite Ludo and myself.

"Then I suppose it is possible," he hesitated "he could be your father. Why do you believe this is the case?"

"My mother died recently and I found some letters. Love letters I suppose. They seem to suggest that Mr. Calnan, Liam was my father."

Doctor Nagpal stood up and paced along the room as he considered his thoughts. He sat down and examined the little paperwork he had in Liam's file.

"Mr. Daly, was your mother Mary Daly?"

"Yes" I answered, intrigued to know how he knew that from the paperwork in front of him.

"Your mother is one of the two contacts in the file for Liam Calnan. People to be contacted in the event of an emergency, you understand. This file has only just arrived and we hadn't made contact with anyone yet."

"Who is the other contact?"

He thought about whether he should answer my question, so I interrupted his thoughts.

"Mary Daly was my mother Doctor. I am her only child. I have inherited her house and anything else she may have

141

including responsibility for Liam Calnan."

"Do you know someone called Gabriella Balcescu?"

"Yes, I met her recently. She was a friend of Liam, not a relative. Well, I'm pretty sure she isn't a relative," I hesitated as I was beginning to doubt most things I knew about Liam Calnan and my mother.

I offered to contact Gabriella and the doctor accepted.

"We need to establish the next of kin," the doctor said almost too quietly to hear and almost as if he was thinking aloud. He realised he had phrased his last words in a particular way.

"Next of kin?" I asked.

He put the paperwork down, closed the file and sat upright in the chair.

"Mr. Daly" he said hesitantly, "Mr. Calnan died last night. I'm very sorry."

In spite of my knowledge of Liam's condition, the statement was still a shock. I didn't know what to feel. I wasn't even sure how I should feel. I thought I should be more emotional but it was difficult to feel anguish or loss for someone I hardly knew simply because he may have been my father. The doctor waited for me to compose myself and to see what reaction would follow the news. There was little reaction except one of disappointment that I had found him so late. Too late it would seem.

We spent the next twenty minutes discussing Liam but Dr. Nagpal had only known him for a short time. I could see that the doctor sympathised with my plight and I wasn't sure our presence there was serving any purpose, other than to waste the good doctor's time. Ludo and I were just preparing to leave when something occurred to the doctor.

"I believe," said the doctor "that the nursing home has received all the paperwork on Liam Calnan. I haven't seen any evidence of other family members." He paused again and was clearly trying to reach a decision about something. We remained silent until he had completed his consideration of the facts.

"Mr. Daly, would you be prepared to take a DNA test?" He explained that he needed to locate a next of kin, if he could and, in the absence of anyone else or, indeed any paperwork to the contrary, I appeared to be the only possible relative.

I looked at Ludo. This certainly wasn't the outcome I had expected when I began the journey to the nursing home earlier that day. Liam Calnan was dead and I was being offered the opportunity to prove that he was my father. The whole situation was surreal. I felt like calling for a 'time out' whilst I considered all the facts.

"Yes, of course he would doctor," answered Ludo emphatically on my behalf, adding, "we must resolve this matter."

"How long will it take?" I asked.

"I'm sorry Mr. Daly, I have no idea. It's not something we do as a routine. I'm sure we have the facility to conduct such tests but I will need to make some calls. Would you like to wait or come back tomorrow? I'm not sure how long it might take for me to establish what the procedure is."

"We'll wait, if you don't mind" Ludo replied again without consulting me and, presumably, rediscovering her patience. The doctor looked at me.

"Yes" I confirmed, "we'll wait."

The doctor left the room and returned about thirty

minutes later looking pleased with his efforts. It was clearly not as complicated as he had feared and he seemed to relish an opportunity to venture into a new area of medicine. A simple mouth swab and some chain of custody procedures and documentation and the process would be complete. He believed he would have the result on Tuesday or Wednesday and we agreed to telephone him on Tuesday to find out.

When we arrived home, it suddenly occurred to me that I should telephone Gabriella. There was a tone of resignation in her voice when I told her the news of Liam.

"I have known him for over twenty years" she said, "and yet I didn't really know him at all."

She asked about the funeral but understood that it was too early to know when this might be or even whether we were entitled to be involved in his burial.

"There's something you should know," I said, and I told her about the DNA test.

"Good" she said. "I hope it is so. It would be too sad that he should be alone in death as he was in life."

"I'll call you when I have some news," I said before putting the handset down.

~~~~~

When the telephone rang at home on Tuesday afternoon, I thought it might be the nursing home calling me with the result. As it was it was PC Etherington saying that, following my family bereavement, they had decided to

144

postpone interviewing Ludo and I about the offences for at least another week.

"Look" I said, "I really don't need this at the moment."

"I know sir" he replied, "that's exactly why we are postponing your appointment. We'll be in touch in a week or so."

I was immediately suspicious of his motives and eventually came to the conclusion that they had postponed the matter in case I won the sympathy of the court through the loss of my mother. I could blame everything on that sad circumstance and walk free. That was their motive, I thought, not one of consideration for my situation but wholly the product of their desire to achieve a successful prosecution.

Impatiently, I decided to call the nursing home and was told by the nurse that the results would arrive the following day so I asked if I could meet Doctor Nagpal in person. The nurse sounded surprised that I wanted to travel all the way there for a result that I could get over the telephone but, on the basis that Doctor Nagpal was on duty, she confirmed it would be in order. Ludo decided to accompany me in the hope that we could achieve some sort of closure to this episode in our lives.

The nurse was probably right in presuming it would be a non-event.

"Mr. Daly" the doctor said as we took our seats in his surgery, "I'm not sure what your expectations are. I'm not sure whether you wish to see a positive or negative result," he added as if he was trying to establish whether he should begin his sentence, 'the good news is' or 'the bad news is'.

The look of indifference on my face was met with some

surprise by the doctor who, unhesitatingly spewed out the result.

"Mr. Calnan is not your father Mr. Daly."

Ludo and I looked at each other and my mind raced. What did those letters from Liam to my mother mean then?

"However" the doctor continued, "he is a close relative. My guess, based on the information I have now been given, would be a first cousin or uncle."

"I'm pretty sure that neither my mother nor father had brothers or sisters," I said. "I would say I was certain" I added, "but certainty itself seems a distant relative at the moment."

I came to the nursing home that day looking for resolution, for closure. What I received was even more doubt, even more confusion. Liam was my uncle or cousin, yet neither of my parents had brothers or sisters. How was that possible?

The drive home was completed in near silence. We were both contemplating what all the evidence suggested. But that's all it was doing, suggesting. Nothing was certain anymore. Ludo and I discussed the events of the past week over dinner that evening. It seemed bizarre that Liam and my mother should die within days of each other. They had been at the very least very good friends. Perhaps they believed I was Liam's son. There probably wasn't any way of knowing back then. But that still doesn't explain how I am related to Liam. After we had finished the meal, we sat drinking a bottle of wine and, eventually, had the contents of the shoebox and my notes from the meeting with Liam spread on the table.

I began to read again the two letters. Ludo examined the

old newspaper cutting, the green rosary, and the Mass card with the face of St Jude. A marriage certificate, two birth certificates and a black and a white photograph awaited examination.

We both rummaged through the evidence. Ludo discarded the Mass card and picked up the black and white photograph, then went off to get some other photographs of my dad, Bill.

"This is definitely your mum," she said giving the photograph a closer look. "And that is clearly your dad. Just look at this photo of him taken, what, a few years later?"

She was right. It was my mum and dad in the photograph.

"And the other one is Liam. He is very young but it is him, isn't it Jack?"

I wasn't certain but had to admit it looked very much like him.

The three of them were standing outside a pub. I handed the photograph back to Ludo. She looked at me, and then looked back at the photograph. It was slightly out of focus.

"Who took the photo?" she asked.

"I don't know I answered." I picked up my notes from my only meeting with Liam. "Mr. Levy, someone called Terry, Nora? I just don't know Ludo. As Liam kept saying over and over again: who knows? Who knows?"

~~~~~

Later that week I received another telephone call from the nursing home. In spite of the fact that Liam was not my father, they still pressed me to take responsibility for the body. After all, the DNA test had proved I was a close relative and, as I was the only relative they were aware of, I became a solitary candidate for the job. For my part, there was no reluctance to accept the duty and Ludo supported that view. Furthermore, we had recent experience in handling a funeral and my only regret was that the Catholic Church didn't have a two for the price of one offer on at the moment.

I was considering publishing an obituary in the national press but knowing what media interest that might generate, keeping the service to Liam's few remaining friends seemed the more sensible course if the funeral was to retain any degree of dignity.

I was keen to run an obituary as it appeared to be my only hope of someone stepping forward with some more information but, in the end, I was persuaded against it by the ever-sensible Ludo, who was being her highly organised self. 'Mum' was the obvious floral tribute for the last funeral, but what was appropriate now? I don't suppose there was a big call for question marks at the florist and a hearse with 'Dad?' might raise a few eyebrows in the quiet lanes of Beadsman's Cross.

5

Ω

Mary's story

The sun was setting on the last day of my life. How many people can know when their final hour has arrived? My beloved John probably knew it, when he stormed off into that summer evening all those years ago. No, I do him an injustice. Time is memory's enemy, as Liam says. He didn't storm off. His decision, and the action he took, was measured. His countenance was frighteningly unemotional; I remember that now. He was calm and his steps calculated. In that frame of mind, surely he would have understood the consequences of that considered act. Surely, he would have known the reaction that would follow his action. So, perhaps like me, he did know that it was his final day on God's good earth. And Bill certainly knew. I think he knew what my intentions were that day. He didn't look into my eyes. He wanted to save me that last look of condemnation.

I finished my tea, washed up the cup, checked the time of Jack's return flight and telephoned Pat Joiner to ask her to call over for a cup of tea in the morning. She was pleased to do so, having given Jack her promise to keep her eye on me in his absence.

Pat had been ill herself lately but was refusing to go to the doctor. She had an aversion to doctors and hospitals since the death of her husband. He had died of cancer like Bill but, unlike me, she didn't care for him at home. She wanted to, if only to avoid hospitals but she simply wasn't able to do it. And, when Tommy had gone into hospital, it looked like it would be a short stay. He seemed to be on his last legs. But Tommy was a fighter and he just held on for months, teetering on the edge of death. Pat had to go in every day until, in the end, she was petrified of hospitals.

So here she was now, riddled with arthritis and heaven knows what else and she won't go to the doctor. How many people do we know at our age who are not on medication? One is the answer, Pat Joiner. So, out of courtesy and because I thought she was a belligerent old fool I asked her again whether she had made an appointment with the doctor. I got the usual answer and heard the theme tune of her favourite programme in the background, so ended the call by saying I would see her in the morning.

I put on a clean nightdress and climbed between the cold sheets having already determined not to live through the night, let alone the nightmare of Alzheimer's. I wondered whether the clean nightdress would arouse suspicion. I dismissed that possibility, wrapped up my own selfishness, and resolved not to put poor Jack through the anguish of a lingering illness. He didn't have the temperament or disposition to nurse me through this ordeal, and why should he? He had done his best over the last five years but my condition was deteriorating and I realised that, if I left it too long, I would not be sufficiently cognisant to make a reasoned decision if, indeed, suicide can ever be considered a reasoned decision.

I sat there looking at the items on the cupboard by the side of my bed, wondering why people ever decided to take themselves off to Switzerland to commit suicide, or felt the need to pursue their right to die with dignity through the courts. Why couldn't they simply just do it? And, if you can, do it without your children knowing it was suicide. Don't make them live with your decision. Don't publicise your intentions, but be brave enough to take responsibility for your actions. No, Jack must never know it was suicide. Why should he pay for my mistakes and the mistakes of John, Liam and Bill? Jack was a victim of what we did. He doesn't deserve to suffer any further. We four must all share the blame, me no less than the others.

I should have walked away from what Michael did to me. But that is all in the past now. It will all be put to rest this very night. Only Liam remains and he has never spoken of it. He will take our secret to the grave.

All I then need is a resource that is both fatal and undetectable and, with the doctor's knowledge of my condition, it was likely that he would simply put my death down to natural causes.

I remember what the doctor said to me when Bill was dying. 'There's only one thing going on his death certificate,' he said referring to the cause of death. His reassurance was provided at a time when I asked about accidently administering too much morphine. And, indeed, due to loss of sleep, I could quite easily have mistakenly administered too much of the drug. I'm sure there are doctors out there who choose to do the right thing. The right thing by everybody, the deceased and those left behind.

After all, what loving wife would take the life of her devoted husband? Except I wasn't the loving wife to his devoted husband.

I thought for a moment, about the alternatives, but concluded that I could not go on like this. My whole purpose in life expired when I was still a young woman. Everything since then has been a falsehood, a pretence, and an imitation of life.

What son should be responsible for bathing and nursing his elderly mother? Not mine I decided. I didn't know when the next opportunity would occur or whether I would be sufficiently capable to make such an important decision. So all I need to do now is reach over and take a few pills. There is a degree of justice in my action. After what I did to Bill, I deserve to die, even if it isn't in as much agony as Bill suffered. No, I will go gently into that goodnight, not screaming in pain like Bill. I mistakenly thought too much morphine would have the opposite effect. I expected him to fall into a peaceful sleep. Instead, I witnessed the frightening and painful experience he suffered. And still I remained silent. He reacted like a heroin addict who had overdosed. Ecstasy followed by an agonising death.

I sat there, by his bedside, holding his hand, listening to his ravings. I didn't leave the room. What I felt for my husband was not love, nor was it sympathy. My emotions had been suspended since John died. All the sadness in the world felt like a yoke across my shoulders from that point. I carried the sadness with me and, when Bill died, there was nothing left.

The first rule for the perfect suicide, as with the perfect murder I suppose, is not to tell anyone. Take the secret to your grave. Much easier in the case of suicide, of course, because all you have to do, presumably, is to resist writing any sentimental goodbye notes. Who would I write such a note to? Certainly not Jack. I have kept so many secrets from him already that to invite any revelations through a suicide note would be unthinkable.

The idea of suicide occurred to me quite early on in my illness. In the case of Alzheimer's disease, by definition, suicide requires some forethought, some pre-meditation and intent. I had that intent. Only the timing needed to be determined. I just needed to be brave enough not to postpone it.

The second rule for the perfect suicide, or murder, is patience. Suicide, like murder, should not be a reaction to an event. That's where Liam went wrong. It was too soon after the loss of his brother. If he had waited a few years, nobody would have connected the murder of Charlie and Michael Harrison with Liam. It would have gone down as a gangland slaying, although that was how it had been reported at the time anyway, except Liam was no gangster, just a young man, not much more than a boy, who was angry at the loss of his brother. He was the only one who shared my thoughts, shared my emotions when John was killed. No, if Liam had demonstrated patience he may have avenged his brother's murder without the loss of his liberty.

So I have to demonstrate patience, but without postponing the event too long. I must avoid the temptation of waiting for Jack and Ludo to have little Johnnie, or Giovanni knowing them. Then little Giovanni, himself, would stop me. There would be someone else to love. Someone else to steal my life from me. No, the decision could not be deferred any longer.

Hope is poisonous. It poisons the soul and destroys the mind. I speak from personal experience. A life spent hoping; a life of unchanging love and unrelenting, misplaced anticipation of a joy that was never forthcoming. How I wish I could have been like Liam. We were both prisoners. He, a prisoner of hopelessness, trapped by a steadfast grip on his own righteousness; held firm by the rectitude of his actions. And me, a prisoner of hopefulness, trapped by an unfaltering unjustifiable belief. A belief that, in truth, seemed to justify my cowardice for I should have followed John with Jack inside me. It should have been spontaneous. I should have followed him into that black hole; that monolith of hope, the ever after. That promise made to me by the nuns and teachers at St. Andrews Junior School. The thought did not go unconsidered. In those terrible days after John went missing it was, perhaps, my only thought. Sitting there with the green rosary, he had given me dreaming of a union in the afterlife.

I stare aimlessly about the room and remember the story of Romeo and Juliet from school. One dying because they thought the other was already dead, then that one returning to life to discover the other one was dead. That story, that hope, had prevented me from committing suicide back then. That thought that John was still alive. Well, that and the stirring of little Jack in my womb. Thinking that John would return. Thinking that he might not be dead. I have postponed the event for too long. I want to die. I am ready to die.

More frequently, I notice myself waking up, or rather coming round, not knowing where I had been or what I had been doing for the last hour, or day in some cases. So it had to be now. And, when Jack said he was going away overnight, I said a little prayer for John and Jack and for the, as yet, unborn Giovanni, or maybe Mary.

But I certainly didn't think about going to Switzerland or making some political point about suicide or the right to die with dignity. I had been denied dignity all my life, what would I do with it now? Anyway, there was enough information around to enable a do-it-yourself suicide. I just needed to select the least detectable method because I wouldn't want Jack to be distressed or, worse still, wondering why I would want to end my life. Autopsies, I found out, are the exception rather than the rule and only occur in about ten percent of cases. So, as Bill would have pointed out to me I'm sure, it was ten to one against them discovering I had committed suicide. Then there are the doctors, as I found out in Bill's case. Any patient in an advanced state of terminal illness, and Alzheimer's is considered terminal, receives little consideration when the Death Certificate is produced. After all, the person was dying anyway. And who else would be interested? Coroners, ambulance men, the police? I'm sure they have enough to occupy themselves without worrying whether the body of a terminally ill patient was the result of a suicide or not. That must create ten times the amount of paperwork to be completed.

So, as long as I didn't hang myself, throw myself off a tower block or put a polythene bag on my head, there was little hope of anyone realising it was suicide. So what's left? Sleeping tablets are the most common means according to the movies. But they are more likely to cause unconsciousness for a few days before death occurs and, if someone discovers you before you die, you may just go into a coma. So not the most reliable choice if you are expecting visitors that week. Paracetamol is fatal within about twelve hours but you don't actually die for a couple of weeks, so no better than sleeping tablets. I ruled out alcohol, bleach, carbon monoxide, caffeine, rat poison, drowning in the bath, electrocution and falling under a train or bus.

Eventually I arrived at a suitable solution. If I could find 500 milligrams of cyanide salts, I simply needed to drop them into the bottom of the toilet bowl, producing Hydrogen Cyanide as it hits the water. Then inhale the fumes and you just have time to flush the toilet before you die. Certain death in twenty seconds. You need to have an empty stomach apparently, as a full stomach can delay death for up to four hours. Almost undetectable and all the evidence is flushed away. The perfect solution it would seem, except I had no way of obtaining even a small quantity of cyanide without attracting some attention.

Just when I thought all was lost, I was reading a gardening book and came across some advice about the beautiful, but quite deadly, it would seem, Foxglove. If only I had time to grow a sufficient supply of Foxgloves in my garden, the extract from the plant will give you an undetectable heart attack. Recommended on the internet as the perfect self-deliverance for those who don't want anyone to know it was suicide. Again, the problem seemed to be one of supply, except that it was available as a prescription drug and, by good fortune, was being taken by Tom Anderson, who called in to check on me occasionally. He who had accompanied me to church on Sunday when I actually remembered it was Sunday and was well enough to go. I became aware of this when he visited me with Ivy O'Brien one day and he had to take his afternoon dose of Digitoxin. I simply needed to invite him back one afternoon and relieve him of his medication. Now here it is, on my bedside table. He's probably still wondering where he left it. The medicine bottle is disposed of and only the pills remain in a small heap on my bedside table, my foreseen resource.

~~~~~

I sit upright in bed, with a glass of water in one hand and the pills in the other. As the light fades in my bedroom, I consciously take myself back to a nightclub. I am younger. We are all younger. We are all alive. And we join in with a familiar lyric. *'Life could never be what we want it to be'*. It tortures me and more than forty years later, it is as relevant and as hauntingly germane as ever. The song was written for me, or at least with me in mind. It must have been. And John and, yes, even Bill too. The three of us are on the dance floor. We are smiling, singing, with our arms around each other. Liam wants to join us but sits obediently at the table.

'Can I be satisfied knowing that you love me?' I sing to Bill.

'Each night before you go to bed my baby, whisper a little prayer for me my baby', is John's line to me. And, as I close my eyes and raise my glass, I sing back: *'this is dedicated to the one I love'*.

A long time ago, before my wretched posthumous life

158

began, lived a young woman who enjoyed life, who woke up each morning with a desire to live life, not necessarily to its excesses, but at least to its limits. A young woman waiting patiently for the arrival of her Prince Charming like most girls of her age. But this was not to be the fairy tale of a young girl's dreams. There was not to be the happy ending that accompanies such tales.

And what would Jack make of it. It is all best left unsaid. That is exactly what my mother said when I told her and dad that I was pregnant. "It's all best left unsaid," she advised my father. Things between me and my father were always best left unsaid. What he felt about me and what I had done with my life. And what I felt about him and how he favoured Linda. I was insignificant to him. It mattered not whether I was pregnant, or whether I got married to John or lived in sin with John. Just as long as he had his precious Linda, that's all that mattered to dad. I'm glad they emigrated. It severed me from my past. My family gone, John gone, Liam as good as gone. And what was I left with? Bill. *Can I be satisfied knowing that he loves me* as Mama Cass sang? Well I suppose I must have been because I spent nine years of my life with him before getting time off for good behaviour.

Satisfied. Yes, that sums up my life. Adequate, no more than adequate. The same way it sums up what my father thought of me. Adequate, no more than adequate. *Life can never be what we want it to be.* The Mamas and Papas were right. As the night finally seizes the day and appropriately suffocates the remaining life from it, Bill, John and I all sing together: '*In the dark hour before dawn*'.

I lay frozen to the bed waiting for death, knowing it

would come soon. But this was not a fearful ending. I had been expecting my life to flash before me, but no. My remembrances play out patiently before me, capturing moments from my early life. That life which began with John and ended with John. The rest was simply purgatory, somewhere between heaven and hell. I had been like a flower cut from the root and placed in a vase. Slowly, by degrees, realising my fate. Life itself taken from me, and then left to exist as if nothing had changed. But it had changed. Life itself had been severed. It was that song's fault, that anthem to my posthumous life. Its significance haunts my waking nights. I read into those lyrics the prophetic ending of my life, my real life, not this one; not this posthumous one. And so I did say a little prayer each night. And it was dedicated to him, or 'Himself' as Liam called him. It became a ritual. I could not go to sleep until I had prayed for him. Not to do so would have somehow betrayed, not just John, but God Himself, who reminded me of my duty through those Bass and Pauling lyrics. They wrote nothing else, or nothing else I ever heard of. Perhaps they were put on God's earth for the sole purpose of haunting me through those words. Why else would they have written 'whisper a little prayer'? It had to be whispered because Bill declared that it should be so. Bill said we should keep that secret in our heart, so the prayer had to be whispered. But how could Bass and Pauling have known that unless God had willed it so? So it wasn't just our song. It wasn't just about John and me. Bill was lurking there, in the lyrics, a shadowy figure hiding behind that whispered prayer. Bill, poor Bill. For just as I had eked out the days of my life, made endless by John's spontaneous actions and musically endorsed by Bass and Pauling, so Bill had lived that same wasted life too. Waiting for a love that would never arrive. The only difference was that my love had at least existed, albeit briefly. But the love Bill wanted had never been born. No, Bill had not been left out by Ralph Bass and Lowman Pauling. You see, I know those words by heart and they had Bill covered too. My destiny was the lyrics but Bill's was the mirror of those words. I was the chorus and Bill the verse. *Life could never be exactly like we want it to be.* And it certainly wasn't for Bill, he wanted life to consist of me loving him. But it couldn't, for I loved someone else. *Can I be satisfied knowing that you love me?* No Bill, your love was not enough for me. A marriage doesn't exist because two people declare it to be so, even in the eyes of the Catholic Church. Nor can it exist because one person loves the other. Unreciprocated love is a worthless thing. *One thing I want you to do especially for me and it's something everybody needs.* I knew what he wanted me to do especially for him and I knew it was what he needed me to do too. He needed me to love him, but I couldn't. His love was not enough to make it right.

I didn't even love him enough to stop him smoking. All those years he waited. Wanting me to insist he should stop smoking. To say that I wanted us to grow old together. But I never did. And he knew I wouldn't. It was a marriage of convenience. Convenient to him because he loved me. Convenient to me because I was having a baby and needed his protection. So, no, I never pleaded with him to stop. And when I sat outside that consultant surgeon's room waiting for him to come out, knowing the outcome, there were still no tears. I didn't even go into the room with him.

161

Cancer. Tumour. Malignant. Three months, maybe six. No growing old together. No pleasant retirement. No summer days together in the garden watching the approaching of autumn. Winter arrived early for Bill.

Nine years we had been married. Jack was eight. That sounded better. Nine years married and a son of eight seems to suggest an early consequence of love. An immediate realisation of a romantic union. And nobody in Beeding suspected anything different. Poor Bill. There are only two tragedies in life and dying too young isn't one of them. The first of the ill fated are those never to have loved. But Bill had loved, I was certain of that. And the second are those who have loved and not had that love returned. Poor Bill. A victim of unrequited love. He was never under any illusion about that fact. He just presumed, hoped, expected that I would grow to love him as much as he loved me. But my love lay elsewhere. I just didn't know where. Charlie Harrison saw to that.

Bill loved to gamble. Each Tuesday evening would be spent locked in the kitchen as he painstakingly selected the most likely football matches to end up as a draw the following weekend. And each Saturday he would be occupied by frequent trips to the betting shop. He never gambled very much but he thought he was successful. No gambler I have ever known has been successful, except perhaps Bernie Woolaston, who treated it as a profession. Bernie had the necessary singular characteristic of a successful gambler, self-restraint. Billy couldn't resist a bet but Bernie could walk away unless the odds were heavily stacked in his favour. I'm convinced that this is why Billy did what he did. Why he ended up marrying me. He was a gambler and he gambled that I would learn to love him. He lost, just like he lost most Saturdays. The best gamblers, like Bernie Woolaston, have patience. Patience to wait for the right bet to come along. Billy couldn't wait for the right bet; he couldn't wait for the right woman. It had to be me and he lost everything.

The people that lived in the East End of London, at least at that time, had patience. They had patience to wait for a Labour Government that would actually do something about their living conditions. They had patience to wait for somebody to do something about employment for those who survived the war. Apart from those lucky few who lived in the new Lansbury development built as part of the Festival of Britain, almost everyone I knew lived in a street, which had been partially bombed in the Blitz. The inhabitants of Poplar and Stepney would never vote against Labour and they were patient enough to wait until their party was elected.

Just around the time John and Liam arrived, the East End got its long-awaited Labour Government. MacMillan might have thought we had never had it so good, but it certainly didn't feel like it. Apart from the feeble attempts during the Festival of Britain, most of us were still sharing Victorian housing, with outside toilets, or living in pre-fabricated boxes whilst those in power decided what to do about the wrecked homes and families that formed London life at that time.

That summer of my youth was warm and exhilarating. I remember sunny days visiting Greenwich Park. Taking the bus around the docks towards Millwall and walking through the foot tunnel, past the Cutty Sark to the biggest park I had ever seen.

Alzheimer's is a strange disease. It gnaws away at the memory but leaves large sections of that memory intact. I remember, as if it were yesterday, walking up Greenwich Hill with John on my arm and Liam running up the hill in excitement. Every day seemed sunny. I don't remember much of the winter, just those long summer days.

~~~~~

Dappled sunlight scatters through the branches of an apple tree until that same sunlight conspires to wake me from my daydreaming. I don't know how long I have slept and I have to think about where I was. My thoughts are scrambled, like the splintered rays of sunlight on the mossy green lawn. It is a sunny day and most of the regulars are outside the pub, which suited John as he could sit with Liam. England had won the World Cup and the locals were enthused by the moment. John looked serene against the noisy background. I realised where I was, on the grass lawn that separated the pub from the road. I must have been dreaming. John's incessant questioning had prompted my dream. Bill, Liam, John, what difference did it make now.

I remember that first day I met John. Remembrance comes as naturally as leaves to a tree. I have nothing else. How could I lose my prized possession? My former friend, my memory, the enemy of time, and now my enemy too.

It was a hot August day and a few customers were standing outside the open door of the pub, but most were inside, shading from the blistering heat. Business had been erratic during the World Cup but since the celebrations, people had taken to going to the pub. Dad was even thinking of taking on extra bar staff but, for the time being, I would do.

Michael Harrison sat, with three other young men, in the farthest corner from the bar. He waved at me and pointed to the almost empty glasses on the table. I started to pour four pints of Red Barrel but my father took over from me. He looked at me, then at Michael, and thought he could see trouble looming.

As I looked around the bar, I saw those standing outside the door part to allow someone in. The tall muscular young man was followed by someone who was clearly under age. Without speaking, the older one pointed to an empty table and the younger one sat down obediently. He came to the bar and ordered a pint of Guinness and a bottle of Coke with a straw.

"Is he allowed in here?" he asked as he sorted through his change.

"As long as he isn't drinking alcohol and he doesn't cause trouble. He looks like someone who could cause trouble," I added sarcastically.

Liam was sitting innocently. John smiled at my remark.

"He'll behave himself alright," he assured me.

My father was taking the tray of drinks over to Michael Harrison's table.

"I haven't seen you in here before" I asked.

"Sorry" he replied, "I'm John and this is my little brother Liam." That was the end of the conversation. He was a man of few words. John took the drinks back to his table but as he turned, I saw a look on his face as he caught sight of Michael. Not the fearful look that most faces showed when they caught sight of a Harrison but one of recognition, one of impending trouble.

I sometimes think that the Gods saw my fear that day and decided to make it a reality. Michael and John were destined from that point to engineer my future. From the look on my father's face, he may have suspected it too. In fact, you didn't need to be overly intelligent to forecast that danger lay ahead with this relationship. But I really would have to possess the skills of an oracle to have predicted that young Liam would cause the trouble he did. Nothing happened between Michael and John that day but there was an inevitability about it. Trouble slept lightly in the East End that summer and these two wouldn't need to do very much to wake it.

"How old is the boy?" asks my father.

"He'll be sixteen next birthday," replies John.

"So he's fifteen" my father corrected him bluntly.

"He'll be no trouble," said John. I see the irony in that remark now. It sits taunting me. But I can't lay the problems on Liam. He simply closed the chapter. He closed the book actually. 'Still waters run deep,' my mother always said. But she referred to people like Billy Daly. She wasn't wrong. Liam was uncannily like Bill in that respect. Whereas John was different. Shallow waters, far from still. Nothing was hidden; emotions, intentions, outcomes.

~~~~~

166

Death seems such an unthinkable event to the young. I thought nothing of it until, of course, John died. Then I thought of little else. Death and I have not conversed for so long. To me it can only be one of two things. If it is simply an end; the lights are switched off and then nothing, then what is there to fear? It is merely a reflection of my life. If, on the other hand, the glory of God awaits me then, again, I have nothing to fear. Except perhaps meeting John. What would I be to him? An old woman? And he to me? Still a young, handsome man? No that doesn't make sense. How could he love me now? That moment, that feeling, is passed.

No, death is simply the end. The alternative is unthinkable. I will not meet John again. Nor Bill I hope. And what of Michael Harrison? Why would I want to open all those old wounds again? Life is not the dream and death the awakening. How did we come to invent such fantasies? We live, we die. And, if we are fortunate, our memory will live on for a generation. Then all is lost.

What does Jack know of my life? Why would he want to know? It is best he knows nothing. I'm sure Bill didn't tell him anything. And if he did, he would have forgotten it. Just the ramblings of an old man. Although he wasn't old. Not that Jack would appreciate that. What did I know of my father? He lived. He ran a pub, he emigrated and he died. Or my mother? She lived, she got married and she died. Well so did I. What else matters? My life was brief. Two summers in the sixties. Nothing. Just like death. Then nothing. And what good would it do to fill Jack's head with those two summers? He probably wouldn't believe his mother was capable of such things anyway.

Truth screams at me from the darkness as it draws near me. So what is truth? What if everyone was told the truth? What good would that do Jack now? Bill is not your father. The truth. But truth only provokes questions and I have neither time, nor tolerance, for questions.

The fact that I lived, even for two summers, would probably be a shock to him. And then it would be one shock upon another. No, a life conceived from a lie should remain a lie.

People are either planets or suns. Jack is a sun; people revolve around him. So was Michael. But John and Liam were planets - always thinking of others, mainly each other, but sometimes me. It was that attention that gave me life. Ludo doesn't have that, of course, she is another sun. That's why she and Jack have problems.

~~~~~

Death comes so slowly, more slowly than I expected. God of mercy end it now. But I cannot clear my head of memories. What a paradox Alzheimer's is. Bill knew the brothers before me. It may even have been him who first brought them in The Crown and Sceptre. Bill had certainly been a regular for some time before I met John and Liam. Bill was older than me, and so I took little notice of him. I search my memory and I remember that day I first met John and Liam. Bill joined them shortly afterwards. He obviously knew them because he went straight up to them and started talking. He had a new Kodak Instamatic camera that he had just bought and he and the boys unpacked it and rolled in the film. Liam was fascinated and John and Bill allowed him to set the camera up.

"Can I take the first picture?" asked Liam, and Bill, generous as ever, allowed him to take one of the two of them drinking their pints.

As I recall, none of the photographs that Liam took were in focus. I seem to recall that there were only two good ones from the whole roll. John took one of Bill, Liam and me and, although I'm sure I kept it, I don't remember the last time I saw it. The other was taken by Bill, after he had read all the instructions. I think he gave it to Liam as a consolation for not taking one decent photograph himself.

I now know why he gave that particular photograph away. It showed John and me in an embrace with Liam peering over the top of us. I remember that picture well. We all looked so happy.

The following Saturday evening the two brothers were back in the bar with Bill. The weekends saw a group of regular customers. Ronnie the Gold would be fencing stolen jewellery in one corner. Ronnie was a stocky guy with a seriously false tan and wrists playing hosts to gold watches and bracelets. Anything you wanted Ronnie could get. My dad bought me a 24-carat gold gate bracelet from him for Christmas. He insisted it was straight otherwise my father wouldn't have bought it.

Sitting on his regular stool at the far end of the bar was Terry Hoon, a little weasel of a man He worked at the other end of the supply chain. Terry would dispose of things that people didn't want found again. Guns, evidence, witnesses and even bodies. He had the smell of death about him. Whenever Charlie Harrison was in, he would always buy Terry a drink, although he would never invite him into his company. Terry was a parasite who lived on the fringes of East End society. The Harrisons did not always come into the pub on Saturdays. Charlie would be at his club or wining and dining celebrities at a boxing tournament.

The weasel stepped down from his stool and walked over to Bill and the boys.

"Hello Billy my boy and how are you this bonny day?"

"I'm in the pink Terry" replied Bill, then tentatively introduced the boys.

"If I can ever be of assistance to you boys, you must let me know. Just ask anyone for Terry Hoon and that'll find me."

"What is it you do?" asked Liam politely, attracting a remonstrative glare from his older brother.

"A bit of this and a bit of that my lad. I help people out." He turned to John, giving a greasy smile. "A pleasure to meet you both." He hobbled back across the room like the vulture he was and perched himself back on his stool. Not having been offered a drink by Bill or the boys he ordered one for himself.

I think it was me who asked John out the first time because, if it was left to him, it may never have happened. For our first date, John took me to a cinema in Stratford to see a James Bond film. We went out together regularly after that, sometimes in the company of Liam and Bill and, at least once each week, on our own. It was Christmas before we made love for the first time. He was my first lover and I think I was his too. I never asked him. Neither of us knew what to do with a condom so, in the end, we didn't use them. It was less to do with our religion and more to do with how he felt about me, and how I felt about him.

Without deliberately trying for a baby we both, subliminally I suppose, concluded that the arrival of a baby would allow us to marry. Well, it would allow me all the antagonism I would get from my father and my mother too probably. Linda would never get herself pregnant. Presumably, she was waiting for Prince Charles to come of age anyway, after all she was a princess wasn't she? No, a pregnancy represented my ticket out of there. It would let my father off the hook too. He wouldn't have to go through the pretence of giving away his beloved daughter, because I wasn't his beloved daughter. No, he could then save all his cash for his beloved Linda. Yes, I would be doing him a favour by getting pregnant. But, in the end, it was intentional, it was a conscious decision. It simply simmered away in my head and I think it occurred to John too. So we didn't use condoms. We used the safe period of the month and then, eventually, the unsafe period too.

It was when I told my father I was pregnant that he first mentioned about emigrating, as if it was a punishment. He didn't care where. Canada, Australia, anywhere to get away from me. Somewhere where he could have his precious Linda all to himself. Life at home became unbearable for me and I continually implored John to get me out of there.

So, whilst my parents were preoccupied with researching their plans for a new life, John and I were queuing at a local Labour Councillor's evening surgery trying to get a flat or Council house to live in.

Three offers we received. The first two were slums, in

order that we were forced to accept the third and last one. Anything would look better after the first two. It was a two-bedroom maisonette on a main road. We had planned to let Liam use the second bedroom until the baby was old enough to need its own. Liam wanted to stay with Nora in Plimsoll Street but, after a long discussion into the night, John convinced him to move in with us. There was some talk about Liam returning to Ireland but he wanted to stay around long enough to see the new baby. To maybe take some photographs back to his Mammy. I think he stayed in touch with Nora. She was a surrogate mother to him.

John and Liam decorated the flat in the evenings and Bill also came round to do some painting if he was on shift work too. In the end, it was habitable. My parents never visited. John was treated like no more than a customer at the pub when we visited there. I got bored with the endless talk of emigration and John and I eventually went to different pubs to avoid it.

Once the flat had been decorated, we decided to hold a party. The boys finally completed the job over a bank holiday weekend. Whitsun it must have been. We were all too tired to host a party, so, after some discussion, we went back to Diamonds nightclub after many months of absence.

I don't think Michael knew that John and I had moved in together and I don't know how he found out. But the Harrisons could find anything out if they put their minds to it.

I don't remember exactly what happened in Diamonds that night. We didn't visit the club too often and my memories of each of those occasions have merged into one event. I remember John having an argument with Michael and I can actually remember Michael being courteous and generous. He sent a bottle of champagne to our table. But something happened that night, I just can't remember what it was. It involved John and Michael as was foreseen from their first meeting in The Crown and Sceptre. I'm not sure what triggered Michael's actions but presumably it was borne out of his jealousy of John. Whatever happened that day it remained simmering, almost out of sight.

~~~~~

It was a hot day at the beginning of June. I was in the bedroom of the flat trying to decide what dress to wear that evening because John was taking me to see *Doctor Zhivago* in London. It was a Friday and John would be home by five o'clock. We probably wouldn't see Liam before we went out because he normally worked late on Friday. I don't know whether I left the door open or whether he broke in but Michael was suddenly standing there in the doorway of our bedroom.

"Fancy a dance?" he asked and I struggled to understand what he meant.

I don't remember screaming. My response was pleading, rather than screaming. We had been to school together. We had been friends. Surely, he wouldn't force me to have sex with him if I told him not to. But he did. My pleading turned to sobbing, my sobbing to loud crying.

"I have a baby inside me Michael. Please."

He didn't speak after the initial remark in the doorway,

or I don't remembering him saying anything else. I'm not sure if he was trying to hurt me or John. I wasn't sure why he would want to hurt me. He held both my wrists in one hand and ripped my knickers off with the other. He shook my legs from side to side and eventually lay on top of me to stop me escaping. When it was over, he rolled off me and dressed himself. I just lay there, on the bed, clothes in disarray, crying loudly.

"Give my regards to Johnnie," he said as he went downstairs.

I heard the door close and lay there still crying into the pillow, not thinking of anything. I'm not sure if I thought about covering the incident up. I'm not sure I thought about anything. I was still lying on the bed crying when John came home

"Who did this ting to ya Mary?" he asked as he sat on the bed and held me to him. I answered immediately.

"Michael. It was Michael." If only I had not said those words. If only I had considered the consequences. I allowed Michael to take away my dignity but I shouldn't have allowed him to take the rest of my life away too. If only we could live again one moment in our lives for me it would have been that moment. If only we could change one day, it would have been that day. And yet I tried, for the rest of my life, to remember that moment because it was the last time that John held me in his arms. The one moment I would like extinguished from my life is the one I treasured and held on to as his memory faded.

I took a bath and got dressed. I felt I should go and look for John. Just as I was getting ready to leave the flat, Liam arrived home, whistling as he came along the landing,

174

unaware of what had happened. In my desperation to keep the truth from him I only managed to confuse and concern him more. He became as agitated as I did as he learned, little by little, of what had happened that afternoon. We discussed what course of action we should take. We had no telephone, so John couldn't call us. But, what if we went out and John returned home?

"He told me to stay here," I told Liam, but Liam wanted to go to Diamonds nightclub to find John. I held on to him to stop him from going.

"Just a few minutes more," I pleaded. "Let's just wait a few more minutes Liam, he'll be home soon."

We sat, silently, in the living room as the sun went down. Suddenly there was a loud banging on the front door and Liam rushed out, thinking it was his brother. But it was Bill.

"We must leave," he declared as he barged into the living room. "It's too dangerous to stay here."

Liam looked as confused as I did.

"We can't leave," he told Bill. "We have to wait for Jack."

"Look," said Bill firmly, "we haven't got time to discuss this. John isn't coming back."

"What?" asked Liam while I sat silently on the couch.

"Probably," added Bill, "John probably isn't coming back."

"Why" asked Liam, "where's he gone?"

Bill grabbed Liam by the shoulders to hold him still because he was fidgeting, not knowing which way to turn.

"It's too dangerous to stay here Liam, we must go. Think of Mary. It's not safe for her. We must leave. Put some things into a bag."

"No" said Liam, "I've run away before and it doesn't solve anything."

"For Mary's sake Liam. This isn't about you or me. It's about Mary. We must save Mary. It's what John would want. John wants you to protect Mary. We have to leave here now."

My heart was pounding. I went upstairs to get a holdall and started putting some clothes into it. At that moment, all I remember was wanting someone else to take control. I wanted someone else to make the decisions, so I responded by doing exactly what Bill was telling me to do. Liam looked confused, so I found another bag and started putting Liam's clothes into it. Bill was still holding Liam and trying to convince him of the great danger we were in.

"I'm not leaving my brother," shouted Liam "I owe him everything. I can't leave him now."

He pulled away from Bill.

"Where is he? Why isn't he here?" he screamed at Bill.

"Liam" said Bill calmly, "I don't know how to say this but John is dead, Liam, he's dead."

"No" said Liam, "how can that be? He can't be dead. It's not true."

"Liam" said Bill, "The Harrisons have killed your brother. Michael raped Mary and Johnnie has killed him probably."

"How do you know all this?" asked Liam as he rediscovered his composure. "How do you know?"

I remember looking at Bill because I hadn't thought about how he knew John was dead.

"It's all over the street," said Bill. "Liam, in all probability, your brother's body is in some flyover somewhere. Now I'm sorry to be so blunt with you, but we have to act and we have to act now. If he is alive he'll find us."

I entered the room with two bags and dropped them on the floor.

"See Liam, Mary's leaving. I'm leaving. You must come with us. Mary won't go without you Liam." I stood next to Liam and put my arm round him. He was starting to cry and I suddenly realised I had stopped crying.

"Look," said Bill, talking directly to the two of us for the first time, "I know what you feel in your heart. But, for this one day, lock those feelings away. For John's sake lock them away and look at them another day. Think on it another day. Not today. Today we must make our escape. Charlie Harrison won't stand by and let Mary implicate him or his son in Johnnie's murder. We must get out of here. Do you understand?"

I remember thinking about poor John concreted up in a flyover somewhere. How do I keep that feeling locked in my heart? There had been no warning. There had been no threat. It was a normal Friday and John had simply disappeared. He had gone to see Michael and not returned home. Rumour and gossip had spread that John had nearly killed Michael Harrison that evening.

"What you're feeling Liam is dangerous. It's not safe. It's not safe for Mary. Lock that feeling away in your heart for today Liam. Come with us now." He paused. "We have to leave."

"Leave?" asked Liam again, but this time it was less of a question and more of a statement.

" Yes, leave, now, tonight. Harrison is not going to

stand by and wait for you to take revenge," he said to Liam.

"Revenge for what?" asked Liam naively.

"John is dead Liam," said Bill again and I started to cry again.

"Mary," he added, "resign yourself to that darling. We must pack those feelings away now. There's no time to cry, no time to remember. You'll have the rest of your life to remember, but not tonight."

So I decided to suspend the emotions of love and exercise the virtue of love. To leave my home and, without ever seeing a body, try to start my life again without John. Eventually to drift into a convenient marriage with Bill and to devote myself to a relationship that was both hypocritical and a poor substitute for the real love I felt for John. It wasn't fair to John; it wasn't fair to me, and it certainly wasn't fair to Bill. But that's what he wanted.

I decided that Bill loving me would be enough. It would have to be enough because I would never love anyone other than John. Well real love, romantic love. Of course I loved little Jack but the love of a mother does not replace the yearning inside. It does not appease the emptiness I felt without John.

When Bill fell ill, I decided to nurse him at home. It was the least I could do for him. I may never have loved him but I owed him something. He respected my dignity and I now had the opportunity to protect his. I would ensure he died with his dignity intact. An extra dose of morphine and he, generous as ever, looked away, not wishing me to feel any guilt at an act of kindness to him. Maybe, if he were here, he would have crushed these digitoxin tablets for me and administered them with the same kindness.

178

Suddenly a jagged sharp pain, like an electric shock, rose from my stomach into my chest. And in a moment of intense pain, the pain that haunted my life, I wondered whether I would see John again.

6

Jack's story

A fragile, tenuous and overcast April Fools day welcomed the undertakers as they arrived outside the house with Liam's coffin. The date seems wholly appropriate, as Liam appears to have fooled all of us. His letters to my mother gave every indication that he was my father. Perhaps he believed he was my father. But what about my mother? Why would she not correct his misunderstanding? He was younger than she was. Almost too young. Yes, mother was just twenty when she fell pregnant but Liam would have been about seventeen. It seemed an unlikely scenario, which had now been proved false.

A noisy, and presumably lost, seagull hovered above. It's loud bellowing mocking my inability to solve such a simple mystery. Ludo, Sebastiano, Mama, Gabriella and I sat in silence in the solitary funeral car that followed the hearse to the cemetery. Behind us drove Gigi and Tonka, looking like two bodyguards enlisted to protect a dead murderer. I recalled newsreels of famous mobster funerals with the cortege flanked by black-suited bouncers. Fortunately, the press was not represented at the funeral. So, at least, the day would go off quietly. The killings back in the sixties were old news. Liam's long-term prison sentence had gone largely unnoticed by the media and he was to be laid to rest in peace.

The funeral had given Ludo's family an excuse to make a return visit. Clearly, they didn't know Liam but the sense of 'family' that binds the Italian culture required their attendance. Sebastiano seemed to think he needed an excuse to visit his sister and he was not deterred by the fact that it was less than a month since his last trip.

The journey took us along the familiar country lanes we had travelled for my mother's funeral just a few weeks ago. The landscape was slightly greener and cow parsley now inhabited the roadside. Mother had been buried in an old part of the cemetery, close to where my father's Rose bush and ashes were – or at least the person I had thought of as my father for so many years. Mother's grave was therefore in a different part of the cemetery from where Liam was to be laid. The cars drew to a halt and we got out.

The new graves were being dug some distance from the internal road and we had to walk alongside some scant woodland. An old Ash tree had fallen some years ago, perhaps in the great storm of 1987, and a crusty black fungus was attracting insect life. We paused to give Mama some time to catch up with us. She was remarkably fit for her age but the path was slippery from an overnight frost that remained, determined to resist the warmth of the sun.

Those trees that survived attracted just a few bluebells and some wood sorrel. The colours of spring were, as yet, the pastel shades of death, rather than the bright yellows of life.

The documentation passed to the nursing home by the prison had little information about Liam but his religion was clearly shown as Roman Catholic. That was sufficient for Father McNally to offer to conduct the service.

Stood around the grave were Father McNally, Sebastiano, Gigi, Ludo and her mother, Tonka, Mrs. Joiner, Mrs. Griffiths who was getting good value out of her big black number, Mrs. O'Brien and Gabriella.

Gabriella wept in isolation, quietly, at the graveside. They had become good friends and she knew, as Liam approached his release date, that she might not see him again. But I don't think it had occurred to her that she might be denied this by his death. Perhaps her tears were as much about others in her past life too. Who had she left behind in Romania? What heartache and anguish had she suffered to cause such tears? What happened to her to create such empathy with Liam? Mother's fellow parishioners joined in Father McNally's prayers and Sebastiano and his mother tried to participate too but in Italian.

Mrs. Joiner got on very well with Ludo's mother in spite of the language barrier. It was strange really, because Mrs. Joiner was a neighbour, not one of mother's friends from the church. I suppose that Mama just assumed that all the attendees at the church were Catholics. Mrs. Joiner even invited Ludo's mother over to her house for lunch the following day. This news was met with undue pleasure by Sebastiano, who immediately declared that he and Gigi would be going sight seeing for the day. Someone with a more suspicious nature than I would think he had an ulterior motive.

It was a day for making new friends it seemed. Gabriella and Tonka were engaged in a long and seemingly intimate conversation in the Horse and Hounds after the funeral, and they arranged to meet for a meal the following evening. Meanwhile I was trapped between Sebastiano and Ludo and was subjected to a subliminal and wholly contrived conversation about children.

By closing time at the pub I was ready to concede defeat, although I did wonder whether I should ascertain who my own father was before I foisted another Daly, or Calnan, onto an unsuspecting world. Ludo's mother caught certain elements of the conversation and it was almost enough to drag her away from her multi-lingual discussion with Mrs. Joiner on the illnesses of old age.

The following day, Sebastiano and Gigi set off with a map of the London underground and a couple of scraps of paper that they had scribbled notes on. It clearly had a plan, as they were deep in conversation about the day ahead, albeit Sebastiano had forgotten his commitment to speak English whilst in the UK. Ludo's mother set off on the short journey to visit Mrs. Joiner, and Tonka and Gabriella had agreed to make a day of it too, rather than just dinner. I was left, not unwillingly I might add, to keep my promise to Ludo from the previous day, hoping that Mama didn't end her visit to Mrs Joiner prematurely.

~~~~~

In the absence of any more information from Gabriella, I resolved to spend what time I had over the next few days reading through any newspaper reports of Liam's trial in case I could turn up any names that might produce a lead of some kind. The gnawing feeling that mother had not been honest with me strengthened my resolve to unravel this mystery.

So I trawled the internet and even telephoned some of my old contacts I had worked with in Fleet Street, but what leads were produced tailed off because the person had died or was simply untraceable. Most of the names mentioned were police officers anyway and there seemed to be no witnesses for the defence, or none that were mentioned in the newspaper coverage of the trial at the time.

I caught up with Tonka again later that week. I called into my mother's house to collect some more rubbish for delivery to the local tip and Tonka was getting ready to go out. He had arranged to meet Gabriella for a third date in just seven days. This was beginning to look serious. Not surprisingly, she had been more forthcoming to the sympathetic and taciturn Tonka than she had been with me. Tonka oozed trustworthiness and the frail Romanian had clearly felt able to tell him her innermost secrets.

Gabriella had been born around the time that Ceausescu became head of state. His disastrous policies had punctuated her young life and made some of the modern day regimes, like Mugabe, seem moderate by comparison. He had made abortion illegal, divorce was impossible, contraception prohibited and childless couples were heavily taxed. In 1974, he declared himself President for life. And, in 1981, rationing was extended to include even the basic essentials such as bread.

Gabriella's family lived in Jimbolia, close to the border with Serbia. Young Serbian men would taunt the young women, suggesting they could help if they wanted a baby.

Then, one night, when she was just 19, she was raped by two men. She wasn't sure whether they were Serbians who had crossed the border, or the border guards themselves. Either she saw little of her attackers, or selective memory had protected her from the details. When the baby boy was born her parents tried to convince the authorities it was their child but they were both too old to be taken seriously and, in keeping with the law at that time, the child was taken away from the single-mother and placed in an orphanage. Despite strenuous efforts, neither Gabriella nor her parents saw Bodgan again.

Life became intolerable for the family and Gabriella's parents resolved to get their daughter out of Romania. Her father was 62 years old and had worked in Timisoara all his life. He had savings, which he kept secret from the authorities and he gradually went about turning this into gold, by buying second hand jewellery. He realised that his daughter was not capable of the more heroic escapes from Romania and he knew she had to succeed first time. Anyone caught trying to breach the borders was soundly beaten. And anyone caught attempting it a second time was never heard of again. Her father knew that the only methods of escape were guile, physical strength or bribery.

It was 1986 and a member of the Romanian Olympic wrestling team had defected to the west during a competition in Greece. Soon after this, two brothers had also escaped by swimming across the Danube at night to Yugoslavia. Neither of these routes was possible for his daughter, so one day, having kept the plan secret her, Teodor Balcescu gave Gabriella some cash and his hoard of gold jewellery in order that she could bribe her way out of

Romania and across Europe. He purchased travel documents and a change of identity. Elana Balcescu became Gabriella Stanasila. She would later reclaim her true surname but retained the name of Gabriella. As I was already aware, the name of Elana evoked too many bad memories as this had been the name of Ceausescu's wife and it was now a name hated throughout Romania.

So, by bribing border guards she eventually managed to make her way to Hungary. From there it was relatively easy to reach Austria and then she finally bribed her way on to a coach containing British tourists returning from a holiday in the Tyrol region. Once she got into the UK, she was recognised as a legitimate refugee and granted permission to stay. Only then could she get a message back to her parents. Over the next two years, the transparency and openness of Glasnost gave her hope that, one day, she may be reunited with her beloved parents. And, three years after her arrival, when the Berlin Wall came down, it seemed that her hope had not been in vain. The world was changing. The Ceausescu regime could surely not hold out against the changes that were sweeping across Eastern Europe. Gabriella's enforced exile appeared to be slowly coming to an end.

A few weeks after the world had rejoiced at the Berlin Wall being toppled, and just one week before Christmas, news reached Gabriella of events in her homeland. Teodor Balcescu, only a few weeks from retirement, was walking home from his workplace in Timisoara. The city was filled with people protesting against the Ceausescu regime. People across Europe had been empowered in these last few weeks. There was an expectation of freedom. But freedom came in a bloody guise to many that day.

The army opened fire on the protestors and Teodor, like many others, was killed that December evening in Timisoara. It was the final act of a repressive President. Three days later Nicolae and Elana Ceausescu were taken into custody and, on Christmas Day, they were executed by firing squad. Gabriella's mother died a few weeks later. At first, Gabriella thought that, perhaps, she had taken her own life. Life without Teodor would have been unbearable and she never held any hope of seeing her daughter again. She had not really understood what was possible in the free society that appeared on that St Stephen's day in 1989. She had lived her life as a prisoner of the state and she could not comprehend the meaning of liberty. The whole tragedy was, of course, compounded by Gabriella's inability to trace her son Bodgan.

Elana Balcescu changed her name to Gabriella because Nicolae Ceausescu's wife was Elana. The once revered couple were, to a much greater degree, reviled by the Country they ruled. Both were executed with the full support of the people. All that Gabriella knew about her son Bodgan, was that he had been taken into one of Ceausescu's infamous children's homes because he was illegitimate. Even if he had survived the intolerable conditions of these homes, his life was only imaginable as a nightmare existence. Her heightened sense of guilt for escaping that awful regime and leaving her child and parents was given some form of release when she met Nora. Nora gave her somewhere to live and welcomed Gabriella into her life. But the young Romanian needed to seek redemption. Tortured by regret and guilt she needed some form of penance to make up for that sense of guilt. She found that escape in Liam and she and Nora visited Liam together until Nora died. Then Gabriella simply continued to visit him on her own. Liam was her reparation, her penance, but she could never forget Bodgan. She thought of him every day and prayed for him every night.

I thought back to Liam's funeral, and began to understand why Gabriella was weeping at the graveside. She had been denied attendance at her father's funeral and her mother's funeral too. Liam was a poor substitute for her parents, but he gave her the opportunity to care for someone. And then there was her son Bodgan. Was he still alive? And, if so, what had become of him in the new Romania? I imagined Gabriella, in her exile, wondering how twenty years of neglect and abandonment had affected her lost son. Her tears had been as much for her own family as Liam.

~~~~~

As Tonka's relationship with Gabriella developed in the days after Liam's funeral, Ludo and I saw quite a lot of them. We had dinner together and they helped us to clear mother's house in preparation for selling it.

One particular dinner was less than successful. I had too much to drink and started asking awkward questions of my best friend. Like whether he ever felt guilty for killing people he had never met before. They were poor jokes, made at the expense of someone I loved dearly. Gabriella

188

was shocked and Ludo was a little more disappointed in me than usual. But Tonka was unaffected by it. The conversation covered war in general and terrorists in particular, and I wondered whether Tonka ever gave any thought to forgiveness.

"For them or me?" he questioned.

"Both, I suppose," I said before changing my mind, "them."

"It isn't for me to forgive. If they want forgiveness, they should go to God. My job is to arrange the meeting," he said in a defiant tone.

Ludo tried to change the subject from the rather paradoxically divisive subject of forgiveness and that was when Gabriella told us the story she had told Tonka the previous week. Tonka later told me that it seemed easier to tell it the second time, so maybe we should encourage her to discuss it. Her own guilt, at leaving her parents and her son, needed to be exorcised.

I eventually managed to change the subject but learned nothing new about my quest for information on Liam.

Because he represented atonement for her perceived sin, the relationship between Gabriella and Liam was less about him than her. She never questioned him but only listened. So she knew little of his past. She believed he came from Ireland and had a brother named John. But, apart from that, his life before prison was largely unknown to her.

"Surely he mentioned someone," I asked, almost badgering her on the subject. Tonka gave me a look that pleaded with me to drop the subject.

"There was someone called Linda. Liam mentioned that his brother John didn't like her. She was a bit stuck up. I think she might have been related to your mum. Did your mum have a sister?"

"Not one she ever mentioned to me," I answered, "I just thought she was an only child like my dad – well Bill."

Gabriella could see it was important to me and thought about it again.

"I'm sure she was your mum's sister. I'm sure I remember Liam saying that his brother didn't like Mary's sister Linda."

"And did Liam ever mention any of the events that led up to his conviction?" I asked almost imploringly.

"His brother had a fight with one of the men Liam killed. The younger one I think. And he also told me, some time back now, that someone was raped." She offered this last remark reluctantly, presumably thinking it might lead on to a discussion about her own experience.

A look from Tonka told me not to go there but I couldn't resist the opportunity to discover something, however irrelevant about what happened all those years ago.

"Who?" I asked, "Who was raped?"

"I don't remember. Liam only told me when I told him about my past life." She paused and I resisted interrupting her. Tonka got up from the table and filled the glasses with wine.

"Was it Linda who was raped?" I continued.

"I don't think so. Possibly. Jack, our conversations were always about me," she continued. "He was a fantastic listener but rarely spoke. It's difficult when two people are both ashamed of their past. Neither of us had any particular desire to unload our baggage. We were just there for each other. I went there to be supportive of Nora and then wanted to be supportive of Liam." She stopped talking for a moment but nobody interrupted her flow.

"But, all the time, he was supporting me. He was listening to my problems. He was unloading my baggage. I know now how much I owe him. I know that now because I know so little about him. I suddenly realise that it was he who was counselling me, not the other way round." She paused again.

"So, Jack, I know very little about Liam. He was one of the few men I spoke to about being raped. He probably mentioned it to me at the same time, perhaps to show I wasn't alone. Liam knew so much about me, and I knew so little about him." She drank some wine in an effort to collect her feelings.

Once I realised she had stopped talking I wanted to keep the conversation going.

"Could it have been Liam who was raped?" I asked. Tonka and Ludo looked appalled at my question but Gabriella did not flinch. "In prison I mean. Do you think it was Liam who was raped?"

"No" she answered positively. "No, I'm certain it was a woman because I was telling him about me and I remember he knew someone who had been raped. I don't think he said who it was. He probably didn't want to betray their trust, just as I knew he wouldn't tell anyone about my terrible experience."

Nothing in Liam's letters suggested that it could have been my mother who was raped. The words came flooding back because I had read them over and over again in my head over the last few weeks. *Those feelings that we agreed to keep locked in our hearts cannot be hidden any longer.* This didn't suggest that a secret was being locked away but their feelings for each other. *'You and Bill might suffer by my actions but it must be done.'* Surely that referred to him killing the Harrisons. *'Jack is my responsibility. I love him too much to deny him this one thing'*. This simply suggests that Liam is my father, but there were no kisses on the letter. Then the next letter in January 1969. Liam wanted my mother to get on with her life with Bill and me. *'Bill is a good man'* he said, so he clearly wasn't responsible for raping her, if indeed it was my mother who was raped. *'It is best that little Jack knows nothing of me. Please grant me this one request. Forget me.'* And, of course, *'A last kiss for Jack. How can anyone not know who his real father is?'* Well me for a start, I thought.

Who else did Liam know who could have been raped? Perhaps it was yet another relative I didn't know I had, mum's sister Linda. Having already spoiled the evening I decided to drop the subject.

"I'm sorry," I said, "it's becoming an obsession with me. It's as if part of my life is missing. I feel like someone who lost their memory for a large period of their life and desperately wants to know what happened."

"That's understandable Jack," said Tonka. "We're your friends. And I think I know you well enough to know that you won't let the subject drop until you have got the answers you want. You're an investigative journalist Jack. You were when I first met you as a kid. You love searching out the truth. Remember the visits to Woolly Fold Wood? In the end, you found out what was going on in that place didn't you. And you'll solve this mystery too."

~~~~~

The following week the four of us met up again and Gabriella and Tonka asked whether we would consider selling mother's house to them as they were thinking of moving in together. Ludo and I were a little surprised but I was pleased the house would remain accessible to me. It haunted my life in a friendly way and I would have felt sad had I never been able to visit it again.

I mentioned Gabriella's case when I interviewed the Foreign Secretary. I was hopeful that he might be of assistance in locating Bodgan but his response seemed shallow.

My train journey into London to meet the Minister was delayed. I was in danger of missing the appointment and made several desperate calls from my mobile telephone to the Foreign Secretary's Personal Assistant. Fortunately, the ambitious politician was as anxious as I was that the interview went ahead. There had been rumours circulating in the national press that he was destined to be the next Prime Minister and a soft interview for *The Daly Report* was an ideal photo opportunity. So, he decided to wait for me in the hotel.

By the time I arrived, he had been waiting nearly two hours and, judging by his appearance and demeanour, he had spent most of the time drinking at the bar. We relocated to his hotel suite and the interview itself went very well. He provided plenty of one-liners that would make a good article. Despite his over indulgence in alcohol he still managed to put over a persuasive argument for a

Conference that I was highly cynical of. Even my question about holding such an event whilst soldiers, around the world, were still giving their lives for a peace that appeared unachievable, was rationally dismissed.

Towards the end of the interview, he began to relax completely in my company. Whether this was the result of alcohol consumption, or the way I deliberately put my notebook back in the briefcase and settled down opposite him with a drink, I cannot say. My intentions were simply to seek his help with Gabriella and her search for Bodgan. He relaxed and even his personal assistant left us alone for a few moments.

When I said I was friendly with a young Romanian woman, he curtly replied that 'we all have one of those dear boy'. This was the first indication I had that he had perhaps relaxed too much. The amount of alcohol he had consumed waiting for me to arrive was becoming clear, hence his less than sympathetic response to my having a young Romanian woman friend. In fact, he completely misunderstood my relationship with Gabriella and, rather indiscreetly, opened up about his own relationship with a young Romanian woman called Adriana Blagu.

Perhaps he believed I would have no interest in such a story. After all, I wasn't a reporter from the News of the World. *The Main Event* was hardly likely to print an expose of the Foreign Minister's extra-marital relationship. By the time his PA returned to the room, he had been less than discreet about his relationship with the woman and admitted that she would be accompanying him to Geneva.

Eventually I managed to get him to appreciate the situation with Gabriella and Bodgan and, on the face of it, he seemed prepared to do something about it. I dismissed any altruistic motives to his promises. It would, of course, be a great news article if he managed to reunite a mother with her child after so many years, particularly a mother and child separated by such a tyrannical regime. Rightly or wrongly, I was convinced of his good intentions by the time we parted company.

At the end of the evening, he grasped my hand and promised, most sincerely, to resolve the matter of the 'lost Bod' as he kept saying.

"Must find this lost Bod Jack. Absolutely. No probs old man."

"That's awfully kind," I said as he personally escorted me to the door.

"No probs. You scratch my back and I'll scratch yours," he said alcoholically. "You have my word as a gentlemen and a Minister of Her Gracious Majesty's Government," he added, swaying as he held on tightly to the door of his suite.

"I look forward to reading the article Jack. I shall be in touch. Trust me. Scouts' honour."

However much I wanted to believe that his intentions were honourable, I had insufficient faith in his commitment to track down Bodgan, to tell Gabriella or Tonka but I did tell Ludo, who was as sceptical as I was.

So, when I called round to see how Tonka and Gabriella were progressing with their plans to buy mother's house, I didn't mention my meeting with the Foreign Secretary. It seems Tonka's extended leave was ending and he was preparing his bag for another tour of duty.

"I thought you told me you were going to be around for the whole of the summer," I reminded him.

"Well you know how it is with me Jack," he answered in resignation. "Duty calls."

"What about the house?" I asked and then regretted it, as it sounded as if I was chasing him. But he was not offended by the question.

"I've put the wheels in motion," he assured me, "Gabby hasn't got anything to do."

"You should do a search and a survey Tonka. I don't want you taking everything on trust mate."

"Ok, I'll do everything properly. 'But I think I'm as familiar with this house as you are."

"Sorry, I didn't mean to hurry you. You go off and save the world. Everything can wait." I put my arms round him and we held each other just as we did when we were kids.

Gabriella had given her landlord notice on her flat in East London and said she was quite capable of moving what little furniture she had. But I insisted on renting a van and moving her properly as soon as she had a weekend free.

While I was there, Ludo called me on my mobile phone to tell me we had to call in to the local police station to see PC Etherington. He was on duty later that week so would appreciate it if we could call in, she said. He emphasised, she added, that we should call in separately as we were charged with two separate offences. I reassured her that we would be visiting PC Etherington together, whether he liked it or not.

Ludo related the latest news, including the call from PC Etherington to her brother that evening. The Skype webcam showed him venting his anger as he handed the line over to his mother.

The next day, I left home before dawn, trying not to disturb Ludo. I was interviewing two jockeys who had been booked to ride in the Grand National and, for some reason best known to themselves, horse racing trainers prefer to gallop their horses before the day begins for most of us. The big race was an annual feature edition of *The Main Event* so I had to find something new each year for my interview.

This year I intended to interview the oldest and youngest jockeys in the race, simply because a 75-year-old aristocrat had decided to risk life and limb to compete. And, as he was a not-too-distant relative of Jonathan Willshire, the interview needed to be handled sensitively. Sir Leslie Aloysius Willshire, was a Judge, so with those initials, headlines like 'law unto himself' sprang immediately to mind. There were many checks and balances to ensure that every racehorse in the Grand National was fit and able to cope with the rigours of the race. A gruelling four miles, and fences higher than Sir Leslie's opinion of himself, placed themselves between success and failure for the horses. Vanity and insanity placed itself between Sir Leslie and his belief that he could succeed. Unfortunately whilst the horses had to meet a stringent vetting process, the jockeys simply needed to pass a medical. The doctor didn't live, apparently, who could tell Sir Leslie that he wasn't up to the challenge that awaited him.

It was an interesting interview. Sir Leslie's great-great-great uncle had served with the Light Brigade but was, in the old man's words, unlucky enough to miss the 'big one' made famous by Alfred Lord Tennyson. Sir Leslie was willing and able to make up for his ancestor's good luck. By comparison, the youngest rider in the race was from a very poor background. He was raised on a farm in Ireland, the 'runt' of the family as his less than politically correct father had described him. He was, indeed, a tiny young man, who sat precariously on the horse to have his photograph taken for the magazine.

In order to avoid incurring the wrath of Titus, I decided to wait until Declan O'Mahon visited England to ride at Cheltenham, a month or so before the Grand National, rather than make an expenses-paid trip to Ireland. I then followed up the face-to-face interview with an extended telephone conversation before the big race at Aintree. Declan was a modest and interesting individual who lived for his work. He loved horses and riding. I tried to get him to make a comment about his elderly counterpart, Sir Leslie, but all he could say is that he hoped he would still be riding competitively when he was 75 years old. He was very flattered that he should be interviewed for *The Main Event* and wanted me to visit him and his family in Ireland.

Having completed the interviews, I was just left with the challenge of writing something new and interesting for the readers.

That weekend Ludo and I helped Gabriella move house. She didn't have much furniture and she asked me to make a diversion to the recycling depot to dump some of that. I had already told her that she could keep what furniture she wanted from my mother's house and agreed to dispose of what she didn't require. In spite of my protestations, she kept assuring us that all the paperwork would be completed when Tonka returned.

"We shall have a nice house warming party when Tonka comes home," she told Ludo. Then we all sat in silence, presumably all wondering where Tonka was and when he would be home.

When we had emptied the van Ludo and I made sure Gabriella was settled in to her new home before leaving for our own home.

"If you need anything Gabriella, you must call us," said Ludo, adding "anything at all. And don't worry about Tonka, he always comes back." I looked at her with a silent reminder that we had avoided mentioning Tonka all day.

"And if you find any photographs or letters," I called out, "let me know. I think we retrieved everything from the loft but it wouldn't surprise me to find that my mother had even more evidence hidden away somewhere."

I received a derisory look from Ludo.

"Don't go climbing into the loft Gabriella. Jack assured me he cleared it out thoroughly, so if there is anything else up there, let it stay there."

Gabriella waved us goodbye and we called out that we would see her again in a few days.

7

Ω

Bill's story

The dubious warmth and dull brightness of a heartless sun wakes me prematurely from a drug-induced sleep. Light without warmth seems somehow like a marriage without love, unnatural. It is morning or, at least the passing of darkness, with the night leaving just the remnants of another pain-ridden and haunting interlude of loneliness and anxiety. Each night, each sleep, the source of empty memories, distant subdued noises and the ever-present threat of death.

Perhaps it is the creaking floorboard or Mary's soft tread on the stairs that stirs me from my tortured slumber. Perhaps it is she who rescues me from my inner dread. Or maybe I am not awake at all. Maybe death has come unnoticed. An unremarkable life followed by an unremarkable death. Perhaps it is Mary coming to administer the fateful dose of morphine that will take me out of this world. What odds would I have got on that happening? I should have placed an ante-post bet on that. Mary, whose life I ruined, with Nemesis sat on her shoulder in the act of ultimate revenge. If only she knew the

200

significance. If only she knew my guilt. The justice of providence. The ultimate outside bet.

I reach across towards a glass of water on the bedside table but I don't even have the strength to raise my arm. My lips are chapped and my tongue dry. I look at the glass and it stares back at me teasingly. Beside the glass lay two books that Mary has placed there. Untouched, unread, just like me. I had hardly read a book in my lifetime. Indeed these may be the only two that I had read. One was a biography of Muhammad Ali that Mary had bought for me a few Christmases ago. It had a strange connection with the other book. *Sting like a bee* had been written by a boxer I admired, Jose Torres. But he had been helped with it by Budd Schulberg, who was the writer of the other book, *What makes Sammy run?*. This book I had purchased myself out of egotism.

I told Mary to take the books away in case Jack picked them up. I also told her to stop him coming in to read to me at night. I'm not sure who it is upsetting more, me or him. He only serves to remind me of my failings. The way I squandered the last ten years of my life. Every time he calls me 'dad' it's like a knife to my side. No sooner than John had been removed as the obstacle to our love and little Jack arrived to carry on his work. I thought, at first, that it would make us a family but he just acted as a constant reminder to Mary. I even, stupidly, agreed to name him Jack but I was prepared to do anything at that time to have Mary as my wife. That was my one dream, my one aim in life. I conceded everything else, willingly, for that one concession. Concession, yes, that's what it is.

There are no dreams anymore, only fragments of

memories to remind me of my imperfect life. Sleep eventually becomes death, it seems, as easily as truth becomes lies. In these brief, salient, moments before Mary administers the morphine, I should tell her. Tell her the truth. I should at least meet my maker with the truth on my tongue. I always knew the right thing to say. The sweet-tongued Billy Daly she would call me, but never the sweet Billy Daly. The selfish-tongued Billy Daly more like. The let's make sure Billy is OK hypocrite of a friend. Always looking after number one but giving the impression of helping others. The disingenuous World Champion of insincerity. Please meet, or at least say goodbye to, the artful and artificial Billy Daly.

I cough. My chest ratchets up and the beast inside me eats away at another piece of my lung. The door opens and Mary is here. I sense a look of disappointment. I have lived too long. I should speak but I question who the beneficiary of the truth might be. Truth is over-rated. Truth is weak. It is better to take that truth to the grave, and all the other unspoken lies with it. Why cause her any more pain?

Mary spoons the morphine into my dry, chapped mouth. The relief seems instantaneous. It can't be. She doesn't think I can hear. But I can hear her silence. It screams at me, reminding me that she does not love me. No words of comfort, no joy in my final hours. No hypocritical words of love. She is incapable of deception or lie, even at this late hour. To say she loves me now would simply confirm what I already know. I am minutes or hours, not days, from death. How long is it since my last dose? I have lost all sense of time.

I had heard, and understood, the exchange of words at

my bedside this morning. Or was it yesterday morning? She was tired she said. She was tired all of the time. She had lost all sense of time and slept in short, interrupted spells of sleep. A sleep without rest she called it. She, like me, was awake most of the night. She had, herself, lost all sense of time too she explained to the doctor. What if, in this confused state, she administered too much morphine?

"There's only one thing going on the death certificate," answered the good doctor.

There was a brief silence as she acknowledged receipt of her free pass out of this mockery of a marriage. A real life get out of jail card. I could see the reaction on her face. Shock, at least to begin with. Then a relaxation of the muscles in her face. Any fatal mistake would be forgiven. A sense of relief, almost joy, filled her face. I knew that look. I remember that look from when I first set eyes on her. Working behind the bar in her father's pub. She was nineteen, maybe twenty, or fifteen years my junior to be more indecorous. Innocent, vulnerable, fragile. Those features were still present all these years later.

I fell in love with her from that very first moment I saw her. Long before John and Liam arrived. She may have known and, if she didn't, she probably did when John arrived, because the same look of love that filled my face appeared on hers. And, although I despised his arrival, I knew instinctively that the only way I could remain close to her was through him. Making a friend of John would mean I could be close to Mary. And so, like most things in my life, I simply made it happen.

In everything but love, that year was a lucky one for me. It started back in the spring with a 50-1 winner in the Grand

National. That set me up with my betting money for the year. Then there was my annual ante-post bet on the Greyhound Derby. Bernie Woolaston famously doesn't give free advice. He was a professional gambler, although I doubt he would call it gambling. There was very little risk to any bets he placed. To him it was a job. To me it was a hobby. I just happened to be lucky that year.

After a local dog had won the Derby the previous year, I decided to take up the 66-1 and 100-1 odds available on the Clapton-based dogs, especially after Bernie had told me he thought the East London track's dogs were better this year than last. That was enough for me. And sure enough it came up trumps. After my big National winner, Faithful Hope romped home in the Greyhound Derby at odds of 8-1. I had taken 66-1 several months earlier, before the opening rounds of the competition. I couldn't believe my luck. I was flush with cash, but even that seemed to have no attraction for Mary. I wasn't quite old enough to be her father but I was certainly too old in her eyes to be considered her lover.

In fact I had such a good run of bets that I decided to treat myself to a new suit, a new camera and a new colour TV too.

I look towards the glass of water again and resign myself to remaining dry. I should have asked Mary but now she's gone. Gone, not to return until the next dose of morphine is due. My eyes fall again on the two books. Jose Torres, boxer and author. He may have been the first person I watched on that new TV when he fought against the Scotsman Chris Calderwood. I invited John and his brother round to see the fight. We got a Party Four tin in and some Coca Cola for Liam and settled down to watch the fight.

I had met the boys previously. They had been lurking around the area I lived for a few days looking for a room and desperate for some food. I genuinely felt sorry for them but, to be honest, thought no more of them than any of the other people who arrived intentionally or unintentionally in the East End of London at that time. Jews, Blacks, Turks, Greeks all swilling around with the Chinese who arrived years before. It was only when I saw the way that Mary looked at John that I really became interested in them.

Love enters in by many doors and meets us in many guises but you have to be around to take advantage of it when it does. I never believed in good fortune or bad fortune for that matter. You make your own luck in this world and I was better at it than most. Mary liked John and I liked Mary. So if John liked me, then Mary's love might follow. Making friends with John would be too obvious and, judging by his character, too difficult too. I doubt he had two friends in the world. So Liam was the bridge that could lead me to Mary's heart. And he was an easy person to like. Young, enthusiastic and easily pleased.

I think when Torres fought Calderwood it was the first time the brothers visited my house. They came to watch it on my new colour TV. Liam loved the TV and they soon became 'familiars of the household', as Liam used to say, especially whenever there was boxing on the TV. But that first visit set up our friendship for the future. We had barely settled down for an evening of boxing when it was all over. The Scotsman only lasted until the second round when Torres knocked him out. So, with the bout over, we passed the time chatting about where they came from and how they got here.

Young Liam was fascinated by the new TV and would pop round during the evening if John and Mary had gone to the cinema and he wasn't working late shift himself. I remember Liam calling round on his own the following week and telling me John had gone on a date with Mary. We sat, together, in front of the TV, with him changing channels and me sulking in a silent jealous ire that never left my stomach. I was so preoccupied that I didn't even notice Liam was crying. It was the news of the Aberfan disaster in Wales. I put my arm around him and consoled him. I think it was more about him than the deaths of so many children. He was obviously homesick and missing his family in Ireland. The news from Aberfan gave him an excuse to cry openly. The news was so distressing that I switched the TV off and suggested we play cards. I taught him how to play poker that night and I didn't look at the TV again until the next evening when the news had switched from Aberfan to a jailbreak by the spy George Blake. The TV seemed such a capricious companion.

Neither Liam, nor I, ever mentioned the crying incident to John. Liam just needed to let his emotions out. He either grew up as quickly as he needed to compliment his circumstances, or managed to contain his feelings thereafter. But, whatever changed, he kept his feelings to himself after that evening.

Both John and Liam were regular visitors to my house, especially if they had insufficient funds for a trip to the pub. Some months later both the brothers were back round my house to watch Jose Torres again. This time I had decided to bet against him. The odds on his opponent, Dick Tiger, were so good that I couldn't resist it. Tiger was much older and he had never lost his hunger. He was moving up a weight to challenge for Torres' World Light Heavyweight title. Torres was younger, taller, and heavier. And, as expected, he took control of the fight. Some particularly good, crisp combination punches had no impact on the experienced Dick Tiger who went on to win on points. I think he was only the second man to win both the Middleweight and Cruiserweight World titles. Either way, Dick and I were both considerably richer as a result and I took Liam and John out for a Chinese meal afterwards. The brothers loved boxing and we would talk for hours on the subject.

~~~~~

The Calnan brothers arrived at a time of heightened tension in the East End of London. The murder of George Cornell by the Kray twins produced demands for action by the police and increasing publicity suggesting that senior police officers were complicit in Ronnie and Reggie's dubious affairs through their friendship with the brothers. Photographs of the Krays with Government Ministers and show business celebrities filled the tabloid press. Ronnie had good contacts for exploiting these photo opportunities, which served only to legitimise the brothers' operation.

Photographs of Charlie Harrison in the London Evening Standard with a junior member of the royal family at Diamonds nightclub would only have annoyed the brothers and it was no surprise that Charlie experienced some problems at the club shortly afterwards. Charlie was only a centurion, although his workforce could only be counted at such a number if you included the pimps and prostitutes on the local streets.

Charlie's primary function was to collect protection money from small local businesses. It was necessary that his contribution was seen as collecting relatively small amounts of money from publicans and shopkeepers in order that everyone understood where Charlie fitted in the hierarchy. Although Charlie never actually dirtied his hands collecting money. Even Digger Rhodes and Charlie's other minder, David Sheih, didn't actually act as collectors. In fact, most of the collectors had normal daytime jobs driving delivery vans for the Co-op or working in a warehouse. That way, if they were ever arrested a top brief, paid for by Charlie, would secure a 'not guilty' verdict with ease. After all, what jury would believe a Co-op delivery driver spent his leisure hours working as a mobster? So maybe, with pimps, tarts and bouncers Charlie's part of the empire did consist of one hundred people.

That empire was enforced more through the threat of violence than violence itself. And, even before violence to the person was considered, collateral damage was inflicted first. I remember drinking in the Lord Nelson pub in Poplar one Friday evening when a large group of young men arrived purporting to be a stag party. I recognised some of them, as did the Landlord, who had clearly not paid his protection money to Charlie. The crowd began by drinking pints of beer and dropping their empty glasses on the floor. By ten o'clock everyone was walking on broken glass in both a literal and menacing way.

The local pop group who provided the legitimate entertainment that night began feeling nervous. Their anxiety was not misplaced. At eleven o'clock the place erupted in a highly contrived fight that involved most people in the pub, including many innocent bystanders. The pop group had all their instruments destroyed. All the elaborate and ornate mirrors behind the bar were smashed, along with chairs, tables, glasses, windows and doors.

Such demonstrations of Charlie Harrison's power were apposite reminders to other local businessmen from time to time. In fact, when everyone was paying their dues on time it was bad for business because there was a risk of people forgetting the consequences of not paying their dues on time. So making excessive demands on one or two occasions was sufficient to prompt a reminder. The wrecked shell of The Lord Nelson pub stood as a monument to Charlie's vindictiveness for a few days, reminding everyone of the consequences of non-compliance.

Michael Harrison was just a junior version of his father. A thug who had no fear of reprisals because daddy would always sort out his problems. All Michael had to do was avoid upsetting or annoying Reggie or Ronnie Kray. Whenever he did see them they treated him like a servant just to reinforce their position with Charlie. So they would give him a slap occasionally as a little reminder of their power.

It would have been different had they learned about John Calnan fighting with Michael. They couldn't permit that and they certainly wouldn't allow Charlie Harrison to let such a matter go unaddressed. So Charlie ignored the first two confrontations between John and Michael. I think he knew that John was someone he couldn't frighten off. Anything short of killing John would, he believed, result in an act of revenge on his son. Charlie let it go because murdering John Calnan was a step too far for him. Charlie wasn't in the same league as the Krays, as they reminded him on a number of occasions.

I was present at one such incident in Diamonds when two men arrived at the club for what appeared to be a meeting with Charlie. I was in the bar at the time and drew the conclusion that they must be representing the Krays. Charlie recognised them and got up from his seat to welcome them. But David Sheih remained in his seat. One of the visitors seemed to take offence at this and when the two of them sat down at the table with David and Charlie the tension grew. One of them says to David, 'Charlie doesn't need a body guard today', and David looks to Charlie for instructions. The big guy blew his top. He hit David so hard that both he and his chair spewed across the floor and David was then given a kick to the ribs.

"I fucking said, 'Charlie doesn't need a body guard today', you fucking piece of shit."

Digger picked David up and led him off to the men's room to tidy up his bloodied face. He cleaned away the blood but his card was marked from that day.

As time passed I grew fond of John and his kid brother, despite losing out to the older one in the romance stakes with Mary. I wasn't jealous of him, not in any way that materialised itself. He never knew and she never knew. It was a burden I would carry on my own. Maybe if I hadn't have helped him when he first arrived he wouldn't have stayed. But that wouldn't have made Mary love me. So I helped him to stay. While I was close to him, he was close to Mary and, by default, so was I.

It was no accident that I appeared where he and Liam needed help. A handout for food and even taking, or directing them, to the Circus. And when John took that awful beating at the hands of Digger Rhodes, I saw my opportunity. If he had fought Digger again the following week, John would have won with me in his corner. It wasn't a lack of humility or misplaced confidence. I was not capable of fighting Digger myself. Dick Tiger might be able to step up a weight but I would have to step up three or four to fight Digger.

No, my gift was to notice the weaknesses and failings in others. Digger's weaknesses were quite obvious to anyone who was looking for it. As was Terry Marsden's, the young lad John boxed a couple of weeks later. Digger couldn't think for himself. Terry carried a flaw that would prevent him from making it as a professional boxer; he was an impatient counter-puncher. And then it was simply a question of finding John's weakness and eliminating it. John was, incredibly as it might seem for such a headstrong young man, too soft. He punched with power. He simply needed to punch with menace. Telling him to punch at a point beyond his opponent's face actually helped him. He felt no anger for his opponents, so hitting an empty space beyond them was actually easier for him to do. He just couldn't see it.

"I'm aiming at his fekking head," he shouted at me once, as I leaned over the ropes trying to give him advice.

"Well don't," I said and then I gave him the advice that would unleash his full potential.

211

John was never going to make it as a professional boxer or even, indeed, a reasonable amateur. He was a fighter but he would only ever make pocket money. And when he didn't need the pocket money anymore, he stopped fighting. Once he found permanent employment at the Barbican development carrying bricks, he lost interest in his weekend boxing. In any case, he had met Mary by that time and he wanted to spend all his spare time with her. While she was serving in her father's pub, I could see as much of her as John. But on her evenings off, I would be left with Terry Hoon or Ronnie the Gold to drink with, if I was to avoid a night at home on my own. During the summer, young Liam would join me if he saw me sitting at the tables outside the pub, but he would never come in the pub unless his brother accompanied him.

It was Ronnie the Gold who prompted me to buy *What makes Sammy run.*

"You are Sammy Glick," he said to me once.

"Who's Sammy Glick?" I asked. And he told me about the book.

I bought the book to feed my own ego, which, in all honesty, didn't need feeding. Well at least not until I was rejected by Mary. At first, I thought Ronnie didn't know me at all. I was neither Jewish, nor was I rich, or likely to become rich. And I had no ambition to be a successful movie screenwriter. But Ronnie had seen my true self in that rags to riches story. Sammy was aggressive, selfish and, most importantly, resourceful. I chose to ignore the aggressiveness and selfishness of the character and empathised with the resourcefulness of him. And, when Glick steals the work of an aspiring young writer for his

212

own personal gain, it was as if Ronnie could see into my soul. I still remember the name of the film that Glick stole. How could I forget *'Girl steals boy'*. The opposite could have been my own biography.

~~~~~

Eventually, I had to become friends with Liam, rather than John, to stay in Mary's company. John wanted to keep an eye on his younger brother and so trips out to Epping Forest or Ongar became a regular weekend event.

By Christmas we were rarely out of each other's company. We certainly all celebrated my birthday together in the November and over the festive period we were inseparable. Then came that fateful New Year's Eve party at Diamonds. That triserial of public holidays that was to change all our lives started that New Year 's Eve. Young Michael Harrison tried to warn John off Mary that night. He felt fireproof in his father's club, of course, but as neither he nor John was prepared to throw the first punch, it amounted to little more than a locking of horns. A couple of rutting stags in a men's toilet, and thankfully out of sight of Charlie Harrison. But the stakes were laid that night. The bets were placed and bets can't be withdrawn once the runners are under starter's orders. And they certainly came under starter's orders that night.

The feud simmered and consisted of fierce glances and insincere smiles in pubs. We didn't visit Diamonds again until the following spring. But absence didn't make the heart grow fonder, nor did it stop a fight breaking out between the enemies the following Easter. Something happened that Easter weekend. I know now that this was when Mary fell pregnant and talk of marriage began. But it was more than that. The relationship between John and Mary changed but so did the one between John and Michael. A new determination appeared on Michael's face that signalled the worst.

The next long weekend was Whitsun and John finished decorating the council flat that he and Mary had moved into and he decided that we should all visit Diamonds club to celebrate. I was nervous about visiting the club again, particularly after the fights that accompanied our previous two visits. So, when we arrived, I went directly over to Michael to buy him a drink and to tell him about John and Mary, in the hopes that he would finally accept that she was outside his reach. He seemed to take the news well and asked me for their address so he could send a present to them.

When I returned to John, Mary and Liam, a bottle of Champagne arrived with Michael's compliments. I couldn't believe it was his own idea and assumed it was Charlie who was finally trying to bring the feud to a bloodless end.

So it was me who threw the six to start this bloody episode. I let Mary down. I told Michael her new address. He just had to wait until John was at work. Nobody heard her screams above the noise of the traffic rumbling past outside. But, in that Council block, they wouldn't have taken any notice anyway.

I had already put Mary in harm's way by telling Michael where she lived with John. I had to make up for that. That's why, when John was killed, I had to get Mary and Liam away from the area. Charlie Harrison's revenge for the vicious beating of his son would not end with John's death. We had to run away and run away very quickly. There was no time for goodbyes, although neither Liam nor I had anyone to say goodbye to. And Mary was so traumatised by the situation that she wasn't considering seeing her parents.

I used to read fairy tales to little Jack a few years ago. I remember reading Snow White and the seven dwarves to him when he was a toddler. The way the woodman led Snow White into the forest with the intention of killing her, but couldn't bring himself to do the deed. Whenever I read that story to Jack I thought about that time. That time when I took Mary away from the East End. I didn't have to kill her like the woodman, I had already ruined her life. I had stupidly told Michael Harrison where to find her. I told him where to go to rape her and, if it is possible, I have done even worse than that to her. I destroyed her life.

What happened after we ran away was as incredible as the day that started it. We were fugitives, although we didn't know whether anyone was actually chasing us. We simply didn't have time to look back to find out. Better to be safe than sorry. I don't know what was in Mary's heart, no more than I knew what was in Liam's. But I knew it was powerful. Hatred, anger, vengeance. But, whatever they were feeling at that moment, it needed to be controlled so that we could put as much space between us and the Harrisons. We did not have time to construct a plan. We just had to run.

"Those feelings that you have in your heart at this moment," I said to them, "lock them away. They will not disappear. You will never lose them. You can return to them later. Once we are safe. Don't wreck all our lives by acting rashly now," I told them.

"Lock away the feelings," Mary repeated as she hurriedly packed a bag. Liam stood there mumbling to himself. He couldn't accept that his brother was dead.

The traffic was roaring outside the flat and I kept looking over the balcony, expecting to see someone coming for us. Coming to take revenge for what John had done to Michael.

"For God's sake," I screamed at them, "just gather up what you need and let's get out of here."

Fortunately I still had money saved from my successful year of gambling. I don't remember how we arrived at Ongar. We ran towards the East India Dock Road and jumped on to a Green Line bus outside Poplar Park. I think it went to Ongar, or maybe we caught a train at Mile End. We got on and off other buses heading away from London. It didn't matter where the bus was going, just that it was going away from danger. Thinking back, we should have gone to Victoria Coach Station and simply taken a coach to a place 200 miles away. But then, Charlie Harrison may have been looking for us there. Maybe it was a clever move. Who would ever think about making an escape on a bus? There again, maybe Charlie Harrison wasn't chasing us at all.

~~~~~

Eventually we stopped running and set about starting

216

our new life together. Maybe, in the deepest recesses of my mind, I had conjured the whole plan up as a way of getting Mary to marry me. Maybe it was a subliminal thought resting in the back of my mind. Owning Mary, having Mary to myself was, I suppose, an eternal thought that lurked in those dark recesses for so long I had forgotten it. But, the day after we stopped running, it suddenly occurred to me that John was gone and Mary was alone apart from Liam, of course, who was a constant reminder of her darling John as she called him. But when Liam left, or rather run away, she was completely alone and pregnant. Yes, it was opportunist, but I deserved that opportunity. Maybe I should have waited until she was thinking straight but if I had, she may have said no. She was incapable of saying no at that moment because she could see no future. Therefore a future with me did not represent a lifetime commitment. For Mary, her life was over. She was at her most vulnerable. Miles from home, no John, no Liam and now the possibility of lonely isolation if I left as a result of her rejection. No, it was checkmate. She had nowhere to go.

So, yes, I seized my chance and, before she knew it, we were married. Mary didn't even know what to do about Liam. She actually believed he had left to go home to Ireland. Why would he have waited all that time so he could take photographs of the baby with him, then leave just before Mary and I got married? His note made no sense. No, I had noticed a change in both Mary and Liam in those last few days before he left. I saw them curled up on the sofa, mourning their beloved John. It was John's birthday, or rather it would have been. I stayed out of their way. They both still harboured misplaced hopes that John was still alive. At one point they convinced themselves that it was so and he was out there somewhere searching for us.

"He's dead," I screamed, after losing my patience.

"We don't know that," Mary replied, pulling me out of the room and scolding me for upsetting Liam.

"Maybe John was arrested," said Mary unconvincingly as she closed the door behind her.

"Arrested? What, Charlie Harrison called the Old Bill to have Johnnie arrested for thrashing his son? Are you absolutely stupid? John is dead Mary. We both know that is the truth of the matter."

I went back into the living room to speak to Liam after Mary had gone upstairs to bed, still stinging from my harsh words.

"I'm sorry Liam, but I really can't allow you to put Mary's life at risk by telling people where we are living, just in case your brother is still alive. He isn't Liam, you do know that don't you. He beat Michael Harrison to a pulp. Everyone on the street knew that. So Charlie Harrison would have to kill him. Charlie couldn't exist in the East End if he didn't take revenge. Your brother is dead, Liam. Charlie Harrison killed him. That's the truth Liam."

And it was the truth. I hadn't told Liam or Mary but I would occasionally call Bernie Woolaston from a public telephone box in the village to find out what was happening back home. It showed how naïve Liam and Mary were that they accepted my constant warnings about the dangers of returning to London. Never once did they ask how I knew and, when they even questioned my views, they never realised that I was still in contact with somebody there.

Bernie was, of course, a reluctant informant but once I

had made contact with him he was compromised anyway, as I had to remind him occasionally. It was against Bernie's nature to gamble but he soon concluded that it was a bigger gamble to upset me than take my calls. So he reluctantly kept me informed of developments. The killing of Charlie and Michael threw the East End into a panic. Nobody could be sure that the Krays had not arranged their murders, so it became dangerous to show favour or contempt for the belated Harrisons.

Some of Charlie's mercenaries saw his death as an opportunity to continue his business arrangements but failed to pass on their takings. Digger pleaded his innocence and was forgiven for his temporary lapse. His restoration after this ill-conceived venture was only made possible through his betrayal of young David Sheih. David became the sacrifice that was necessary to restore order to the empire. David had failed to pass on the protection money and his only mitigation was that he didn't know who to give it to once Charlie was killed. So David had to die and it had to be Digger who did the deed, just so everyone knew that power had been restored in the East End.

The death of Charlie Harrison made only a ripple in the lives of the true rulers. Digger simply needed to ensure all the takings were passed on up the chain from that point.

David's body was found in a car park near his home. He had been clubbed to death with a baseball bat that Digger later burned to eliminate the murder weapon. No arrest was ever made and, apart from pulling in Terry Hoon for questioning, the case remained forever unsolved. It took several months, but David paid the ultimate price for upsetting Charlie's two visitors to the club a couple of months earlier.

Everyone knew David was dead. His blood-splattered body lay on view until the police found it the next morning. Digger deliberately chose not to dispose of the body. He needed to provide absolute evidence to the brothers that David was dead and that he had fulfilled his part of the bargain. A simple disappearing act would not suffice if Digger was to be promoted. This was not the case with John. It suited the Harrisons to have John's body disappear. There was too much evidence leading back to young Michael. It was this absence of a body that made it so difficult for Liam.

So, when I sat there simply repeating that John was dead, Liam's countenance slowly changed. It was a slow, painful realisation that his beloved Jack was gone forever.

He sat there motionless, bereft of ideas, or so I thought. No response, just silent contempt as they describe it in the army.

It may even have been this statement that finally pushed Liam over the edge, though how he ever got his hands on a gun has bewildered me to this day. How he ever managed to get at the Harrisons is a mystery too. The trial had been short for a murder trial, lasting less than two weeks. He showed no remorse for the killings and the whole process was a formality.

In contrast to this, Liam protested his innocence at the second trial for the murder of the police officer. But the same gun had been used for all the murders. The trial lasted almost twice as long as the previous one but the result was the same. It was a very difficult time for me. Mary knew, as I did too, that Liam couldn't have killed the police officer.

We could actually have given him an alibi, and, for months, Mary pleaded with me to contact the police. As the trial date drew nearer she raged for days that we were letting Liam down.

"But he's already serving a life sentence for killing the Harrisons," I insisted. "What possible difference can it make?"

"He's going to be found guilty of a murder he didn't commit," she screamed back at me. If I ever held hopes that, one day, she might love me, those hopes disappeared that night. If I was in any doubt before, I resigned myself to the fact that we would be husband and wife in name only. The rest of our life was to be a deception from that point. A deception born out of a deception.

So, in spite of this singularly divisive argument, my plan had succeeded and her kidnap was complete. But she would only ever be a captive bride. She was as much a prisoner as Liam was. She could leave whenever she wanted, but she never did. But she did get remission. The marriage, if it can be elevated to that status, lasted only eight years before cancer stepped in. Referee stopped fight in round eight. The surprise winner was Mary but her victory was a shallow one. She was already a widow when we married, but now she could wear a widow's weeds, and openly mourn the loss of her beloved John, whilst everyone would assume her tears were for me. Life would finally permit her a public show of grief, but the condolences of what few friends we had would only add to the hypocrisy.

Even I can take something from the situation. She doesn't want to kill me because she hates me. She doesn't hate me. She despises me, which is even worse. But her motive is, as unlikely as it seems, pity. It is mercy she wants to deliver today. The additional dose of morphine that will take me from this world will be administered out of a love undeserving of the name. Four lives destroyed by one moment of madness. A chain of events that could be foretold from the outset. Johnnie dead, me dead and Mary and Liam serving out their time until death takes them willingly from this world.

~~~~~

The floorboards creak from Mary's soft tread on the stairs. I look about the room and find nothing to comfort my final moments. No photographs of a happy married life. No smiling children. No romantic mementos of happier times. All the evidence in this room, or the absence of evidence, is indicative of a loveless life. She appears in the doorway and her features betray her disappointment at finding me awake, still alive. She has the morphine in her hand. Does she think I don't know? The sun shines brightly through the window onto her face, the face that I love, and she cannot see the tears in my eyes. My heart, my soul and my mind screams to her to kiss me this one last time but I know that, to do this, she would be acknowledging that this is the final act. I cannot recall when she last kissed me. I am not sure if she has ever kissed me with any sincerity.

She pours the medicine into the spoon and I look away. Seconds pass and, for a moment, I sense she cannot go through with it. Or perhaps she is praying. Perhaps she is saying one last prayer. But is it for me or for herself?

One last act of courage on my part, as I charge my body to rise for a last time. I raise my head from the pillow and the cold spoon touches my cracked lips. I open them and the morphine trickles in. She refills the spoon and pours some more into my mouth. There is an immediate sense of ecstasy, a sudden feeling of elation and, as that brief moment of joy ends, Mary takes my hand in hers and holds it to her lips.

8

Jack's story

A threatening grey sky loiters ominously on the horizon as the train makes its way slowly towards London's Liverpool Street Station. I shuffle in my seat, still a little stiff from helping Gabriella move house over the weekend. She and Ludo are becoming good friends and had even been out together for a meal. I find it difficult to concentrate on my book of Eliot's poems. Their haunting themes lure me once again towards confused thoughts of Liam.

> *Time present and time past*
> *are both perhaps present in time future*
> *and time future contained in time past.*

Eliot's cryptic phrases force me to read it over again as the click clack of the train begins, at last, to pick up speed. I am going to be late again for my meeting with Titus, Jonathan and Richard. Richard had telephoned to ask me to call in to the office without saying what the meeting had been called for.

A clap of thunder could be heard over the noise of the train and darkness swept across the sky. The train shudders to another unscheduled stop. I put the book in my briefcase and take out the article

I was preparing for the Grand National issue. It required less attention than T. S Elliot, although I was still working on the contrast between the old, landed Sir Leslie and the young and peasant-like Declan. I needed to raise it to Ali-Frazier level but should I focus on the age, the wealth or the position in life. Declan's humility fascinated me and this really did seem the distinguishing feature that separated them. I was just pondering the idea when the train slowly moved away to continue its seemingly endless journey towards London.

The consideration for the reader wasn't their background or how much money they had, but the attitude towards fame that each had. I think it was Shelley who said that there is nothing we can do in this life to secure fame. And his friend Keats considered fame a wayward girl. In all likelihood neither of these combatants would find fame this year or, at least, not according to Ladbrokes and William Hill.

One might consider that Declan, because of his age, stood the best chance in the long run. If the Aintree fences didn't kill old Sir Leslie his own stupidity would do it sooner rather than later. I was still considering the possibilities when the train suddenly lurched into Liverpool Street Station and I rushed out to find a taxi.

As it happened the meeting didn't take long and I wondered why we couldn't have simply discussed the matter over the telephone. It was an important issue though, I suppose. But, in spite of Titus's objections, Jonathan asked that he be allowed this little indulgence, as he called it, as it had been something he had dreamt of doing since he made the decision to become a publisher.

I didn't think my article was that controversial but Titus had insisted he spoke with his legal people before it went to press. Richard was ambivalent to the whole thing so, in the end, Titus was outvoted and my article would be published in a couple of weeks to coincide with the long awaited, and eagerly anticipated, Peace Conference.

The rain never arrived but stayed ominously in the background and my return trip home took considerably less time than the outward leg. I was welcomed by a message on the answer phone from Dr. Nagpal. I telephoned him immediately and he asked me whether I could call into the nursing home to collect Liam's personal effects that had been delivered to him by the Prison Service from Sanderlings Open Prison. He sounded uninterested in the contents but eager, as I was to obtain any further evidence of my parentage I agreed to collect them the following day.

Over dinner that evening Ludo and I speculated about what Liam's effects might consist of. What does one keep whilst serving a life sentence for murder? Would he have had flared trousers or was that after his conviction? Would he still have the baseball boots he wore in the photograph? We concluded it would consist of little more than a toothbrush, pyjamas and, if we were really lucky, a photograph that would provide the last part of the jigsaw.

Intrigued by what awaited me at the nursing home, Ludo asked me not to look at Liam's effects until we were together the following evening and, reluctantly, I agreed to do so. Whether she was concerned about me or simply wanted to be on hand at the possible discovery of my real father's identity, I don't know and didn't want to ask her.

So, the following day, I returned home with a black sack of what felt like items of clothing and a small attaché case similar to the one the Chancellor of the Exchequer poses with each Budget day. But this one was battered and worn and clearly dated back to the war, or early fifties at the latest. If nothing else had been achieved, at least I had something to appear on the *Antiques Roadshow* with at some time in the future.

In the interest of hygiene, we emptied the contents of the black sack on to the living room floor rather than the dining room table and, not surprisingly it revealed nothing more than some old used clothes that were presumably given to Liam when he left prison.

Ignoring the bundle of rags, Ludo spread the contents of the attaché case on the dining table, as I attempted to return the ragged collection of clothes back into the black sack. I felt in the pockets before doing so but my intensive search produced no further evidence. The contents of the small attaché case looked far more interesting. Amongst Liam's effects were three black and white photographs, a newspaper cutting that had been cut roughly around the edges and three letters.

Ludo and I contained our eagerness and decided to look at each item together, to try to avoid reaching any premature conclusions about what the items represented. Two sets of eyes were better than one. So we pulled two chairs together on one side of the table and began our interrogation of Liam's effects.

The first item we looked at was a photograph of someone's birthday party. It showed a woman blowing out the candles on a birthday cake with two other women sitting either side of her. On the reverse it simply said, 'Nora's 50th birthday.' We put the photograph down on the table and looked at each other in a disappointed manner.

"Well" said Ludo optimistically, "at least it tells us who she is and how old she is too."

I shared her optimism.

"Is it too much to hope that everything will be catalogued so simply?"

They weren't but at least we now knew what the mysterious Nora looked like. If this was the standard of the evidence, our anticipation of success was greatly decreased. Perhaps Liam had taken the photograph or perhaps Nora had simply taken it with her when she visited him in prison.

The next item was a newspaper cutting, which again, we read together. In view of the previous newspaper cutting found in mother's loft, the discovery of another one did not fill me with optimism. We handled the ragged, delicate piece of newspaper gently. It revealed certain important information. Liam Calnan had an older brother, John who had been murdered, or was at least missing and feared murdered.

Whoever Liam and John Calnan were they were obviously caught up in a gangland feud in London's East End. I recalled to Ludo the stories I had heard about the Krays and the Richardson gang but she was not impressed, having lived with her own gangster brother for too long to be overawed by a tough-guy image.

I couldn't remember a television programme called Police Five and Ludo had never come across it during her avid viewing of daytime TV.

Liam, it seemed, had tried to escape to Ireland after he

had killed two members of the Harrison family but was caught close to the ferry port of Fishguard in Wales. How stupid, I thought to myself. Surely that would be the first place that the police would look for an Irishman on the run. Why did he try to return to Ireland and, if he had to go there, why not try to find an alternative route?

I read the article twice, trying to ensure that I did not miss any vital clues.

Missing man feared dead

John Calnan, who has been missing for over four weeks, is believed to have been a victim of the recent gangland violence in London's East End. Calnan, 22, is believed to have frequented the Diamonds nightclub owned by gangland leader Charlie Harrison, who was murdered along with his son Michael last month. Police have arrested Liam Calnan, the younger brother of the missing man, for the two murders. Although no body has been discovered police believe John Calnan was murdered around the same time and his death either caused the killing of the Harrisons or it was a reprisal for those murders. Liam Calnan, 17, is being held in custody pending the trial. A spokesman for Scotland Yard said that several useful witnesses had come forward as a result of the case being shown on Police Five last week. A source close to the police said that Liam Calnan had been arrested in Fishguard whilst fleeing to Ireland.

The second photograph was one of me when I was about one year old. I recognised it immediately because my mother had one that must have been taken at the same time. Ludo hadn't seen many photographs of me as a child, so she spent a few minutes comparing me with the black and white picture that looked as if it had been taken at a professional photographer's studio. Indeed it was stamped on the reverse: *Allinson's Studio Evestown.* There was no date but this item could be accurately dated too. The third and final photograph was similar to the one I had found in mother's loft but, although this one was of three people, none of them was my father – Bill. The black and white photograph showed mum with her arms around a young man who may have been the one in the previous photograph from mother's loft. He was holding an old ten shilling note aloft, above his head in triumph, as if it was the FA Cup. Ludo wanted me to explain what a ten shilling note was but, after several attempts, I gave up. Behind mother and the man was a younger man. Either of the men could have been Liam but I was convinced he was the younger one standing behind mother.

When we compared it with the photograph from mother's shoebox, it was clear that the younger man at the back was the one who appeared in both photographs. It suddenly occurred to me that that man being embraced by mother was probably Liam's brother, who Gabriella had vaguely remembered him mentioning. The same man referred to in the newspaper cutting, John Calnan.

"That's him," I shouted enthusiastically as if I had found irrefutable proof of my parentage.

"Who?" asked Ludo. I pointed at the man sitting next to mother.

"That's my father," I declared. "I know it."

"How can you be so sure?" asked Ludo.

"It makes sense Ludo. Just think what Dr. Nagpal said about the DNA result. Liam had to be either a first cousin or my uncle."

We both agreed that the younger man at the back was Liam and the man being embraced by my mother was probably his brother, the one Gabriella mentioned, called John. I took the photograph over to the light to look at it more closely, interrogating it for signs of any family likeness .

"It doesn't really help though," Ludo said rather dejectedly. "The newspaper cutting suggests he is either dead or has been missing for fifty years."

I continued to examine the photograph and, in the absence of a response to the last comment, Ludo picked up the next item. She couldn't wait for me to join her, so began relating it to me.

"It's a handwritten letter from your mother to Liam. No date on it I'm afraid," she called over to me.

"Oh, it's the letter that accompanied that photo of you Jack. Your mother must have sent it to Liam by post."

"Can I just read it myself?" I called back but she ignored my pleas.

"If John is your father, why is she telling Liam that you look just like him? I just can't understand that. I think you are Liam's son. You know it make sense." I was continuing to look at the photographs.

"And what about this?" she continued, "we shared a

great love and fate stole that love away. That doesn't sound like she's in love with John. It sounds very much like Liam is the love of her life."

"Well if he was," I assured her, "then she might be on the child offenders register because he must have only been fifteen years old."

"Probably sixteen," she corrected me as I took the letter from her hand and began reading it for myself. I must admit it did seem to endorse Ludo's conclusion."

Dearest Liam

I hope you are well. I enclose a photo of Jack. He is growing up so fast. He looks so much like you. I truly understand the reasons for your actions. We shared a great love and fate stole that love away. I think of him every day. You are the only person who knows how I feel. Bill says we should keep our feelings locked away but he doesn't understand the pain that causes. I wish you would let me visit you. I'm sure Bill would understand. Please write.

Love,

Mary.

I read the letter over Ludo's shoulder and waited until she had finished reading it before reaching across the table for the next item from the attaché case. It was another letter.

Dearest Liam,

Bill has died. I wish I could say it was brief and painless but it wasn't. I could not send him to hospital, so I looked after him at home. There is no reason why I should not visit you now Liam.. Surely you want to see Jack. He is 8 years old now and is growing up to be quite the young gentleman. I don't know how you can go all this time alone. Bill has only been gone a few days and I cannot stand the loneliness. I have walked in loneliness all my life or at least since John died. Do you ever imagine that John is alive, after all, we never saw a body? I still hold that hope in my heart. I believe you share that hope. Please let me visit.

Love, Mary

This letter had been written after the first one and was dated 21st December 1976, so we stood some chance of dating the first one too. More significantly for me, there was no mention of Christmas, which seemed strange considering the date of the letter. So I suggested to Ludo that the second one had probably been enclosed in a Christmas card.

"The opening message isn't something that could easily be written on a Christmas card is it?" I asked rhetorically and Ludo nodded, taking another look at the letter herself to see if she could find any other hidden clues.

"You're quite clever aren't you?" she said and pecked me on the cheek.

"Well it is my job I suppose. I know I don't always see the most obvious things, but I do notice the nuances. Hopefully, in the absence of so much evidence, it is the nuances that will tell us what happened here."

"And who your real father is," added Ludo.

233

"I'm pretty sure it must be John. Liam would have been a child. I just can't see my mother having sex with a boy as young as the one in that photograph."

"I can't imagine your mother, or mine, making love to anyone," she answered with a laugh. "But they must have done at some time Jack."

"Look at the way she is cuddling John. It must be him Ludo. It can't be that innocent faced boy in the background."

"I'm not sure innocent is the right expression Jack. He murdered three people."

"Well we don't know what drove him to it," I pleaded in his defence. I picked up the remaining letter.

Dear Liam

I will respect your wishes. I will not visit you again, but I will always be here if you change your mind. Your solicitor says an appeal is out of the question, as the evidence is overwhelming. But you can still shorten your sentence if you show remorse. Hopefully by the time parole is considered you will have reconsidered this. What harm will it do to simply say you are sorry. Of course, I know you won't mean it. I have kept your earlier note. It is true we did share a great love for John. You were the only one he permitted to call him Jack. He loved you so much. Perhaps one day I can tell young Jack everything but Bill agrees with you that it is best if it is not spoken of. Please write to me again. I pray each night to St Jude for you.

With all my love

Mary

Apart from a rather formal looking prison service form, the attaché case contained nothing more than this third letter, which clearly preceded the last one but was, again, undated.

"Who is Saint Jude?" Ludo asks as she finishes reading the letter again.

"He's rather famous over here Ludo. He's the patron saint of lost causes. I think he might very well be adopted as a figurehead for the Daly family too," I added.

Ludo seemed to have missed what was clearly to me the most significant reference in the letter, that Liam referred to his brother John as 'Jack'. Surely this provided the best evidence yet that John was my father, rather than Liam.

The prison document that remained gave brief details of Liam's date and place of birth. As Ludo read through the documents again, I searched the web to see if I could find out where Ballycraich was and learned that Liam had been born about twenty miles outside Cork in Ireland. Quite how Liam managed to get to London at the age of fifteen or sixteen is difficult to fathom. Perhaps he travelled to London with John or maybe he followed John there. I began to think that we might never find out.

Ludo and I began preparing our evening meal in the kitchen and discussed whether a trip to Ballycraich might throw some light on the mystery. In a brief moment of optimism we even contemplated the possibility of finding a relative of Liam's still living there. But before making any travel arrangements, I suggested we should show Gabriella Liam's effects to see if it jogged any memories.

I considered whether I might claim the cost of the trip

against my interview with young Declan but decided that Titus would never authorise it.

Gabriella was still unpacking after moving to mother's house at the weekend, so she was pleased to join us for one of Ludo's special seafood risottos the following evening. It was evident that she was concerned about Tonka. This was Tonka's life I told her and it is something she will need to get used to if she wants them to remain together. I was convinced that nothing, even his love for Gabriella, would make him leave the SAS, at least while he was fit for duty. Ludo was less tolerant of love-struck females but made an effort and managed to console our visitor. Gabriella occupied herself with Liam's effects while Ludo stirred the fragrant pot of rice. But none of the contents prompted any immediate recollections.

I picked up the photograph of Nora and the two other women and showed it to Gabriella.

"So this is Nora?" I said expectantly.

"Nora," replied Gabriella, giving the photograph a cursory examination, "no, that's not Nora."

"Not Nora," I questioned her, "well who is it then?"

"I don't know," confessed Gabriella, now looking intently at the photograph, "I don't recognise any of them."

It seemed that every time I made some progress towards solving this mystery it simply became more complex and confused. If this wasn't the Nora who visited him in prison for all those years, who was it?

Whilst Ludo and I busied ourselves in the kitchen, Gabriella looked through my mother's effects again and read through my notes from my meeting with Liam.

Eventually, Gabriella appeared in the doorway of the

kitchen with the notes in her hand.

"There is a guy called Terry, I think, who lives in the East End who must have been around when Liam was there. Nora introduced me to him one night in the pub. He is a greasy, disagreeable man who spends most of his time in the local pubs or at the bookmakers. He's probably older than Liam though. I haven't seen him lately but he may still be around."

Gabriella and I returned to the dining room and she sat quietly for a few moments trying to remember his last name. She was sure his first name was Terry.

"Terry Moon or Noon," she guessed. "No. Hoon. Terry Hoon" she exclaimed.

It sounded familiar to me too but I couldn't place the name. I was sure Liam had mentioned it in his ramblings. So I took the notes from Gabriella and read through them. I didn't need to read very far when it suddenly hit me. I jumped up from the chair and kissed Ludo and Gabriella on the cheeks.

"That's it," I declared. "Not 'who knows?' but 'Hoon knows'" I told them knowingly. "Don't you see?" I said to two puzzled faces. "Liam wasn't saying 'who knows?' but 'Hoon knows'. Terry Hoon knows."

"What does Terry Hoon know," they asked in unison.

"I don't know" I confessed, "but that's what he was trying to tell me. Hoon knows. We just need to find out what it was that Terry Hoon knew."

"Well" said Gabriella, "he may drink in the same pub I suppose. He certainly seemed a creature of habit."

"Well, it's about time we had some luck" I said hopefully.

We speculated about the possibilities as we enjoyed Ludo's risotto and it was agreed that Gabriella would stay with us that night so that we would drive off to the East End early the following morning. If a tour of the local pubs at lunchtime didn't work we would simply continue through into the evening until we found someone who knew Terry Hoon, or could provide any information about the mysterious Liam.

~~~~~

The three of us left the following morning and Gabriella just needed to call into my mother's house for a quick change of clothes before we set off in search of Terry Hoon. When we arrived in mother's street, there was considerable activity across the road. A police car and an ambulance had mounted the kerb outside Mrs. Joiner's house. Gabriella went off to change and Ludo and I decided to make enquiries. Having convinced the young police officer standing outside the house that we knew the resident very well, we were allowed to stay until we had learned that Mrs. Joiner had died suddenly. The policeman was waiting for the doctor to confirm it was natural causes before releasing the body to the ambulance crew.

We decided to wait and were there so long that we were eventually joined by Gabriella. The policeman was just about to release the body to the ambulance crew when Mrs. Joiner's daughter arrived. I had met Julia at a pensioners' Christmas party last year when we were acting as chauffeurs. I introduced Gabriella and Ludo, offered our condolences and decided that we could be of little further assistance, so went on our way. I gave Julia my telephone number and asked her to contact me when she had time.

By the time we reached the East End of London, it was lunchtime. The fates were certainly with us that day, as we struck gold at the first attempt. It was not entirely luck because Gabriella remembered the precise pub that Terry Hoon frequented most often. She remembered it because Nora stopped going there in order to avoid the 'weasel' as she called him. He was a contemptuous individual as I learned personally when Gabriella introduced me to him at the bar.

Dressed in an ill-fitting suit that had never seen a dry cleaners, he was precariously perched on a stool, drinking scotch and water, whilst scanning the racing pages of a newspaper. He was probably seventy years old but looked ten years older. His face was rough, reddened and deeply creased. His eyes were translucent with age. And what hair he had fell, unkempt from his balding head. He smelled of tobacco and his fingers were heavily stained with nicotine.

I asked him if he wanted a drink and he unhesitatingly ordered a scotch directly from the barmaid.

"A large one please, Irene" he shouted bawdily in her direction. "You remember what a large one looks like don't you darling."

He was clearly fond of the coarse innuendo, particularly his own, and he laughed himself into a coughing fit, that I prayed would not take him until he had parted with some useful information.

He spoke with a grating, gravelly voice and his throat

gurgled violently between words. I recalled that sound from my childhood, sitting at the bedside of my father or, at least the person I had always considered to be my father.

"Jack here is a reporter Terry," Gabriella explained, "and he was hoping to find someone who could tell him about someone I think you used to know."

"And who might that be?" he asked.

"Liam Calnan," I answered.

"Well, there's a blast from the past," he said smilingly, almost in anticipation of some recompense. "Well I'm yer man Jack," he continued, "but you need to answer a question from me first."

"Go ahead" I answered, almost guessing what was coming next.

"What's it worth?" he laughed out loud. Then, clearing his throat into a closed right fist, he continued.

"I mean them Fleet Street reporters pay real dosh don't they. Ten grand for some soap star's story last week," he added, directing his comments towards Gabriella rather than me, as if she was some kind of broker for the deal.

We haggled, with me telling Terry that I could get whatever information I wanted from the internet nowadays, and with him telling me that he knew things I could never find on the internet. We finally agreed on £50. I nearly said 'and all you can drink', but it occurred to me that he looked like someone who was capable of drinking quite a lot, so I stopped at £50.

I called to Irene to refresh our glasses and we removed ourselves to a quiet table in the corner whilst Terry began to recall the events of the mid-sixties.

Liam and his older brother John arrived from Ireland, he

explained. Terry didn't know what caused them to leave their homeland but he assumed they were on the run from the Irish police, the Garda.

"Why else would they come to London? It wasn't the bloody potato famine was it? We didn't want 'em 'ere did we?" he continued. "Fucking blacks and Micks taking our jobs. No, it must have been the law."

I looked at Ludo and Gabriella to see if his language offended them but they were both absorbed by the lecher's tale. I was simply doubting that he had ever done a respectable days work.

"The older one, John, started going out with Mary Travers, whose father managed a local pub. It's not there anymore. The Crown and Sceptre it was called. It's a bleeding gastro pub now", he added. "The three of them went round with an older bloke called Billy."

Terry couldn't remember his last name.

"Daly" I told him.

"That's right son. Daly," he replied, having clearly forgotten it was my name too.

Terry continued his meandering version of my mother's life before I knew her.

"Mary and John became an item as they say now," Terry added. "The youngster was always in tow," he said, referring to Liam. "They became friends with Billy Daly and the four of them were always together. One of the brothers fancied himself as a boxer. The older one it was."

"John" I suggested and he nodded as he took another gulp of scotch.

"Handy with his fists" Terry confirmed. "That's probably why he ran away from Ireland."

Terry then told us about a local gangster called Charlie Harrison and his son Michael. The Krays had controlled a large area of the East End but allowed people like Charlie to manage smaller parts. Charlie looked after Poplar, up as far as Mile End, where his nightclub was.

"Diamonds nightclub it was called. Reggie and Ronnie were often in there," Terry recalled. "Of course, I knew the Twins very well. Then it all started to go pear shaped," he explained. "1966 it was. A couple of months before the Calnan boys arrived. That idiot Georgie Cornell went into Ronnie's local, the Blind Beggar in Whitechapel and asked where that 'fat poofter Ronnie' was. Well, Ronnie had to kill him didn't he. He couldn't let Georgie get away with that could he?"

Terry looked at his empty glass and made a slurping noise as evidence that it was empty. I reluctantly called to the barmaid to bring us another round of drinks.

"Listen Terry" I said, "I can get all this from the internet. George Cornell, Reggie and Ronnie Kray. Bloody hell," I added, "they made a bloody movie about it."

"Well" continued Terry ignoring my protest, "once Ronnie had topped someone, Reggie had to do it too. By the time Liam and Johnnie arrived the East End was becoming like the fucking killing fields. If Charlie wanted to stay in with the crowd he had to top someone too didn't he. So why not Johnnie. After all, the Paddy was always goading young Michael." He paused to take a drink. "No Johnnie had it coming probably. Rumour had it that Johnnie gave Michael a good hiding."

If that was so, I wondered, what had happened between them. Gabriella had said that she thought it started with someone being raped. Is that why John beat up Michael? Was it Mum's mysterious sister Linda. What was it that happened between these two young men that began this chain of events. If John didn't like Linda, as Liam had told Gabriella, why would he put his life on the line for her? Just when I thought I was making sense of it all, I was drawn back into the, very probably, embellished memories of Terry Hoon.

"Well," continued Terry, "Charlie could hardly stand by and let that pass could he? Some Mick giving his wonderful son a slapping."

Terry took another mouthful of scotch from his replenished glass, fumbled with his tobacco tin then remembered times had changed and he would need to go outside if he wanted to smoke. He decided to resist anything that might cause us to leave and cost him the opportunity of a further free drink.

It was clear that Terry had realised that, as long as he could keep talking, he could continue enjoying free drinks. I was thinking about leaving when Terry offered to tell us a lot more but it was going to cost another £50. After some shuffling of chairs and an exchange of views, I decided to pay, which seemed to worry Terry. He was brash and indiscreet and I thought there was a good chance of him telling me something very useful now that the scotch was beginning to take effect. Unfortunately a visit to the toilet refreshed him slightly and he returned to the table with more vigorous suspicions.

"Here, Gabriella," he said as he returned to his chair, still talking to her as if she was the broker between us. "He's not a bloody copper is he? You wouldn't tuck me up would you darling?"

"No, he's not a copper Terry. I told you he's a reporter," she answered.

"Nothing will come back to you Terry," I confirmed.

"Oh yeah" he said as if he had suddenly remembered something, "this is all off the record, son. I don't want to be quoted."

"You've been watching too much telly Terry," I replied.

Terry slumped into his chair, took another drink and decided to continue with his recollections.

"Right" he said gathering his thoughts. "So, Charlie topped Johnnie Calnan for beating up Michael. Rumour says it was at the club. Diamonds, where the cinema is now. The only thing that is for sure is that Johnnie is supporting the Bow Flyover." He coughed and laughed into his scotch. "Charlie made sure that nobody would find the body. No body, no conviction. They were the rules you see. Clever bloke that Charlie. Just as hotheaded as Ronnie and Reggie but smarter. Didn't take chances. Know what I mean?"

We nodded and waited for Terry to continue.

"Next thing I know is Billy, young Liam and Mary have done a runner. Well, who wouldn't with Charlie on the rampage and determined to take out any witnesses that might lead the Old Bill back to him. Then, out of the blue, Liam turns up one night asking me if anyone could get him a shooter." Terry realised that he was about to implicate himself in a murder.

"I told him I couldn't help him, of course," he added unconvincingly, almost as an afterthought. Nobody sitting around the table was fooled by this obvious lie.

"Anyway, the fucking idiot only bought a red hot piece

that had been used to kill a copper. Double bubble for the clever bastard who sold him that gun," Terry added winking at me. "Got shot of a murder weapon, pinned the killing of a copper on an enemy of Charlie Harrison and made money out of the transaction as well. Problem was that, whoever it was, forgot to tell Charlie that young Liam was walking round with a fucking gun." He paused and took another mouthful of scotch. "Still Reggie was getting fed up with Charlie anyway. The boys reckoned he even denied killing young Johnnie at one point. 'Save that one for your brief' the brothers told him," he continued. "No, the boys thought he didn't have enough bottle to manage Mile End after that. So, bish, bash, bosh. Everyone's a winner. I mean Liam was going away anyway wasn't he?"

I got up out of my seat and threw the second £50 note at Terry.

"It was you wasn't it, you fucking little weasel. You sold Liam that gun didn't you?" Ludo looked appalled at my language.

Terry pushed his chair back, becoming increasingly convinced that I was a policeman.

"Me? No," he protested, "where would I get a shooter from?"

"Liam told me before he died" I insisted. "'Hoon knows'" he said, "Hoon knows. Hoon knows I didn't kill that copper. How else would you know Terry? If it wasn't you who sold him that gun, how would you know? No it was you Terry," I continued as I picked up my coat and ushered the girls towards the door. I turned and pointed at him. "You sold Liam Calnan that gun. I hope you fucking rot in hell."

We walked round to the car.

"Did that make you feel better?" asked Ludo disapprovingly.

We sat in silence as I started up the car. As we drove back past the pub, Terry Hoon was standing outside puffing away on a rolled-up cigarette. He caught sight of us out of the corner of his eye and turned away.

"Guilty as sin," I declared before the silence returned.

~~~~~

When we arrived home from our investigatory trip to London's East End, Ludo telephoned her mother and told her about Mrs. Joiner. Sebastiano took over the conversation from his mother and insisted that he and Gigi would accompany his mother to Mrs. Joiner's funeral. Ludo insisted that they did not have to come but Sebastiano was resolved on the matter. Mrs. Joiner was a very good friend of his mother and she really wanted to attend the service. Ludo said that mother seemed less convinced of her unshakable friendship with Mrs. Joiner but Sebastiano would hear nothing of it. I assumed that he was just happy for yet another excuse to visit his little sister.

I telephoned Julia the following day and she gave me details of the funeral, which Ludo passed on to her brother so he could book their flights to England.

Much to the surprise of Ludo's mother and Sebastiano, Mrs. Joiner was not a Catholic. So it was not a Catholic funeral.

"Why are we going to a different church?" asked Ludo's mother. I tried to explain with Ludo translating.

"Not a Catholic? What is she then?" asked Mama.

"Church of England" I explained.

Mama looked confused. She had never heard of the Church of England, let alone been to a C of E service.

Sebastiano and Gigi went missing just before the service and I later found out that, in a private ceremony, they had urinated up the outside wall of the church.

"We had to consecrate the church before the service," Sebastiano explained. "We baptise it and Mrs. Joiner stands a better chance of going to heaven."

Back at the Horse and Hounds after our third funeral in just a few weeks, the landlord was becoming suspicious. Either we were the unluckiest family in England or the black plague had decided to wipe out our entire social network. Meanwhile, Sebastiano and his mother were wondering whether the Catholic Church would ever forgive their attendance at a heathen ceremony.

"You cannot go-compare that service with the Roman Catholic one," explained Sebastiano.

The following day Sebastiano and Gigi decided to continue their sight seeing tour of London and were gone for most of the day. In fact they only got back in time for a family dinner before packing for the return flight the following day.

"No more funerals" called Sebastiano as Ludo drove them to the airport.

"Baptism only next time. And in a Catholic church," he added threateningly.

Ludo had conveniently forgotten to remind Sebastiano

about our appointment with P C Etherington, which we rushed off to after she had dropped her family at the airport.

~~~~~

The police station was adjacent to the local Magistrates Court in Evestown. It took some time to locate Constable Etherington who eventually ushered us into a small room.

The tall and rather despondent looking policeman told us that we would be formally charged with the offences of assault and robbery respectively. He emphasised the word respectively, presumably in case we mistook it for respectfully, which it wasn't.

"If you each admit the offence you are charged with, we are prepared not to take this to court. You will then be given an official warning by Superintendent Bagaert and, if you stay out of trouble for the next year your record is clear." He didn't wait for a reply and started preparing the necessary documentation.

"And if we don't?" I asked, which seemed to stop him from filling the forms in. He sighed, placed his pen firmly and deliberately on the desk and looked at us with growing impatience.

"But you can walk out of here today," he said, as if he was granting us a plenary indulgence.

"Yes, but I'll be walking out of here a guilty man."

"Well hardly," he said.

"Well what else does pleading guilty mean?"

"Look Mr. Daly, it's a formality. You get your wrist

slapped and we all get on with our lives," he explained rather brusquely.

"Yes and you improve your clear up rate by finding an innocent man guilty."

"And an innocent woman too," added Ludo as she stepped alongside of me, showing support for our position.

"Well if you don't see Superintendent Bagaert, then you'll have to attend court."

"Yes" I said, "and receive justice I hope. You seem to be forgetting PC Etherington that we didn't commit the crimes that you have accused us of."

He placed the documents back into the buff folder, put the top back on his pen and mumbled that some people couldn't be helped.

"You're not helping me by finding me guilty of a crime I didn't commit," I insisted.

"Or me" added Ludo.

The Constable walked to the door and opened it for us.

"I don't think there's anything more to say Mr. Daly," he paused, "and Mrs. Daly," he added to be politically correct. "You will be hearing from the Crown Prosecution Service."

"Good day" I said insincerely as we left the room.

Ludo deliberately changed the subject when we got in the car outside the police station.

"I haven't got anything in for dinner," she confessed.

"Let's eat out then," I suggested, adding, "We'll launch the campaign for the Evestown Two."

"Shall I phone Gabby and ask if she wants to join us. I think she is missing Tonka."

I was sure she had only suggested this to stop me talking about injustice all evening, so I agreed. Ludo telephoned

Gabby and we picked her up on the way to the Darsene Restaurant.

Gabby was making good progress with painting the kitchen and she enjoyed our company for dinner. I think she felt the need to offer further information about Liam. I was just pleased that it was her who raised the subject as Ludo was anxiously trying to talk about almost anything else.

"I remembered something Liam told me Jack," she said without prompting on my part.

"What was that?" I asked, trying to seem uninterested in case I destroyed any chance of producing offspring later.

"He told me that his dad, or his Pa as he always called him was a bit of a bully. I think that's why the boys left Ireland. Maybe he used to hit them when they were young, I don't know, but I think that was why they left home."

Ludo changed the subject and I made no effort to change it back again. I simply thanked Gabriella for her information. But her comments sat restlessly in my head over dinner. Liam and John's father had been ready and able to hit people. His son John had a quick temper too, as was evident from Terry Hoon's story. And Liam killed two people out of revenge. If I was a descendent of this family, as was looking more and more likely, then maybe that answers the disquiet I felt about myself. Why did I hit that guy in the shop? I wasn't defending myself, I simply struck out. Just like every generation of my family had done before me it seemed.

It was too late for Ludo to call her mother when we got home, so she resolved to call them the following evening to update them on our visit to the police Station.

250

9

Ω

John's story

It was Palm Sunday and the sparse congregation shuffled impatiently as the old priest walked around the church sprinkling holy water on his flock as it held up the palms. I felt a large splash on the back of my neck. It felt cold and dribbled slowly down my back. Under stern instruction the noisy Flanagan children in the front pew fell silent as Father Kennedy climbed the steps into the pulpit. I wanted to walk away but was held in place by a severe look from the Mammy. Liam and another altar server stood below the pulpit, holding large candleholders and they gazed at each other in an attempt to stare the other one out. Most parishioners had attended the Vigil Mass the evening before, but those with young children gathered and listened, less than attentively, to the old priest.

"While he was still speaking," the priest boomed, articulating each syllable, "Judas, one of the Twelve, arrived, accompanied by a large crowd, with swords and clubs, who had come from the chief priests and the elders of the people. His betrayer had arranged a sign with them, saying, 'The man I shall kiss is the one; arrest him.'" Father Kennedy

252

paused and looked anxiously at the Flanagan children who were shuffling along the pew.

"Immediately" the priest continued even louder than before. The shuffling stopped. "Immediately," he repeated, "Judas went over to Jesus and said, 'Hail, Rabbi!' and he kissed him. Jesus answered him, 'Friend, do what you have come for.' Then stepping forward they laid hands on Jesus and arrested him. And behold, one of those who accompanied Jesus put his hand to his sword, drew it, and struck the high priest's servant, cutting off his ear. Then Jesus said to him, 'Put your sword back into its sheath, for all who take the sword will perish by the sword.'"

The words echoed in the darkness of my dream. The holy water continued to dribble, relentlessly down my back and I seemed to lose consciousness. Perhaps it was a dream or my imagination. But suddenly there was shouting and I found myself in a large crowd outside the dock gates on the Isle of Dogs in East London.

I was trying to keep Liam close to me, so as not to lose him in the crowd. Men were forming a less than orderly queue to seek jobs for the day. Then I felt this warm moist slap on the back of my neck. My hand reached behind my head to see what it was. Someone had spat on me. The whole crowd were shouting about 'Micks' and 'Paddies' but I could not see who had spat on me. I walked away pulling at Liam with one hand and wiping the spittle from my neck with the other.

In my dream, if it was a dream, it suddenly turned dark again. I felt nothing except that dribble of moisture running down the back of my neck. The dampness grew and it felt warm now. Then the shadowy charcoal mist that filled my eyes turned a darker shade of black and I momentarily lost consciousness.

~~~~~

What would you have me do, dear God? Walk away? I walked away before, leaving my Ma and my sisters at the mercy of that drunken bastard. I wasn't going to do that again. I could barely live with the shame of it. I couldn't walk away again. Were we not put on your good earth to protect the innocent, to stand up for the weak? He raped my Mary and her with my baby inside her.

What I did does not make me my father's son. I am not like him. When I use my fists I do it for a reason, with a purpose, not gratuitously like him. I do it to feed young Liam, to protect my mother, to protect my wife. My father thought only of himself, so please don't liken me to him. Wasn't it my father who started the whole business? If it hadn't been for the Mammy I would have acted before I did. But she kept on telling me to leave it. She would have let him beat her until he killed her.

For my part I was ready to set the matter right the day I started work at the forge. The day I started work I became a man. I was bringing home a wage, so I was entitled to some say in what went on under the roof of the house I lived in.

When I was a boy, I was subject to the old man's rules. I grew up with him hitting Ma like he did. He took his belt off to me and Liam too, and God knows what he did to the girls. They wouldn't say anything but they feared him to

254

such an extent that he must have harmed them all at some time and I dread to think how. Their fear was one born of knowledge, not one born of wild assumption. No, he had harmed the girls I was sure of that.

When the Mammy told us to say our night prayers and Liam mumbled on about the Mammy and Pa and Nora, Biddy and Theresa, I was there praying for God to give me the strength of character to deter the old man from his ways. Four years of standing by and holding my tongue, while he bullied and beat her.

Eventually I could wait no longer for God's divine intervention. I could wait no longer than the end of my first week at work. I was a man with a man's wage packet in my hand. I had a say. Even at the end of my first day, I could barely resist the task I had given myself. But, even then, contrary to my better judgement, I tried to reason with the man. But he would have none of it. He dismissed my pleas that he should stop beating Ma after quenching his thirst to excess every day. Through the insistence of my mother I brooded on my intentions for four more years before my rage got the better of me.

In the end, all I did was to return home after work to find no 'tea' on the table and the Mammy's arm broken by that wife beater. "Every marriage is its own mystery," the priest said.

"There's no mystery about this marriage Father," I said, "Like there's no tea on the table for me when I get home from work Father. Because this big bastard here has broken the Mammy's arm, like he's broken her spirit before it."

And what does he do? Calls the Garda, to arrest his own son for doing no more than his duty. If Ma had not suggested it I probably would have taken myself off anyway. Then its: 'take Liam with you John'.

"But he's fourteen Ma."

"He's sixteen next month," she says. "Take him with you John, fer he's no good widdowt ya."

I think she knew the danger the boy was in, for if my Pa couldn't take his revenge on me then Liam would, almost certainly, be the recipient of his wrath. What could I do? I barely knew the boy. He was so much younger than me that we had different interests, or the same interests but at different times. I was at Secondary school when he was at Primary. We had different friends so, apart from sharing a dinner table with him, he was unknown to me.

It wasn't until I took him off to London with me that I could see how much he looked up to me. 'Jack' he called me, since he was a babe in arms, always Jack, never John. Then it became 'Himself' would you believe? If that isn't putting me on a pedestal what is? The poor young lad didn't speak for the whole 130-mile journey from Ballycraich to Rosslare. He sat there with a little red attaché case on his lap like an evacuee from the Blitz that I'd seen in photographs in the books when I was young. There I was worrying about what might be passing through his young mind when we stop to sup from a roadside water fountain and he asks 'will we be home for Nora's birthday next week Jack?'

"Maybe for the Mammy's birthday in July," I answer, hoping he wouldn't notice the lack of confidence or honesty in my reply.

"Ireland is a country for old men Liam," I told him assuredly. "We're better off making our fortune elsewhere. I mean they've just re-elected Eamon de Valera. And him being 83 years old.   Whoever heard of an 83-year-old President? No, we're better off making our way in England. There's plenty of work there Liam.   We'll be going home rich men."

I waited patiently for his considered response, all the time worrying about the probability of homesickness. But, if he suffered from it then it wasn't evident at this stage.

"Who's Eamon de Valera?" asks Liam innocently.

"God, do ya know nutting about Irish history Liam?"

"Are you sure his Irish Jack?" says the worldly-wise Liam Calnan. "He sounds Spanish or French to me."

"Liam, he's just about the most famous Irishman ever born. Where have you been for the fourteen years you've been on God's good earth?"

"I'm sixteen next month," he muttered tentatively under his breath.

One could always rely on our Liam remembering a birthday. So there was little likelihood of him forgetting his own.

The rain that had lashed the ferry for the entire crossing began to ease when we arrived at Fishguard. A great monolith of false hope greeted us. A rainbow that stretched off towards a new life in England hovered above us, beckoning two young runaways. I had no intention of returning home in time for Nora's birthday next week, nor indeed my mother's birthday next month. In fact, I was entirely convinced that Liam and I would be celebrating my own birthday, on our own, cast adrift in life's stormy sea.

My 21st birthday party at Ballycraich seemed a distant memory. I was the eldest of five children. Biddy and Theresa separated me from Liam and then little Nora was the youngest at nine years my junior. We had a grand time celebrating my coming of age. Coming of age, indeed. I had been working at the blacksmith's shop for the last four years.

I looked at the mournful little waif and pondered on our future. Maybe we would be home for Biddy's 21st next year.

But, for now, I was off to London with my kid brother in my charge. I had heard about the Irish Sea and the fact that it took no prisoners. It showed us no mercy that day. Apart from the few hardened seafarers on board, everyone bestowed their last meal to the sea. The fish eat well in the Irish Sea that's for sure. Liam fared no better than anyone else did and I had to wait for his stomach to settle before feeding the poor lad when we arrived back on shore in Wales. If I remember rightly, he was surprised that he wasn't already in England and I wondered what they had been teaching him during his years at school. Eventually his stomach stopped twisting and turning and he began to feel hungry again. I made no attempt to hide when we arrived in Fishguard harbour. If Pa had called the Garda and the police had been waiting for me at the dock, I was prepared to take my chances. I didn't mind running, but I wasn't prepared to hide for the next year just to satisfy the old man.

As it happened there was no reception party waiting for us, just a steel grey sky and a threatening thunderstorm that had followed our sea journey from Ireland. A local cafe served both as shelter and the provider of a hearty meal that Liam and I consumed with less mercy than the sea had shown us.

I always had in mind to go to London but I hadn't really given any thought as to actually how we would get there.

We certainly didn't have enough cash for the train fare and the money that the Mammy gave us was just enough for the meal at the dockside. Whether it was an unalterable event of providence or the decree of heaven, we found ourselves a lorry driver who was bound for London. He had less conversation in him than I did and I was only slightly more talkative than a Trappist monk was. Liam was too afraid to speak, so the journey passed by slowly and silently. We stopped only to relieve ourselves at the roadside. The vehicle rattled around as it journeyed further and further into the night. The enormous gearstick travelled a foot either way as it shook from side to side, clattering my hipbone every time I moved away from my sleeping brother. The driver drove faster and faster as he feared we might miss the deadline at the vegetable market he was delivering to. If he arrived too late, it would mean waiting another day and getting less for his wares as it would be a day older.

Fortunately there was little traffic in London, or so he told us in one of his rare attempts at making conversation. But it was more vehicles and people than I had ever seen, even on a market day in Cork, so I worried what it might be like when the population had woken up. In the end we did arrive on time and, with Liam and myself helping him, the load was discharged quicker than he could achieve on his own. He was pleased with his takings and, after buying breakfast for us at a nearby café, he gave me some change to see us on our journey. The sun was just coming up as we determined to head east. Liam said it would be wrong to go back the way we just came from and I suppose he was right. So we walked through the city, along strangely named streets until we came to a place called Aldgate. We asked directions there from a newsagent standing by the road. He seemed furtive in his response and almost ashamed of speaking to us. But it was a straight road in any case and we continued through Whitechapel, Stepney and Mile End before deciding to turn off of what appeared to be an endless straight road. The hot sun passed over our heads and warmed our backs as we marched ever eastward. The side streets were worse than the main roads, with rows of tiny terrace houses herded together like cows awaiting milking.

~~~~~

The streets of London were not, unsurprisingly, paved with gold. For a couple of young Irish lads they were paved with prejudice, intolerance and hatred. If you were seeking somewhere to live as we were, there were vacancies but not if you were black or Irish. If you wanted a job your accent was a disadvantage. And, if you were walking the streets, you needed to know who controlled them. It wasn't the police that was certain. Didn't the whole of London know that Ronnie Kray had shot George Cornell in The Blind Beggars pub just weeks before we arrived? But nothing happened to him as a consequence. From what I'd heard of the brothers, Cornell must have either been very brave or very stupid to walk into their local pub and call Ronnie a fat poof.

For every thousand portions of malevolence and wickedness we struggled to find one of decency and kindness in London that summer. But we did, eventually find it, or her I should say. For an old woman who smelled of sweat, urine and hard work, Nora was, paradoxically, a breath of fresh air. She put a roof over our heads and berated anyone that even looked like objecting to sharing a pub with us. Whilst civil rights activists were creating a path in the wilderness of the United States, old Nora was digging up her own road to racial tolerance. She had a heart given by God and a tongue given by the devil himself.

But even Nora couldn't help us to find work at the dock gates. There were definitely no blacks or Irish given jobs there. And shouting out for a job only exposed me as the object of abuse. So just like Ballycraich I had to walk away again with those bastards spitting on me as I went and Liam cowering under my jacket.

It was there, outside the dock gates, that I met Bill. His kindness shone out just like Nora's tolerance. The first money I earned after arriving from Ireland was due to Bill. He introduced me to the boxing at Ludgate Circus. And he was good enough to act as my corner man and clever enough to give me good advice and to tell me things I would never have thought about myself.

"I'm given a minute to tell you what you're doing wrong John," he bellows at me between the rounds of one fight. "And I have to tell you that, if I had ten minutes it wouldn't be long enough. Now get out there and survive for 3 minutes so I can work out how we are going to beat this lout."

When the bell rang three minutes later I sat down in silence.

"Are you an idjut," says Bill, "can't you see it. The big

bastard can't see out of his right eye. His reaction is two seconds slower on that side. Wait until he throws a right and as his head swings to the left, hit him with a left hook. But don't forget, increase the impact value. Don't aim for his head, increase the impact value. Aim for a target about six inches behind his head. Punch straight through the fucker's head."

I took his advice and beat that tattooed seaman in front of a cheering crowd at the Circus. I'm not sure if it was after this fight that I met Mary. Or, perhaps, it was after my very first fight, the one I lost against Digger Rhodes.

Maybe it was later. It was certainly a few weeks before we had any money to speak of, so there was no going down the pub for a while. By the time Liam's much-awaited sixteenth birthday arrived I had salvaged enough to buy three glasses of beer and Nora took us to The Crown and Sceptre. Stan Travers and his wife Carol were working behind the bar, helped by their daughter Mary.

The money I had managed to save was entirely the result of boxing at the pub in Ludgate Circus. I had taken a cynical beating at the hands of that giant South African called Digger Rhodes and my eye was bloodshot and bruised for weeks. I made a pitiful figure, I'm sure and I tried to keep out of the daughter's way for fear it would turn her off me. When Liam and Nora went off home ahead of me, Mary came to clean the table. She gave me a piece of beef steak in a paper bag, which she had concealed in her apron.

"For your eye," she said, and turned to go back to the bar. I held her wrist, tightly enough to produce a fearsome look. I released her arm and began to protest about her charity. But she would have none of it.

"Would you not help a wounded dog in the street?" she asked.

"I'm thought no more of than a dog," I answered. "The signs tell me as much."

"Take it. Hold it on your eye for an hour. It'll take the bruising away."

When I got home, I found Liam listening to an old radio that Nora had given him.

"I've got you some steak for your dinner," I said to him.

"What about you Jack?" he asked, almost not wanting to hear the answer that would force him to share it with me.

"I had some fish and chips on the way home" I lied and fried him the steak. The bruising would go down soon enough and I wasn't likely to have enough money to visit Mary again before it had.

~~~~~

In spite of all the disadvantages afforded to me by my birthplace, London was a great place to be in the summer of 1966. The World Cup was responsible for Liam finding employment, delivering newspaper copy and match statistics around Fleet Street. England's success in the event also cheered everyone up. It was also a great year for boxing, which kept Liam and me happy and we made a good friend through the sport too. Bill Daly proved to be as good a friend as Nora did and he loved boxing too.

Cassius Clay, or Muhammad Ali, as he had become, exploded onto the scene and battered local hero Henry

Cooper into defeat at Highbury a few weeks before we arrived. Plans were being made for his return to England to fight Brian London in August and I hoped that Liam and I might be able to see it, if I could raise enough money for the treat. Wouldn't that be something great to write home about? Liam and I watching the great Muhammad Ali box. The fight eventually took place a week after England had won the World Cup and Liam had a job by then which involved evening work, so we never did get to see the fight. Not that it was much of a match. Ali jabbed London unconscious in less than ten minutes, so that would have been a waste of our hard-earned cash. It was around this time that the Metropolitan Police started taking a firm control of the situation in the capital following the massacre of three policemen who were gunned down in a London street.

Liam and I were at home that night listening, on the radio, to Jose Torres retain his light heavyweight title against Eddie Cotton in Las Vegas. We left the radio on and heard how the police were looking for three men who callously murdered a policeman in a street near Wormwood Scrubs prison. There appeared to be many gangsters in London at that time, not just the Kray twins. Harry Roberts, and his associates Duddy and Witney were probably planning to spring someone from the Scrubs prison. After all, it wasn't long afterwards that the spy George Blake escaped prison. Perhaps it was him they were planning to free. Someone would have paid the twins a fair sum to arrange that because it was in their patch. Anything happening to the north of the Thames seemed to come under the rule of the Krays and anything south of the river was controlled by the Richardsons. Fortunately, neither of the groups had a navy.

The police made some high profile arrests that summer but it made no impact on the streets. I was sitting in the pub with Bill and Liam some three months after we arrived when news broke that the police had arrested Buster Edwards for the Great Train Robbery. The place erupted with laughter. He was a flower seller and small time, petty criminal. Now if they had arrested Charlie Harrison that may have made a difference. Certainly it would have changed my life.

~~~~~

The summer had almost ended before both Liam and I found work. He was kept on by the news agency after his trial period, although his wages didn't increase from the £5 per week he started on. But he was happy enough and didn't mind the unsocial hours the work involved.

Eventually I managed to secure employment with a contractor working on the Barbican development in the City of London. I worked in strangely named places like Cripplegate, Cheap, Bread Street and Farringdon Without, although I never found out what it was without. And the buildings I worked on were incredibly futuristic. They seemed to be taken straight out of that new TV programme *Star Trek* that Liam visited Bill's house to watch each week. One of the tower blocks was 42 storeys high. If it had been built in Ballycraich you would have been able to see it from

Cork.

As a contractor, work was erratic to begin with. Then I found regular employment as a hod-carrier working, of all things, on a massive YMCA building. I told Liam that, if I worked fast enough, we could be living there next year. But he just looked downcast.

"Will we not be going home before then?" he asked sadly.

He was right. I had stopped thinking about returning home. It was never mentioned by me in conversations and I hadn't appreciated the message that he had taken from that. But it must have seemed unlikely to him. Mary and I were talking about getting married, much to the disgust of her father. Although his angst didn't last for too long. He only had eyes for his younger daughter Linda. He was always talking about emigrating to Canada or Australia and taking his wife and Linda with him. But Mary was never mentioned.

Although the Barbican development wasn't far from where Liam worked off Fleet Street, I started work before Liam, even when he was on early shift. And sometimes, I was going home just as he was arriving for work. He would sometimes meet me in the Brown Cow pub off Moorgate, particularly if we hadn't seen each other for a few days.

I was finding it difficult to keep a trace on Liam. One night Bill told me he was moonlighting some evenings for a character called Bernie Woolaston. He was a professional gambler and Liam was working as some sort of runner for him. I went to see Bernie to try to persuade him to leave Liam alone. I know we needed the money but I didn't want Liam getting involved in activities linked to the criminal fraternity. As it was, Bernie made no objection whatsoever. He considered he had a legitimate, if a little questionable operation, but didn't want to lead Liam astray.

With regular income and Liam working evenings I could see more of Mary. She seemed unhappy at home. There was a jealousy between Mary and her sister Linda that I never quite understood. Mary believed her father favoured Linda but I didn't see enough of her parents to have any thoughts on the matter. The less Mary saw of her parents the happier she was. Then, one Sunday, we were sitting over Greenwich Park, looking down on the Maritime Museum in the distance and she asked how I would feel about being a father.

"I feel like I've been a father for the past year," I answered.

"Liam is your brother John, you shouldn't feel so responsible."

"But I am Mary, I am."

"He's a grown man now John. He has a job. No I mean how would you feel about being a real father. To have a child of your own?"

I almost gave the wrong answer but stopped myself as I suddenly realised what I was being asked. We were both sexually inexperienced. I was Mary's first partner and she was mine. But, whilst we knew little about sex, we understood the consequences of not using contraceptives. So, in that split second before I answered, I realised that Mary was pregnant.

"That's wonderful," I said kissing her. "We'll find somewhere to live. Somewhere nice for the baby."

She smiled. For a brief moment I feared that the

pregnancy had been contrived to enable her to escape from her parents but I knew she loved me too much to do that.

Stan's reaction was to ban me from the house and from the pub. He didn't speak to me. He and his wife passed messages to me through Mary, who was resolute throughout. We were getting married whether her parents consented or not.

So we set about looking for somewhere to live. We put our names down on the Council housing list and visited local councillors' surgeries to try to enlist their support. We were low priority but were still given three offers of accommodation. All of which were places that nobody else wanted. After being offered two slums that even the local tramps and drug addicts had stopped using, we felt sufficiently desperate to accept the third and final offer, knowing that the alternative might be to seek help from Stan or, worse still, return home to Ireland with a pregnant wife and less money than I had left with.

We decided to ignore what the outside of the flat looked like, and the noisy main road and loud parties into the early hours of the morning. We were determined to make the inside of the flat a home, where we could raise our baby.

~~~~~

Liam was only slightly more independent than when he arrived from Ireland but he still wanted to stay living at Nora's house. She had become like a second mother to him so I wouldn't have objected if he had been adamant about it.

But, in the end, he conceded and it was agreed that he would live with us, at least until the baby was born. Liam had decided to stay until he had seen his new nephew or niece and then return home to Ireland with photographs of the baby. From that date he had focus in his life and he was a happier person for it. He could see the future stretched out before him like he had never seen it before, certainly not since he landed at Fishguard on that wet day last year.

When Liam and I had finished decorating the flat, with a little help from Bill, we decided to celebrate with a night out. I don't remember who had the idea of visiting Diamonds Nightclub. It may have been me because I had, by now, completely forgotten the fight I had there with Michael Harrison the previous Christmas. Nothing happened, well nothing of any consequence it seemed. But the evening somehow renewed Michael's interest in Mary. He always wanted things he couldn't have, or rather shouldn't have, because in the end he could have anything he wanted. He simply had to ask his dad. But I should have known that a seed had been sown that night. If only we hadn't visited the club. If only we had kept ourselves to ourselves, maybe nothing would have happened.

A few days later I came home from work to find Mary sobbing. I asked her what was wrong although, from her dress and the fact that she was lying on the bed, I knew. In my heart I knew what had happened. I shouldn't have made her tell me. She tried to conceal it.

"Tell me Mary," I said. "There is nothing you can do or say that will ever change the way I feel about you. There's nothing that could ever stop me loving you. Just tell me the truth."

She broke down in tears.

"He, he..." But she couldn't say it. The words lodged in her throat.

"He," she repeated, unable to complete the sentence for sobbing.

"Who did this ting ta ya Mary," I asked again and she finally gives me the answer I already knew in my heart and my mind.

"Michael," she said.

I remained calm. I had to remain calm for Mary. My countenance may have changed, but she would not have noticed through the tears. My mind raced through the possibilities.

"He made me do it," she finally added, as if I didn't know that too.

And, in that instant a black, shadowy inescapable space opened up before me, in which I could see the awful chain of events as if they had been pre-ordained. The inevitable violence and the unavoidable carnage that would undoubtedly follow my actions, beckoned like the reaper himself. Mary was calmly sobbing now but her eyes stared vacantly.

"Don't worry Mary," I said. "Stay here. Just wait for me here."

She grasped the sleeve of my jacket as she saw too that black hole that represented our future. But I gently released her grip.

"Please John," she said. "Can't we just..." But before the sentence had ended I had left her there. I think I considered walking away from confronting Michael but I simply couldn't do it. I could not have lived with myself if I had not acted immediately.

"Walk away," the voices screamed in my ear. "Walk away."

"I can't," I replied to myself, "You know I can't."

I don't remember seeing anyone on my journey to the club. It was a bright sunny day and I was hot after a hard day's work. A bus went past with an advertisement for *Doctor Zhivago* and I thought briefly about how different the day could have turned out. I realised that the events of this day would probably affect the rest of my life, but I was unable to change its course. The nightclub was empty when I arrived. There was nobody in the foyer and as I walked into the main open-plan bar area I was confronted by Digger on the dance floor, halfway between the exit and the bar, where Michael sat on a stool. Charlie was not around and, as I approached Digger, he turned away to seek instructions from Michael. As he did so, I landed a fierce kick in the soft flesh behind Digger's left knee. As his knee gave way beneath him he crumpled slightly downwards, and I swung a left uppercut that lifted him off the ground. He landed heavily slamming his head on the wooden dance floor. Digger lay unconscious and I had hardly broken my stride in doing it. I walked directly towards Michael. He tried to step down from the bar stool he was sitting on but seemed to catch his left leg in the stool. As he stumbled slightly, trying to retrieve his balance. I fired a left hook aimed at a target about six inches behind Michael's head and he fell backwards, his leg still caught in the bar stool. I lifted him up with my left hand by the collar and buried my right fist in his face. I dropped him to the floor, then lifted him again with my right hand and buried my left hand this time into

271

his face. I lost track of how many times I repeated the action. Over and over again I punched the increasing lifeless body of Michael Harrison until his eyes were both closed, his nose seemed to have collapsed on his face and blood was starting to congeal on his nose and lips.

"Who told you where we were living?" I asked him.

As I recall, these were the only words I spoke throughout the entire incident. He didn't answer the first time, so I just continued hitting him. Each blow saw a new piece of pink flesh on Michael's face turn crimson or the nose bleed more, or an eye swell up, or a tooth loosen, or a bump appear. Until, eventually Michael, spitting blood said: "Billy," and he fell unconscious at my feet as I stood up. I turned and walked out of the club, casting just a cursory glance at the giant, still unconscious, figure of Digger Rhodes on the floor.

It was still light out when I came out of the club and the sun had lost none of its heat as it descended in the western sky.

I headed away from the club towards home, totally unharmed and unmarked apart from bruising to my knuckles. It was the longest day of the year and the warm sun felt good on my back as I had walked a short distance towards home. Then I suddenly realised that Liam would be leaving work by now and would need to pass by Diamonds on his way home. So I turned and hurried back to meet him. I had gone a short distance when suddenly Bill turned out of a side street. He looked unusually flustered and I guessed he had seen Mary. He hadn't, but by the time I had realised this, I had told him what had happened to Mary. Under a barrage of questions I eventually told him what I had done. He raged at me, calling me stupid. I tried to walk away and the setting sun glared into my eyes as Bill grabbed my arm and swung me round.

He grabbed my jacket and threw me against a wall. He blamed my father. It was in the blood he said. I was going to destroy everything. Nobody's life would be the same.

I kept walking and was now in the car park at the rear of the club. Bill threw a punch at me. I ducked and hit him in the midriff. He slid down the wall into a sitting position. I should have walked away then but I couldn't leave him there. So I walked back over to him and lifted him from the ground. I was just apologising for hitting him when he pushed me back against the wall that ran down along the rear of the club. Neither of us saw the overflow pipe that jutted out of the wall and I felt something puncture the back of my head. There was a look of shock on Bill's face. Something wet ran down the back of my neck, under the collar of my shirt and down onto my back. For a moment I was in a crowd outside the dock gates and someone had spat on me from behind. The crowd were shouting and jeering but I couldn't see who was responsible. Then I was in the church in Ballycraich with the Mammy, and Father Kennedy was sprinkling holy water. I could hear his footsteps behind me and a droplet of holy water struck my neck and trickled down, under my collar and onto my back.

The last thing I saw, as I fell between some rubbish bins at the rear of the nightclub, was Bill running away.

10

Jack's story

Memory is a strange thing, as I had seen with mother. Why is it we remember some parts of our past life and yet not others? I have two memories from my childhood. Moments in time, frozen, like a photograph capturing an eternal thought in the record of a person's life.

The first is a day when my old English teacher described me as vacillate. Mr. Kelly often did that. Not call me vacillate, but use a word that he knew I would have to look up. Delivered with the intention of enriching my understanding and appreciation of the English language I suppose. He meant it, unusually for him, in a derogatory way, for he was rarely critical of his pupils. He encouraged rather than admonished. But, in any case, I failed to take offence at it. What is wrong with being vacillate, I thought, after looking the word up in the dictionary?

At first I thought, rather naively, that it meant that I physically swayed from side to side but I soon realised it meant I dithered or changed opinion. He was right of course, but I couldn't understand what was wrong with dithering. Surely every decision in life is worthy of a moment's thought. Due consideration cannot always be considered a bad thing, although Mr. Kelly, with his usual authority and great collection of anecdotes, referred me to a famous American Football star who, when asked for his motto in life said: 'when you come to a fork in the road, take it'.

It was true, of course, I was vacillate. The fact that I spent so much of my childhood with Tonka set such a characteristic in stark contrast because he never lacked urgency. He was deliberate and I represented deliberation.

And that contrast is again apparent when that episode in my young life is seen against the other lasting memory I have, indeed the only memory I have of my father or, at least the person I thought was my father, Bill. I remember, when he first fell ill, how I would sit by his bedside and read to him before going to bed myself, a role reversal that should have warned me that our relationship was changing, if not ending. But I was too young to see the signs. I was too young to understand the permanent nature of death. But, in my heart, I knew my father would not recover. This was no normal illness.

On their deathbed one expects people to be more forthcoming, more truthful and candid, and my father didn't disappoint me. He spoke of many things, most of which I didn't understand. I wish I could remember them now, as I'm sure they were lost parts of the jigsaw I was currently working on. Little did I know that I probably had all the pieces to this particular jigsaw at some point in my life but, like most of my childhood toys, they had been lost. Or, perhaps I missed all the obvious signs whilst I concentrated on the subtle nuances.

But one evening, he started talking about books, perhaps because I was reading from one. He confessed that he had only read a very few books in his life. So few, it seemed, that he could remember the titles of them all. I can't remember them all but I do remember the book by the boxer, Jose Torres, who he liked. The other was a book about a man called Sammy Glick. I've never forgotten the name because there was a phrase from the book that people used to describe him: *'Sammy Glick is good and quick'*. Anyway, my father, or Bill, for I'm not sure how to address him anymore, had been compared to this character.

It was flattery that caused him to read the book, an act of penance it would seem because he disliked reading as was evidenced by the few times he exercised his ability to read, other than to read the race card or the football results. That last comment comes back to me now like something my mother said.

So, eventually, sometime after he died, I read the book myself, hoping to find some similarity between me and Sammy or, more importantly, between me and my father. I found none. In fact Sammy had more in common with Tonka than me. More importantly, if Sammy was, indeed like my father, then I was as dissimilar to him as I had always feared. The reality of this is now apparent to me. I was not like my father because he wasn't my father. It was as simple as that. Now all those same questioning thoughts return to haunt me about my real father. If I wasn't like Bill, then presumably I am like John or Jack as Liam called him.

My thoughts dwell on that failing on my part and I wondered how we nearly missed the fact that Liam called his brother Jack and I was named Jack. Gabriella even recalled this fact later and we all saw the significance now. I was named after my father, who Liam always called Jack.

Some clues stare you in the face I suppose. This was particularly true of me. Sometimes, missing the obvious, in a fevered search for the nuances. The longer you look the less you see.

So I had the same name and, I fear, hold the same temperament, as was demonstrated in Langton's store. Generations of rash, violent behaviour distilled into one moment of uncontrollable rage. I am no longer vacillate but hot-tempered, rash and impetuous; not slow and considered, but spontaneous and thoughtless.

'I am the family face' said Thomas Hardy, 'flesh perishes but I live on'. He wasn't referring simply to facial features, of course, but to that genetic material that makes us who we are.

Perhaps John was vacillate when he was young. After all, we all change. None of us remain the same. If we are the same at forty as we were at eight years old, then we would have wasted a life. So perhaps I am growing to be like my real father, hot-tempered. I thought about resisting it but how could I resist what is, after all, part of my DNA? The inherited characteristics passed down through generations expressed not just through my physical appearance, but also through the metaphysical elements that make me who I am, a microcosm of my father and his father before him.

But, if I do share those same impetuous tendencies, why can I not understand what drove John to do what he did? To bring the house of Calnan crashing down about his head. I felt that, if only I could understand this, my patrilineal endeavours might reveal my true self. I recalled what Gabriella had told me about John's father. Violence begetting violence. If the only example he had been shown as a child was violence at the hands of his own father, then it is not unreasonable that he should follow the same path himself. He met violence with violence.

~~~~~

The following week I returned to work on a full-time basis after three funerals. It was a pity that the Co-op no longer gave stamps or paid a dividend because between us we had paid a small fortune to the Co-operative Funeral Service in recent weeks. It hardly seemed appropriate to suggest a frequent flyer club.

The Grand National issue of *The Main Event* failed to identify the winning horse. Favourites floundered at rain-swept Aintree that Saturday and only the most fortunate of punters would have found the winner who romped home, almost unopposed.

Sir Leslie kept with family tradition and flew off at a gallop as soon as the tape went up. Indeed, in his impatience to lead the charge he almost broke the tape and created a false start. His mount left the rest of the field a distance behind and the High Court Judge needed only an outstretched sabre in order to recreate his ancestor's charge into the guns.

As he reached the water jump at the end of the first circuit, Sir Leslie's mount suddenly ran out of steam. Horse and jockey landed heavily in the water but managed to stay upright. The rest of the field swept past the tired partnership, which only managed to climb over two more fences before the horse, much to the dismay of Sir Leslie, pulled up, unable to even attempt the next fence.

Undeterred by his mount's unwillingness to proceed further, the old man made several attempts at the fence before conceding defeat and cantering back to the stables, head bowed.

In the meantime, the remainder of the field that had stayed upright had accelerated up to the speed that Sir Leslie had started the race with. At the finish, half the runners that began the race had fallen and there were, thankfully, no injuries, other than to Sir Leslie's pride.

Youth triumphed over doggedness and young Declan managed to finish the course at his first attempt. Interviewed by a TV reporter after the race, he appeared happier than even the winning jockey, having overcome one of the most challenging of horse races. The future was bright for Declan and one can only hope that Sir Leslie will hang up his saddle before he damages anything more than his ego.

Most of the articles I needed to write over the next few weeks were straightforward, so I still had some spare time to continue the investigation into my own parentage.

After my first day back at work, Ludo and I were sitting at home, scanning the Internet for more information about Ballycraich and the elusive Calnan family, when the doorbell rang. It was PC Etherington with a young policewoman. The bright fluorescent police car sitting immediately outside our house was causing curtains to twitch eagerly along the street.

Neighbours impatient to take over the late Yoda's

chairmanship of the local Neighbourhood Watch, were looking round their curtains, presumably saying 'God, there must be another death over there'. After three funerals and rumours of violent crimes, we had become dubious celebrities in Beadsman's Cross, although the local newspaper had not yet covered the Evestown Two.

PC Etherington explained that Radovan Stodkovic had voluntarily attended the local police station a couple of days ago and confessed to the shop lifting offence at Langtons Department Store in town.

"That's great news," I said enthusiastically, adding "no need to apologise."

"I wasn't going to" he quipped back at me. "In fact, I don't suppose this is news to you is it Mr. Daly?"

"Sorry, but I don't understand what you mean," I said convincingly enough to produce an expression of surprise on his otherwise featureless face. The young policewoman nodded knowingly in support behind him.

"Mr. Stodkovic had clearly been subjected to a severe beating, Mr. Daly, and we all know how handy you are with your fists."

"I am not *handy* with my fists," I insisted. "I hope you're not suggesting that I...."

"I'm not suggesting anything," he interrupted, "but in the circumstances we are dropping the case against Mrs. Daly and, a little more reluctantly, dropping the assault charge against you. It seems two wrongs do make a right," he added sarcastically.

I decided to be vacillate rather than impetuous, so deliberately chose not to respond to his invective remarks. Ludo too remained calm.

"Mr. Stodkovic," The Constable continued, "insists that Mrs. Daly was not his accomplice and you are not known to him. And, perhaps more importantly, that his injuries had been caused by walking into a door." This last remark was reinforced with a shaking of the head in disbelief.

I could restrain myself no longer.

"Or maybe it's because I'm not known to him," I protested vehemently.

PC Etherington firmly believed, he said standing his ground, that Mr. Stodkovic's explanation of how his injuries were sustained was inconsistent with the injuries themself.

"Quite how a door would cause both facial injuries and bruising to the ribs Mr. Daly, seems a mystery."

"Perhaps it was a rotating door," I replied with equal sarcasm, adding "I can assure you..." but he stopped me from saying anymore.

"We'll leave it there Mr. Daly. I hope we don't have cause to meet again."

"Suits me," I said as they walked back towards the flashing lights on the police car that continued to attract the attention of my neighbours.

After they left, I poured myself a Jameson and ice and asked Ludo if she wanted a drink too. She did and we sat staring at each other for a few moments. I must admit that my first instinct was to blame Tonka. After all, he was always turning up when I needed him. But this wasn't the equivalent of taking care of some school bullies. Whoever did this used persuasion as well as a sound thrashing.

Then, suddenly, the identical thought occurred to both of us at the same time. Synchronised intuition I suppose.

"Sebastiano!" we declared together.

"And Gigi too, I imagine" added Ludo.

"Sightseeing indeed," I added.

Sebastiano denied any knowledge of the affair when Ludo called him later that evening. Their conversation was in Italian but I could understand the subject matter and it sounded like a trip was being planned. After she finished the call, Ludo sat me down to tell me about a suggestion that her brother had made.

"Sebastiano" she said, "thinks we should go to Ireland to try to retrace your family history. He is right, Liam and John may well have family still living in Ballycraich or close by."

It sounded a good idea because I was certainly not making any progress using the World Wide Web.

The correspondence in Liam's personal effects clearly suggested that it was John who represented the love that mother and Liam shared. And it now seemed equally certain that it was John, and not Liam, who was my father, but I needed to understand what had happened back then. Who was raped? Why did John feel the need to give everything up to avenge that offence? Was it just because he was hot-tempered and, if so, am I that way too? Or did he think it through and decide that, whatever the consequences, he simply couldn't live with the shame of walking away from the fight?

We talked it through that evening and it was decided that we would take a holiday in Ireland in a couple of weeks. Ludo was very enthusiastic and went into planning mode. She trawled the internet looking for flights and hotels. As the plans progressed in the ensuing weeks, it became more like a pilgrimage, with Ballycraich as the holy

282

shrine.

When Gabriella joined us for dinner one evening, she had heard from Tonka and he was expected home in a couple of weeks. We suggested that they might want to join us on our trip to Ireland, insisting that the search for my family would not dominate what was, after all, a holiday. Gabriella agreed, saying she would tell Tonka if she got the opportunity to speak with him again.

Unfortunately, due to the nature of his work, Tonka was often out of contact for long periods. However, Gabriella felt sure he would want to join us and so we booked the flights to Cork and made a tentative two-night reservation in the City. We decided to simply see where the holiday took us from that point.

Having found Terry Hoon so easily our expectations of finding a relative of John and Liam rose as the holiday drew nearer. For my part, I needed to know whether John Calnan was my father. Ludo agreed, reassuring Gabriella that it would not occupy all of our time. Gabriella didn't seem to mind. She was preoccupied with the return of Tonka. She was a very strong and determined character but even she found it difficult to deal with the absence of her newly found boyfriend.

~~~~~

Gabriella telephoned the week before the holiday was due to begin, to say that Tonka would not be home in time for the outbound flight. However, he expected to return around that time and, if necessary, would meet us in Cork.

The evening before our flight Gabriella joined us for dinner and slept in the spare bedroom. She was obviously agitated and anxious about Tonka despite my reassurances that he always comes back and he always will come back. He's indestructible I told her. That's why we all called him Tonka at school, after the Tonka toy trucks that were unbreakable. I didn't tell her that Tonka had, in fact, managed to smash such a toy into small pieces as a boy and that was really how he got his nickname. I also omitted to tell her that the strap line for the famous toy was 'built for boyhood'. Tonka was, indeed, built for boyhood, rather than manhood, but it seemed to me that he was getting closer to the point in his life when he might settle down and give up his game of soldiers.

Before retiring for the night, the three of us sat up, after dinner, sorting out which items from Liam's personal effects, and which items from the shoebox, that we would take with us. In the end it was just about all of it, for they took up very little space.

Liam's effects contained the photograph of someone called Nora. After a long discussion, we concluded that the Calnan brothers might have had a sister or cousin called Nora who sent Liam the photograph of her and the two other women at Nora's fiftieth birthday party. Perhaps the brothers had three sisters. Even with our current mortality rate, that would give us a reasonable chance of finding one of them still alive.

So, with the photograph of Nora's birthday party safely tucked away in my hand luggage along with the other artefacts from Liam's belongings and the shoebox in mother's loft we left for the airport. We flew to Cork Airport, hired a car, and decided to drive the short distance to Ballycraich before we checked into the Best Western hotel on the outskirts of Cork.

The sun shone brightly as I drove slowly in the direction the car rental manager had told us. He assured us that we would find a sign to Ballycraich near a large detached house that stood in its own grounds. We followed the instructions and soon found the very sign he spoke of.

Taking the turnoff, we past the occasional pub, and the less occasional church and the narrow road headed in a winding, southerly direction into the tiny hamlet of Ballycraich.

My heart beat faster as we found somewhere to park the car. This was an uncomplicated village, so small that nothing could be hidden. If the Calnan brothers had come from this place, even though it be forty years ago, they would be remembered. The buildings, although few in number, had been here for longer than forty years and remained untouched by history itself.

We left the car and walked back towards the village shop. Nobody spoke. We simply looked at each other, encouraged by the stillness and simplicity of the place. We appeared to be the only people in the village, although the door of the pub was wide open. We looked at each other and decided, silently, to visit the shop first.

There was no name on the shop and it would have been too much to hope that it was owned by a Calnan. It wasn't, as we found when we entered the establishment through a glass door.

Mrs. McAuliffe was genuinely pleased to see us. Her

shop acted as newsagent, grocery store and post office to the tiny community it served. The old woman reflected the pace of the village and her responses were contemplative and considered.

"Good morning," I said once the loud doorbell that signalled our entrance had stopped ringing.

"And good morning to yerselves too," she answered politely, before adding, "are yer staying at the big house?"

The puzzled looks answered her question and she continued without reply from us.

"Oh, I'm sorry, I'd heard that there were guests up at the big house."

"No, we've just arrived today," explained Ludo, "we're from near London," she added, not wishing to confuse the old woman further with a detailed explanation of where Beadsman's Cross was.

"Now, if I might say," prompted Mrs. McAuliffe, "you don't sound like you are from England my dear."

"No," answered Ludo, "I am from Italy. Gabriella here is from Romania, and Jack is from England."

"May the saints preserve us," says an impressed Mrs. McAuliffe, "To be sure, Ballycraich has not had so many different nationalities visiting it in one day before. Is there a purpose in your visit or are yer just enjoying our fine country?"

"Well both," I replied. "You do indeed have a lovely country but the main purpose of my visit is to trace my family history and perhaps even find some living relatives," I continued in a hopeful tone.

Her ageing eyes brightened at the possibility of being of service to us.

"And what is your family name young man?"

"Calnan," I answered.

"Well," she answered, "you won't need to stretch yer legs too far around these parts before finding yerself a Calnan."

Before we had time to speak, she ushered us out of the shop and paused only to button her cardigan and tidy her hair in the reflection provided by the glass door. For a moment I wondered whether the Calnans may have offended her in the past and she was dismissing us from the premises. But her demeanour was enthusiastic rather than offended. She reversed the sign inside the shop door to indicate it was now closed but made no attempt to lock the door as she pointed us back towards the place where we had parked the car.

I quickly realised that she wanted to join us on our journey of discovery, rather than simply give us directions.

Events of this kind were obviously rare in such a small village and she was clearly not going to miss the action. For all her years, the woman could walk briskly and did so without providing an explanation for her actions. She walked a few feet in front of us and we tried to keep up. We past a small cottage and a woman aged about fifty appeared at the gate to ascertain what was happening. She was soon spotted by Mrs. McAuliffe who called over to her to go and find Theresa and Bridget, and to be sure to tell them to get themselves over to the pub as quickly as they could. The woman went off immediately and we continued on our way towards the main building in the village, The Bull Pub.

Despite the door to the pub being open, Mrs. McAuliffe knocked forcefully on it and called even more loudly to the inhabitants.

"Hello in the house," she began. But, on not seeing anyone, she called louder still.

"Nora, will yer come and meet my visitors," she said claiming us for her own.

"We have visitors from half the countries of Europe," she added, "and their looking for you Nora."

A man aged about seventy years old stepped out from behind the bar as we entered. He wiped his hands with a bar towel and approached us.

"Thomas, Thomas," said Mrs. McAuliffe with growing impatience, "will you be off and get Nora for I've already sent for her sisters and she wouldn't be wanting them to be meeting this young man before her."

The man was the archetypal, unflappable Irishman. He chose to ignore the instructions and held out his hand, which I took in mine. He had a strong grip and I waited eagerly for an introduction. Was he Thomas Calnan I wondered?

"Yer very welcome I'm sure," he said, adding "I'm Thomas; Thomas Flynn."

My heart sank and I introduced myself as Jack Daly, before adding "and my wife Ludo and this is Gabriella."

He nodded but remained silent.

"Well," I added "Jack Calnan actually." This didn't appear to confuse him or at least not as much as Mrs. McAuliffe, who called out loudly, "Nora, will yer get yerself down here to meet this young man with two names."

There was still no sound of movement from upstairs and I began to wonder whether there was anyone else in the pub. Then Thomas finally obeyed his instructions and called up the stairs.

In a composed, and almost serene voice which was hardly raised at all, he called into the stairwell.

"Nora, will you get yerself down here, for yer brother John's boy has come to see yer."

I felt like dropping to my knees in praise of God and good providence, and heard the toilet flush upstairs.

I retrieved the photograph of Nora's birthday party from my pocket and looked at it as the very same woman, albeit it a little older, arrived at the foot of the stairs. She looked at me, began to cry, then walked the few steps over to me and held me in her arms.

The same good fortune that led us directly to Terry Hoon, remained our travelling companion and, within a few hours of leaving England, we had found John and Liam's sister.

Nora needed no convincing that I was her brother John's son.

"To be sure he is," she exclaimed when she had stopped crying, "Yer look just like him."

I introduced her to Ludo and Gabrielle.

"The Mammy told me things you need to know. About the brothers. Ma missed our John and Liam so much," Nora added as she began to cry again.

Two more aunts arrived a few minutes later. Theresa and Bridget were just as emotional as their sister was. Then, almost as quickly as they had arrived, they both left, promising to return with even more relatives.

We continued drinking in the pub after the normal lunch closing time and Nora insisted that we stay with them, rather than drive back to our hotel in Cork. Nora told us so much about her brothers. She knew, she said, from an early age that her brothers were devoted to one another but in different ways. Liam's love was born out of admiration for an older brother. John's love of Liam was born out of responsibility. But the common factor, Nora added, was that there was nothing either of them could do to stop the other one loving them. Their only fault was that they loved each other too much. For, if the fates had reversed their roles, Nora was convinced that John would have done exactly what Liam had done, only probably much sooner. John didn't think too long about matters before taking action. But that delay was all that separated them.

Later that day Nora's sisters Theresa and Bridget, who they called Biddy, returned along with their husbands and assorted children and even one lovely grandson named Sean. From being an only child with no cousins, I had suddenly become a member of a very large family.

"I didn't know I had such a large family," I whispered into Ludo's ear as I sat there with little Sean on my lap.

"And getting bigger all the time" she smiled back at me, looking down at her tummy.

"Can I?" I began to ask.

"Too soon" came her answer. "Keep it to ourselves for now," she suggested.

Gabriella, Ludo and I sat entranced as we learned about my real father, John Calnan who was known as Jack only to his younger bother Liam. Nora had corresponded with Liam throughout his imprisonment. Clearly he had not kept her letters but Nora had kept Liam's and shared the contents of them with her sisters over the years.

"Your mother was raped Jack," explained Nora

sympathetically. "She and John had set up home together when she found herself pregnant."

"What, as the result of being raped?" I asked nervously

"No, no, no," she said, "not at all. Your mother and John were having a baby and managed to get themselves a little flat, nothing special, but Liam liked it. He was terribly homesick you see and made very few friends. Those he did befriend were probably best given a wide berth," she added.

"And did he mention the other Nora, the one who shared their first house?"

"He did indeed," she said cheerfully. "Wasn't she a wonderful woman?"

"I don't know," I admitted, "I didn't know her, but Gabriella did," I added as I pointed towards Gabby.

"Oh yes, I know about Gabby. Liam was always mentioning her in his later letters." Nora hesitated as she tried to gather her thoughts.

"Anyway, just as Liam was settling in at the new flat with Mary and John, and just at that time of his life when he felt most happy, his world disintegrated in a second."

She paused again for a moment as little Sean decided to run off to his mother. Then Nora continued relating the story of her brother.

"There were many gangsters it would seem in their neighbourhood at that time and one of these awful persons raped your poor mother. It was a terrible ting that nobody recovered from. John found her, you see, and set straight off to see yer man. He was like that our John, couldn't hold his own counsel for a second. Straight off down the road to sort this fella out." She paused again as those awful events came flooding back, and her eyes welled up.

291

"And he succeeded it would seem. Liam said he must have whipped him to within an inch of his life and then some. Then events took over, as they say."

I sat enthralled as she went on to explain that John went missing and they concluded that the gangsters, the Harrisons had killed him. Liam was beside himself with grief. He and Mary weren't thinking straight, she explained.

"They were incapable of thought. But Bill was. He took charge of the situation, or what was left of it. Otherwise Liam would have gone the same way as our John. Eye for an eye, tooth for a tooth and a life for a life."

But Liam couldn't get over it. She said he brooded on it from that day. He thought about avenging his brother's death every day. He had told Nora as much in his letters. Circumstances seemed to build to a crescendo and when Bill told him that he and Mary were going to marry, he just decided to do it. It was around the time of his brother's birthday, so that surely contributed to it.

"Liam was always one for a birthday party. He remembered all our birthdays. We always received a letter on our birthday," she added. "John missing his birthday like that must have pushed Liam over the edge, as they say."

"So that's what happened Jack. Your father, your real father was John and it was he that punched and beat Michael Harrison to within an inch of his life for the young gangster's attack on Mary. Charlie Harrison inflicted immediate revenge and, if the rumours were to be believed, our beloved John was buried unceremoniously in the Bow Flyover in London's East End, which was under construction at the time."

In spite of the advice from Mary and Bill, it seems that

Liam could not accept his brother's murder and somehow, he managed to get his hands on a gun and killed both Charlie and Michael Harrison in Diamonds nightclub before escaping back to Ireland.

"Trying to escape," I corrected Nora, but she had chosen her words well.

Apparently, Liam had made it back to Ireland and all the way back to Ballycraich. He told his mother everything but was sent back by her to England to give himself up.

"Liam wanted to escape," Nora, explained "but the Mammy said he should turn himself in. When he was arrested at Fishguard, he was on his way back to London, not trying to get away. He never received parole because he would never say he was sorry; he never showed any remorse for his actions."

Nora explained that Liam absolutely refused visitors. She and her sisters wrote many times but he would never change his mind. I explained how Gabriella met Liam through his surrogate mother Nora, and we spent the rest of the afternoon learning more about Liam and his brother.

I apologised for not contacting them before the funeral but explained that we only found the letters after Liam had been buried.

In her ignorance, their mother had convinced herself that Liam's actions would be considered a crime of passion and he would serve only a token sentence. She could not be aware of the maliciousness of Terry Hoon or the subsequent decision by Liam to cut himself off from all his friends and family, who he felt should not trouble themselves with his welfare.

While we were in the pub, Gabriella received a call from

Tonka on her mobile phone. She had to go outside to take the call because of the noise inside the pub.

She returned in very high spirits to say that Tonka was apparently back home in the UK. Gabriella couldn't quite understand what he was saying but it seemed that he hadn't been on active service.

"So what's he been up to?" I asked

"Attending to some personal business he said."

I didn't take much notice and simply assumed that the mission was so secret that he couldn't talk about it in any way whatsoever. Asking whether he was unhurt when he had just told Gabriella that he hadn't been on active duty would have been indiscreet, so I changed the question.

"So, is he at home then?" I asked

"Yes," she said "and he is flying out to join us in the morning."

It was another great excuse for a family party and Nora began making preparations to receive my best friend Tonka.

"Maybe" suggested Ludo quietly to me as we walked the country lanes the following morning "he went off to buy a ring."

"Ludo, it doesn't take several weeks to buy a ring. He just can't tell her about his work. I've got used to it and now she will have to as well."

"But he's lying if he's saying he hasn't been with the army. That's no way to start a relationship."

~~~~~

Our first morning in Ireland was greeted with birdsong and a rural view of extraordinary splendour that had remained unchanged for generations. I imagined Liam and his older brother walking these same lanes. They both now lie in a foreign land bereft of the love of their family. I resolved to promise the sisters that I would not forget them. Those who are remembered never die and I would not let their memory die. Young Liam had a grave but a flyover in London's East End marked his brother's tomb, miles from his homeland. Tears and floral tributes cannot help either of them now but this should not deter us from mourning their loss.

Nora and I spoke about birthdays and the significant part they had played in the events back in the sixties. Liam loved birthdays she had told me, so it seemed appropriate that I should mark Liam's and my father's birthday each year. Nora, Theresa and Biddy would be pleased that someone laid tributes at the places where their bodies rested. Dying too young is not the greatest tragedy and, in itself, is no great source of sorrow. The true root of sadness and the greatest tragedy is never to have been loved. Neither brother suffered this fate and I would see that they were not forgotten.

Maybe one day I could clear Liam's name of the murder he didn't commit. My experience of the press told me that the world would see him no differently for it. To be falsely accused and wrongly imprisoned for that murder was part of Liam's penance. I doubted whether the uncle I had met all too briefly, and had come to admire, would appreciate my interference.

And then there was mother. She took her love for John to

the grave, without telling me the true identity of my father. Such an act was not born out of ill-conceived wisdom but of the protective love of a mother. I cannot reproach her for an act of maternal kindness, however misplaced such an act was.

As Ludo and I explored the lovely countryside of Ballycraich on that fresh morning, we were joined by the youngest member of the family, Sean. The rain was disappearing into the Western sky, taking some dark clouds with it, and a warm sun crept slowly in pursuit. A rainbow began to rise up from a distant field, offering hope to the hopeful.

Having made sure he was up in time to join us for the walk, Sean latched himself on to his new Auntie Ludo. He seemed greatly pleased to have gained himself a new uncle and aunt and was soon asking whether he could visit us in England.

The countryside around the pub was even quieter than Beadsman's Cross and, after our walk along the country lanes I visited the local newsagent to buy a copy of *The Main Event* and eagerly read my interview with the Foreign Secretary. Our publication wasn't a big seller in Ireland but extra copies had been produced as it covered the much-heralded Peace Conference.

Despite his assurances to the contrary, the Foreign Secretary had done absolutely nothing to try to find or reunite Gabriella and her son Bodgan. So I felt no regret whatsoever when I read my own exposé that Jonathan and, more reluctantly, Titus had agreed to publish. Under Jonathan's witty headline: *'Peace on the side'*, it gave explicit particulars of the Foreign Secretary's affair with a Romanian girl, who had accompanied him, first class of course, to Geneva for the Peace Conference. Any hopes of being short-listed for the Prime Minister's job disappeared under a barrage of unhealthy tabloid interest in his private – now largely public - life

Later that day, just as the lunchtime party was about to get into full swing in the pub, Tonka arrived with a young friend who stood timidly behind him. He had never introduced us to any of his SAS colleagues before so I was surprised to see he had brought one to Ireland. Perhaps he felt in need of support for a trip to Ireland, particularly to the Republican area of Cork, where Her Majesty's forces didn't normally receive a very warm reception.

"Well, introduce us then Tonka," I shouted above the music and chattering voices. He leaned over and whispered in my ear.

"Can we have the music off for a moment Jack?"

He looked serious and I anticipated bad news. I shouted to my new Auntie Nora to ask her to turn the music off for a moment.

The feet-tapping Irish fiddles ceased their encouragement to dance and Tonka prepared to make an announcement from the doorway. The sudden silence attracted the attention of everyone and Tonka found himself with an attentive audience.

"I think he's getting married," Ludo whispered to me, with a confident look in her eye.

"It'll make a change from bloody funerals," I said.

"I'm sure we all remember singing Amazing Grace at Mass on Sunday," began Tonka, and this cryptic opening gained everyone's attention.

"I always well up when you get to the part where we sing '*I once was lost but now am found*,'" he admitted. "It seems we have been inundated by people who were lost and now are found lately," he continued, "including my best friend here Jack, who it seems was lost to his family for far too long."

There was a spontaneous cheer and then silence allowed Tonka to continue.

"Well, my young friend here has also been lost," he added, pulling the embarrassed tall, dark young man forward to face the multitude of strange faces.

"But now he is found too." Tonka paused and a few seconds passed before he finished his sentence.

"Everyone, particularly you Gabriella, this is Bodgan."

Released December 2016
The sequel to Deathbed Confessions

Deathbed Betrayal

An old friend of the Daly family is murdered in a crowded Romford betting shop and yet there are no witnesses. The police are convinced that this is a vigilante killing of a paedophile and the only way to prove them wrong is for Jack Daly to find out who killed Bernie Woolaston and why.

The cold-blooded murder triggers a chain of events that takes Jack back to the east end of London – back to that perilous world where his life could be in danger if the wrong person finds out who he really is.

Not everybody is who they seem in this fifth book in the Jack Daly series and, in a bloody and taunt ending Jack comes face-to-face with his past.

Deathbed Confessions is Peter Larner's most popular novel and followers of the Jack Daly series of mysteries have waited eight years for the sequel. If you liked *Deathbed Confessions,* then you will love *Deathbed Betrayal.*

Deathbed Betrayal is the tenth novel from Peter Larner and the fifth book featuring Jack Daly, which follows on from the very enjoyable *Harpoon Force,* but with an intriguing storyline that successfully picks up the threads of *Deathbed Confessions.*

Made in the USA
Charleston, SC
05 December 2016